Recent titles by Alys Clare from Severn House

A World's End Bureau mystery

THE WOMAN WHO SPOKE TO SPIRITS

The Gabriel Taverner series

A RUSTLE OF SILK
THE ANGEL IN THE GLASS
THE INDIGO GHOSTS

The Aelf Fen series

OUT OF THE DAWN LIGHT
MIST OVER THE WATER
MUSIC OF THE DISTANT STARS
THE WAY BETWEEN THE WORLDS
LAND OF THE SILVER DRAGON
BLOOD OF THE SOUTH
THE NIGHT WANDERER
THE RUFUS SPY
CITY OF PEARL

The Hawkenlye series

THE PATHS OF THE AIR
THE JOYS OF MY LIFE
THE ROSE OF THE WORLD
THE SONG OF THE NIGHTINGALE
THE WINTER KING
A SHADOWED EVIL
THE DEVIL'S CUP

THE INDIGO GHOSTS

Alys Clare

This first world edition published 2020
in Great Britain and the USA by
SEVERN HOUSE PUBLISHERS LTD of
Eardley House, 4 Uxbridge Street, London W8 7SY.
Trade paperback edition first published
in Great Britain and the USA 2020 by
SEVERN HOUSE PUBLISHERS LTD.

British Library Cataloguing in Publication Data
A CIP catalogue record for this title is available from the British Library.

ISBN-13: 978-0-7278-9027-6 (cased)
ISBN-13: 978-1-78029-685-2 (trade paper)
ISBN-13: 978-1-4483-0410-3 (e-book)

All Severn House titles are printed on acid-free paper.

Severn House Publishers support the Forest Stewardship Council™ [FSC™],
the leading international forest certification organisation.
All our titles that are printed on FSC certified paper carry the FSC logo.

MIX
Paper from
responsible sources
FSC
www.fsc.org   FSC® C013056

Typeset by Palimpsest B
Falkirk, Stirlingshire, Sc
Printed and bound in Gre
TJ International, Padstow

For Jon, Hannah, Imogen, Phoebe and Reuben;
happy memories of the Mary Rose on a *very* hot day,
with much love xxxxx

ONE

The autumn light was fading as I rode into Plymouth. The men on the north gate knew me and nodded a greeting as I hurried past. The streets were lively with townsfolk on their way home, and my horse and I had to draw into the side more than once as vast carts emptied of their produce slowly trundled out of town. Each delay was a stab to my conscience, for I should have been there earlier and, but for the desperate plight of a small boy who had fallen off a haystack and cut his head open on a sharp piece of granite, I would have.

The congestion in the narrow, winding streets showed no sign of easing, and in frustration I slid off Hal's back and led him down a narrow side alley to an inn I'd often used where they know how to care for horses. Leaving him with the ostler and a few coins, I told the lad to look after him until my return.

Whenever that might be.

I was faster on foot, able to utilize the double-backs, the dark alleys and the little-known stairs, and soon I knew the sea was near. I turned a sharp corner, leapt down a short flight of steps and emerged onto the quay.

Like everywhere else in Plymouth, the waterside was crowded and noisy, the activity focused on the line of ships tied up, gangplanks down and commercial transactions still in full swing. As it was late afternoon, the nature of these transactions was already beginning to alter. I spotted at least three women who had nothing but their own bodies to peddle, and exchanged a glance with one of them. She was a handsome, wild-looking young woman and a few weeks back I'd treated her for the pox. Now she scowled at me, as if fearful I would betray her secret to her potential customers. *It's all right*, I said silently to her, *it's the diseased ones I'd betray if I could, before rounding them up, treating them and trying to make them understand how to increase their chances of staying healthy.*

But prostitution is as old as mankind, and without doubt the resultant diseases are too. I would be fighting a losing battle.

I stared up and down the line of seagoing craft.

And there, at the southern extremity of the quay and separated from her nearest neighbour by a good ship's length, was the vessel I sought.

For a few moments I stood and simply looked at her.

She had always been a beautiful ship and in my eyes she still was, despite the scars and the depredations of her long years of fighting. I felt the familiar lift of the heart as I ran my eyes from her bows to her stern, but then another emotion seemed to insinuate itself into the elation, as if a desirable woman had smiled seductively and displayed a mouth full of rotten teeth.

And I recalled what I was there for.

I broke into a run and pounded down the quay until the steep wooden side of the *Falco* rose up above me.

They must have been looking out for me, for even as I'd approached, the gangway was being run out – why had it not been already in place? – and it thumped down on the stones of the quay at the precise instant I had need of it. Looking up, I called out to the figure standing at its other end, 'Gabriel Taverner, physician. Permission to come aboard?'

I was close enough to see the extremity of relief on the young sailor's gaunt face, and it gave me the same premonition of dread I'd experienced on noticing the absence of the gangplank. But the young sailor had already run down to meet me, and, looking into his wide, frightened eyes, I guessed it was only discipline that kept him from grabbing my arm and urging me to hurry.

He leaned towards me, muttering words I barely made out. '*What?*' I demanded. 'Speak up!'

But he shook his head.

As he slunk away, leaving me to make my own way to the captain's cabin – he appeared to know who I was, and that I knew my way there – I didn't know if to be irritated or relieved at his reticence. For what I thought he'd said was, *Thank God you've come. We're all going mad here.*

*   *   *

It began when Sallie brought me a note that morning as I was finishing my breakfast. Receiving notes is nothing unusual, for it is how some of my patients choose to communicate, presumably finding it easier to reveal complaints of a personal and embarrassing nature by letter rather than face to face with their doctor. Sometimes the notes contain money in settlement of my bill.

I held out my hand. Even as Sallie put the folded piece of paper into my hand, my hopes of it containing money faded.

'It must have been left very early, afore I was up and about,' said my housekeeper. She was peering over my shoulder; I could sense her avid interest. 'I've been to and fro across the hall I don't know how many times, and I heard nothing,' she went on. 'Either they were here when it was still dark, or else whoever left it walked on air.' I turned in time to see her shudder and surreptitiously cross herself.

'No need to start conjuring up supernatural beings, Sallie,' I said briskly. 'Will you bring more bread? Celia will be down soon.'

Sallie muttered something and, turning, left the room.

My housekeeper has the rare ability to show disapproval and irritation in the very way she puts her feet to the floor.

With a smile, I spread out the missive on the table before me and began to read.

And, even as I did so, a flicker of superstitious dread ran through me and I wondered at Sallie's prescience . . .

This was what it said:

Aboard the *Falco*, Plymouth.
the eighth day of October in the year 1604.

To Gabriel Taverner, Rosewyke, Physician:
Gabe,

I urgently need your counsel and your help.

We are recently returned from the Caribbean and the Spanish Main. I shall not here describe to you the excess of assaults, both to our corporeal entities and to our spiritual wellbeing, that have been heaped upon us; for I pray that, in short time, I may recount same to you in person. In brief, I am close to despair.

I shall await you at midday in the inn known as the
Tamar Rose on Plymouth quay. If this time is not to your
convenience I shall return every day subsequently at the
selfsame hour until we meet.
    Your erstwhile captain
    Ezekiel Colt.

I had not managed to present myself at the Tamar Rose at midday,
nor at any time vaguely approximating it. As I was hurrying
back to Rosewyke from the last of my morning calls – all of
them local, which was why I was on foot and only then going
to fetch my horse in order to set out for Plymouth – the urgent
summons to tend the lad with the split head had turned up. And,
despite the desperate tone of Captain Zeke's note, despite my
intense curiosity to find out what had happened, despite
my growing dread for whatever fate had overcome my former
ship, I'd had no option but to answer it. The lad's life was starting
to slip away along with his pumping, streaming blood, and I
had only just been in time.

Now, ducking from long memory at the spot a few paces from
the door to the captain's cabin where for the first few days
on the *Falco* I had always banged my head, renewed guilt at
having ignored Captain Zeke's summons for almost a whole
day surged through me. But now, actually on board his ship
and aware even in these initial moments that something was
very wrong, the guilt was several times more powerful.

I tapped on the closed door and a well-remembered rasp
shouted, 'Enter!'

I opened the door and went in.

I had expected him to have changed to some extent, for it was
more than half a dozen years since I'd seen him. But as I stood
staring down at him, I felt my face drop in astonishment.

He met my eyes, his holding amusement. 'As bad as that?'
he said. He was seated at his table, and with a foot pushed out
the chair on the opposite side. 'Sit down before you fall down.'

I went on staring at him.

He was a short, stocky man, and had always been inclined
to fat. He did everything with enthusiasm, from killing the

Spanish through sleeping with pretty women to eating and, in particular, drinking, and his appetites were reflected in his face and his body. In my memory his thick hair was reddish chestnut, his spade-shaped beard pure red, his eyes light grey and deeply embedded in the wrinkles and pouches a sailor develops from staring at the sun on the bright water, yet nevertheless full of life and sparkle.

My memory was false. Now his hair was widely streaked with white, the plumpness had fallen off him and the lines of laughter around his eyes and brow had been replaced with the deep furrows of a habitual frown.

I sank into the chair. I said, 'Good God, what's happened?' And, before he could answer, I added almost angrily, 'And why did you need to summon me when surely you have a surgeon on board?'

He had been rubbing his face with his hands as I addressed him. Now as he bared himself before me, I saw the desperate pain in his expression and regretted my words. I began an apology: 'I am glad to be here, whatever the circumstances, and—'

He didn't let me finish. He said quietly, 'Gabe, you were with us in the Caribbean.'

It wasn't a question, for he knew full well I'd sailed in those magical deep-blue waters several times. 'I was.'

'Then maybe you'll understand,' he muttered. Before I could pounce on that he went on, 'That's where we've been. Dominica, Trinidad, Maracaibo, Portobello.' He glanced up at me. 'Paid our respects to Sir Francis while we were there, and *that* was a weird moment, I can tell you . . .' His eyes slid away and for a moment his face wore a strange, almost awe-struck expression. Grief, perhaps, for he would have followed Francis Drake to hell and back and had not forgiven the admiral's officers for ignoring his dying wish to be buried on land and instead sending him in full armour inside his lead-lined coffin to the bottom of the sea.

'Then on to Guatemala, and the plantations,' Captain Zeke resumed. 'We were watching out for our own ships, keeping the filthy hands of the Spanish and the Portuguese off what doesn't belong to them, reminding them whenever we needed

to that just because they've decided the whole fucking Caribbean
and all the lands encircling it belong to them, the rest of the
world doesn't necessarily see it that way.' He paused, waiting
while the sudden angry blood drained from his face.

I remembered him back in the days when I'd sailed with
him. He'd been a predator like no other, the combination of his
extraordinary seamanship and the swift, responsive, highly
manoeuvrable *Falco* making him invincible. So he believed – or
he'd acted as if he believed it, which amounts to much the same
thing – and so his crew believed, his ship's surgeon included.
The flames of our fury at the Spanish needed little stoking then,
for the Armada was a very recent memory and all of us were
still outraged at the cheek of the enemy for imagining they
could simply sail to our precious island and take us over. (We
might have felt differently, of course, had the elements not lent
a hand in making our victory so easy and so overwhelming,
but they did, and there it is. You don't meet many sailors – many
Englishmen at all, come to that – who won't point out that God
controls the weather as he does everything else, so whose side
was he on, then?)

In Captain Zeke's straightforward philosophy, one of the best
ways to maintain an advantage over an enemy was to keep his
pockets empty. A huge proportion of Spain's wealth came from
the Caribbean lands, so the job of the *Falco* and her sister ships
was to interrupt the flow of gold, silver, jewels and trade goods.
In the case of the near blockade that was imposed in some
places in the last years of the previous century, *interrupt* could
be translated into *stop*, or, more accurately, *take away and stow
safely in English ships*.

Captain Zeke gave a great sigh. 'So, we've been away near
a year, we've sustained damage here and there, we've lost crew
members to injury and sickness, and we're ready to sail for
home. More than ready – you can patch up a ship so she's
seaworthy out in those unholy, godforsaken places, Gabe, but
to do the job properly you need a home port, English oak and
English craftsmen.' Ezekiel Colt was a patriot to the last drop
of his rich English blood. 'We've left the Yucatan behind and
our course passes south of Cuba and Hispaniola before we
sail out into the Atlantic. Only we don't, because a storm comes

out of nowhere and, helpless before it, we're blown straight back to the western end of Hispaniola.' He shook his head, his expression full of horror. 'God's teeth, Gabe, I never saw anything like that storm. I thought it spelt the end of us, and I'd have been quaking in my boots because there was no priest on board and I was terrified of dying unshriven, only we were all far too busy mastering our horror and keeping the *Falco* afloat for room in our heads for anything else.' He stopped, and shot me a swift, calculating look; almost an assessing look, it struck me. Then he said very softly, 'There was something unnatural about that storm, Gabe, I'm telling you. It had – it was as if it had a purpose for us, and that was to stop us pursuing our chosen course and send us back into that accursed deep blue sea.'

'The Caribbean,' I murmured.

He gave an exclamation of impatience, as well he might. 'Of *course* the fucking Caribbean,' he muttered.

'It was just a storm,' I said mildly. 'You have weathered storms before, and not seen the malice of the supernatural acting through their violence.'

He gasped, crossing himself. '*Stop*,' he hissed.

The mood in the captain's cabin was strange, and suddenly I realized I was cold. Yet it had been a warm day, and the early evening was mild . . . Enough, I thought. 'So you found shelter and waited out the storm?' I prompted briskly.

Captain Zeke looked up, and there was a flash of his old humour in his eyes. 'We did,' he agreed. 'Our hosts were none too pleased at our presence, but they'd learned it's best not to antagonize the English and they helped us when we asked. They were as eager for us to be gone as we were to go, however, and we sailed as soon as the *Falco* was seaworthy, the holds full of fresh supplies to see us safely home. Or so we believed,' he added ominously.

He was silent for so long that it became obvious he was reluctant to continue. I waited. He would tell me in his own time; he had sent for me for that very reason and he was no coward. However long it took, I would hear the tale.

In an abrupt gesture he got up and lurched for the brandy bottle that stood on a shelf beside his bunk, collected a couple of fine crystal glasses and poured out two very generous measures. He shoved one across to me and picked up the other, gulping down about half in a few swift mouthfuls. Then he said, 'It began as soon as we left the last sight of land behind us.'

'What did?'

He shook his head. 'I don't know, Gabe, and that's the truth. It – the men—' He shrugged. 'There was an unease at first; just that. Unease. We should have been a cheerful ship, for we were going home, we'd done well out of the voyage, there'd be good profits for every one of us, the losses to our ship's company were tolerable and no more than to be expected, and there were neither badly injured nor sick men among us. Not then,' he added ominously. 'Yet for all that, there was grumbling, complaining, arguments and even outright fighting almost from the start, and although I was reluctant, for the crew were good men and we'd all been together a long time, I had no choice but to hand out discipline. Oh, nothing terrible,' he added before I could comment, 'nothing worse than cut rations and a couple of minor floggings.'

'And did those measures improve the mood?'

'No, they made it worse. And—' He paused, rubbing fiercely at one eye with the knuckle of his forefinger. 'And I saw something beneath the moaning and the squabbling. I saw what was causing it.' He looked at me, and the white of the eye he'd been attacking was red. 'They were afraid, Gabe. My men, who'd been through so much with me, who'd stood fast amid battles, storms and the worst the oceans could throw at them, were scared.'

'Of what?' I said.

'I didn't know at first,' Captain Zeke admitted. 'Then I sensed a whisper of it myself, and I understood.'

'A whisper? What do you mean? Was someone muttering imprecations?'

Captain Zeke smiled grimly. 'The down-to-earth Doctor Taverner, always so literal,' he murmured. 'No, it wasn't an actual whisper, although God knows there were other noises nobody could explain . . . I was being poetic, Gabe. To put it more plainly, I wondered if what was frightening the men so badly emanated from a part of the ship inhabited by them and not by me, so late one evening I went down into the lower decks and made my way straight through the ship from bow to stern.' He reached for the brandy and poured himself a second measure. 'I found all was pretty much as I expected, although some of the crates of supplies had shifted slightly and I issued a reminder to myself to send someone to see to it the next day. Otherwise there were the usual sights and smells, quite a lot of water slopping around, rats. Then—' He stopped, drained his glass and said very quickly, as if he needed to take a rush at it, 'Then I saw the shape of a man.'

'A man? One of the crew, no doubt, come to assist you in your—'

'Shut up, Gabe,' Captain Zeke said wearily. 'Of course it wasn't one of the crew. It – he – was skeletal, huge eyes in a dark face, barefoot and just the remains of tattered garments hanging on his bones, and his skin was blue. He was there one moment and gone the next.' He leaned his elbows on the table and pushed his face close to mine. 'There one moment and gone the next,' he repeated. In case I'd missed the point, he added very softly, 'He wasn't real, Gabe. He was a ghost.' He paused. 'And he wasn't alone.'

I said, and it was an unthinking, automatic response, 'I do not believe in ghosts.'

My brave assertion hung in the silence for what seemed a long time. Then Captain Zeke nodded. 'So I have always assumed. Which is why I wanted your counsel, and why I am reassured to have your presence on my ship. My *haunted* ship,' he added very firmly.

'You want me to reassure your crew,' I said, determined, I think, to ignore this wild talk of ghosts and hauntings and remain firmly in the realm of the logical and the tangible. 'To see if perhaps they are all suffering from some ailment that might cause visual and auditory hallucinations, and thus have given rise to these unlikely beliefs. Possibly there is some dietary deficiency, and I can very easily look into that, and into other possible causes for—'

Captain Zeke was watching me, a strange expression on his face. It was as if he was waiting for me to wind to a halt;

or, more likely, to work out something that he knew and I
didn't . . .

And after a time I knew what it was.

For I had recalled a question I'd asked him at the start of
our conversation: *why did you need to summon me when surely
you have a surgeon on board?*

So in a different form of words I asked it again: 'So, Captain
Zeke,' I said, 'why not ask your own doctor to advise you?' He
didn't answer. 'You do have a ship's surgeon?' I persisted.

'Ashleigh Winterbourn Snell,' he said. 'Young, eager, full of
book knowledge and desperate to show it. Set out right from
the start to demonstrate that he was ready for anything, that he
would be right beside the men in the worst of their ills and
their injuries and do his best for them, that he could pick up a
sword and wave it around to fairly good effect when required.'
Captain Zeke paused, glancing at me. 'He wasn't you, but he
was all right. He had courage enough, until he had to face
something he couldn't deal with.'

I was beginning to have a deep concern about Ashleigh
Winterbourn Snell. 'He's dead, isn't he?'

Captain Zeke muttered something, which I thought was *God
rest him.*

'What happened to him?' I demanded.

'He took your view, Gabe, that ghosts didn't exist and the men
were suffering some mass delusion. He made them spend their
time on board in the good fresh air, as he phrased it, doing exercises. Exercises!' he said scathingly. 'As if a seaman's life is
anything but exercise. He got them on additional doses of lemon
juice, he tried other variations to the diet, he tried taking their
minds off their fears with evening entertainments, as he called
them – getting them telling stories, having jolly sing-songs.'

'He sounds like a good, conscientious man,' I said, stung on
my fellow doctor's behalf by the captain's sarcastic tone.

'He was, he was, and I'm not belittling either him or how
hard he tried,' Captain Zeke said swiftly. 'Only, perhaps, his
utter refusal to open his mind a little. To ask himself whether,
if a single man in a ship's company believes one thing and
everyone else believes another, the man who stands by himself
ought not to look a little deeper.'

'He could not do that,' I replied. 'He would have taken the view that he alone stood for reason and sanity; that he as ship's surgeon was responsible for everyone else's physical and mental well-being and must at all costs hold firm.'

'That was precisely the view he did take,' Captain Zeke said sadly. 'Even when others could *see* the blue ghost flitting right across in front of him, he shouted out that it wasn't really there, it did not exist, and he held up his two hands in the shape of the holy cross like a shield as he advanced towards it. But then—' Captain Zeke faltered. 'But then something happened: I don't know what it was, whether poor Doctor Ashleigh saw, or heard, or maybe even smelt something, but he gave a great cry and his face suffused with blood, and he fell back onto the deck and we all heard the crack of his head on the wood.'

'He was dead?' I asked, my voice barely above a whisper.

'No, although it would have been better if he'd died.' Captain Zeke's voice had faltered on the words, and he paused for a moment. 'He came round after a few hours and we all realized he'd lost his wits,' he went on dully. 'We'd got him down to his bunk and when he woke up we had to restrain him, for he was wild. His eyes had gone huge, he was foaming at the mouth and he kept screaming, "I see you! I see you!" Jesus, Gabe, I can still hear him now.'

'Then he's alive?' I was half on my feet. 'But I thought you just implied he was dead! You must take me to him, the poor man needs—'

But Captain Zeke put out a very strong arm and shoved me back in my chair. 'He's not here, Gabe. He – it was hard to keep watch on him all the time, for we were all exhausted and nobody was prepared to stand guard over him in the depths of the night, for that was when his mania was at its height. I made sure he was firmly tied and couldn't move from where we left him, but he must have had a blade hidden somewhere and he managed to cut himself free.' Then, his voice almost a sob, he cried, 'We were nearly home, Gabe! That's the pity of it.'

'What did he do?'

'It was early in the morning – a beautiful dawn, the rising sun ahead of us painting pink and gold spangles on the water, the breeze soft and the sea calm. The lad up in the crow's nest called out that he'd sighted land – we were past the Scillies so it would have been the tip of Cornwall – and we were all so relieved. Dear God, I can't tell you how good that moment was. But then there was a sudden clamour from below, and the sound of pounding feet, and Ashleigh Winterbourn Snell appeared, laughing like the madman he was and crying out that he was an Englishman, a Devonian, true and loyal and would lie in English waters, off a Cornish shore, and before anyone could get a hand on him he seemed to fly across the deck and he threw himself into the sea. He disappeared, Gabe. We circled and searched for hours, convinced we'd find him, but we didn't.'

After a very long silence I said, 'What do you want me to do?'

TWO

C aptain Zeke stared at me in silence for several moments. I thought he was mentally forming his response, but it turned out I was wrong. When eventually he spoke, he said in a conversational voice, 'Have you noticed something?'

I had no idea what it was that I should have spotted. His ship was weary and in need of a considerable amount of repair, but that was to be expected after a long voyage. His crew, by his own account, were in a poor state; perhaps with a bodily sickness with which I could help, perhaps with some strange mass malfunction of the mind, but he and I had just been speaking of that so it couldn't be what he was referring to. With a shrug, I said, 'What?'

'You have been on board the *Falco* now for some time, Gabe, yet you sit here with me with no sign of unease or discomfort other than the frown of puzzlement which, I imagine, has been put on your face by what I have just told you.'

Of course.

In his note he had summoned me to a meeting ashore, in a quayside tavern, and it was only because I had failed to arrive that I had come hurrying to the *Falco*. He would not have suggested it, knowing better than any man save myself what happened nowadays when I went on board a ship. He had witnessed my terrible seasickness as we sailed home from the Caribbean the last time I went to sea; he was there when I first began to realize that the blow to the head I'd sustained in port had done some damage to my sense of balance which would never be repaired. He had watched as time after time I'd gone out again on the *Falco* to test myself, each time with the same result. He had sat with me in the worst of Plymouth's filthy drinking places when self-pity overcame me as finally I faced the brutal truth that I would have to leave the seagoing life I loved.

Now, as understanding dawned, I sat very still, sending out

imaginary feelers to my head and my stomach. Just for an
instant there was a flash of queasiness, but I told myself it was
my imagination, and it passed.

He was watching me intently. 'Well?' he barked.

I shook my head – carefully – and still there was no vertigo,
no nausea. 'I'm all right,' I said cautiously.

He began to smile.

But I couldn't let him believe something that wasn't true.

'We are in port, Captain, and it is a fine, calm day with the
sea as flat as a village pond,' I said firmly. 'From the little I
understand about my complaint, I deduce that it is set off by
motion. Today there *is* no motion.' I stood up abruptly, for I
could not bear to speak of this any more. 'Again I ask you:
what do you want me to do?'

He rose to his feet. 'Ah, well,' I heard him mutter. Then,
fixing me with a hard stare, he said, 'I want you to search my
ship with me. I want you to walk in the places I have walked,
pause in the dark spaces where my crew have seen and sensed
things that have terrified them almost out of their wits and where
they won't go back to even if threatened with a flogging.'
Suddenly he banged his clenched fist down on the table, the
loud sound making me jump. 'Sweet *Jesus*, Gabe, how do you
think it made me feel, to tell a man I'd have him whipped because
he wouldn't venture into a black space where I myself was afraid
to go? God alive, whatever haunts this ship has turned me into
a coward and a hypocrite!' His furious words echoed round the
cabin. Then in a quieter voice – and I could see the effort it took
to bring himself under control – he said, 'I want you to do this
with open senses and, more importantly, an open mind, and then
try to tell me that evil does not dwell aboard my ship.'

I rose to my feet in exasperation, glaring down at him. 'I
will tell you that right now!' I cried. 'I am a physician, not a
witch-finder or a ghost hunter! Instead of crawling into the
deepest and foulest reaches of the *Falco*'s lowest decks, let me
instead see your men, talk to them, examine them, hear what
they have to say about their symptoms. Then, armed with all
the information I can gather, I shall return to Rosewyke to
consult my books and my diaries and see if I can work out
what ails the crew and how to treat it.'

Captain Zeke looked at me. 'I will make a bargain with you,' he said.

'Go on.'

'Do as I beg you, and search the ship. Then, if you find nothing to back up what I now fully believe to be true, I will let you loose on my crew.'

It was the best – probably the only – deal he was going to offer. I stuck out my hand and we sealed it.

The *Falco* was eerily quiet.

It was true that many of the men had gone ashore, for in port only those on watch or with specific duties to perform were required on board. I could not help but wonder how many of those who had slunk away would decide never to come back. But this was not the quiet of a deserted place, for the ship was far from deserted. All over the topmost deck, where the captain and I began the tour, teams were working on repairs. There should have been the usual sounds of an adequately paid work-force with a satisfying job to do, yet it seemed to me that the men spoke in whispers, their mood subdued, and many kept glancing over their shoulders as if sensing they were watched by unseen eyes. One man wore a heavy wooden crucifix around his neck. Another crossed himself repeatedly. A third was muttering under his breath: words from the Paternoster, repeated over and over.

Deliver us from evil.

The strange silence intensified as we began our descent through the ship. One deck down, we began at the bow with the shot locker and progressed past the heavy guns. Again, men were at work; again, nobody spoke. In one place, they'd even set a lad on watch, as if they were fearful to bend to their labours without someone to keep his eyes on the approaches.

On that same deck we came to the surgeon's cabin.

I stopped – I couldn't help myself – and stood in the doorway. Doctor Ashleigh had placed his chest precisely where I used to keep mine. The work space was set out with care and an eye for efficiency, and my sense of fellowship with him increased. I pictured him here, that poor young man, and for a moment I thought I could even see him, a tall, gangling figure bending

his long back over a table as he studied some small puzzle, the
mutter as he talked to himself under his breath . . .

I shook the fancy away and followed the captain on
towards the stern.

We continued our descent. A handful of men were busy
on the next deck down, removing some empty water barrels
and starting on cleaning out the space where they had been.
There was a rustling of rats from somewhere out of sight. The
men paused to touch their foreheads as the captain passed.
Nobody spoke.

Below, the galley was cold and deserted, the cooking fire
out, the storage spaces empty. It was dark down here, and
I was glad of the lanterns Captain Zeke and I had brought
with us.

We went through the narrow little opening between the galley
and the first of the holds beyond. We went on, presently coming
to the place where the great mast bored down through the ship
on the way to its roots in the keel. More storage spaces. There
was a smell of rotten meat. The space was airless and chill.
Our lanterns illuminated a circle round us, but the further spaces
of this deep place were dark and sinister, and I felt a sense of
dread creeping over me.

Captain Zeke was working his way past abandoned barrels,
a pile of broken buckets, a three-legged stool missing a leg and
lying on its side like a dead dog. He went on through a low
opening into a second hold, a third, a fourth, and, afraid to lose
his light and his presence, I went after him.

I'd been the one to say there was no such thing as ghosts,
that it was mere fancy to claim a ship could be haunted. Yet
there we were, Captain Zeke and I, and it was he who forged
ahead, I who had to force every single step as I followed his
lead.

We must have been close to the stern now. We had crawled
into increasingly small spaces, moving aside stacked crates that
looked as if they'd stood there since the *Falco* was launched
and covering ourselves in a disgusting mixture of dust, very
old cobwebs and a sticky, moist, clammily cold substance that
seemed to adhere to absolutely everything. And the smell was
becoming intolerable.

Captain Zeke stopped, straightened up and held his lantern at arm's length. We were in a cramped, dark hole of a place, and I had no idea of its original purpose: now it seemed to be a receptacle for bits of junk that nobody knew what to do with. The floor seemed to be on a slant, and with a faint sense of unease I realized that we were well towards the stern, above the rudder, at the place where the lowest deck began to slope steeply up and away from the keel. I held my lantern beside his, and slowly we turned in a full circle and stared into every corner. At the rear, immediately opposite the narrow entrance, was a roughly-stacked pile of broken bits of wood, some the remains of furniture damaged beyond repair, some offcuts from ancient maintenance jobs. We moved towards it, and the stench grew almost overpowering.

'What *is* that?' Captain Zeke said. I sensed he had intended to speak loudly, in defiance, perhaps, of the awful conditions, but it was as if the intelligent darkness all around us drew in the words even as he breathed them out. I felt a shiver of sheer dread.

'It smells like shit,' I replied, my own words sucked away just as his had been.

'Not down here.'

'I'm not saying it *is*, just that it smells like it,' I protested in a harsh whisper. 'A lot of things smell like shit.'

He had bent down to the loosely stacked woodpile, and now was poking at it. I wished he would stop. 'There can't be anything under all that,' I began, even as he gave it a sudden shove.

The stack collapsed, pieces of raw timber and worked wood of various sizes and weights rolling towards us and several crashing into us. Both of us leapt back, and Captain Zeke muttered a sharp curse.

'Are you injured?' I demanded.

'Nothing serious,' he replied, briskly rubbing his shin.

The smell was appalling now.

Holding out our lanterns, we illuminated a low, roughly circular opening in the bulkhead against which the wood had been stacked.

Our free hands over our noses and mouths, we lay down and

edged through it on elbows and knees, Captain Zeke going ahead.

I was bent double and still restricted by the sides of the opening as he emerged into whatever lay beyond. His gasp of utter disgust made me straighten up instinctively and very unwisely, so that I cracked my head violently on a beam right above me. Bright lights flashed across my vision and I felt a wave of nausea. The stench was making me retch and, fleetingly, there was another smell as well, and it had elements that I knew I ought to recognize. But then, dizzy and reeling, I fell, both knees crashing on the sloping wooden boards with an echoing crump like cannon fire.

I felt his hands on me as he dragged me out into the hellish space beyond. The smell was far, far worse now and I wished he'd pushed me back the other way.

I managed to stand up. Shaking from the sharp pain inside my skull, I followed the line of Captain Zeke's pointing arm as he held his lantern over what he had just spotted.

It was a large, squat barrel, perhaps half a man's height and roughly two to two and a half foot in breadth. It stood in the corner, leaning against the bulkhead through which we'd just crawled, roped firmly in place even though the sloping floor worked in its favour, forcing it back against the wooden wall. I puzzled for a moment over how it had come to be in that tiny space with its low, narrow access – I'd just had a blow to the head and wasn't at my sharpest – and then I realized: it had gone in the same way Captain Zeke and I had, on its side.

We stared at it, our hands firmly over our faces. The lid sat askew so that the contents were visible, glittering as they caught the light from our lanterns.

And I thought that one thing was sure: it wasn't going to be taken out the same way it went in.

For it was full almost to the top with bodily waste. Unless the lid could be sealed in some way that would be totally leak-proof, it wasn't going anywhere until it had been emptied.

I spared several moments' compassionate sympathy for whatever poor sod got landed with *that* job.

I said, 'Captain, I believe your ghosts are now explained. You've had illicit passengers down here.' I kicked my foot around the detritus on the floor: meat bones, a rock-hard heel of bread, a little pile of rotten vegetables.

He didn't reply.

I thought perhaps he was embarrassed. He had all but sworn his ship was haunted; he had been utterly confident that he would prove it to me. Instead we had just found evidence of a far more rational explanation, pretty much as I'd known we would.

But then he turned to face me, and I saw his expression.

His eyes were wide, the whites showing all around the pupils. His mouth was open as if he was halfway through a huge yawn. He was shaking, and beads of sweat stood out on his deathly pale flesh.

'*Listen!*' he hissed.

But I could hear nothing except the slap of water from somewhere close by. 'I can't hear—' I began.

Then something hit me. I flinched, my upflung protective arm expecting to encounter bone and sinew, but there was nothing there.

Nothing there.

But I'd felt it, heard it . . .

There was evil in that dark and horrible space, humming like a hive of furious hornets in a chimney, the sound rising in pitch until it beat against my head and I cast down my lantern, crying aloud and stuffing my fingers in my agonized ears. I screwed my eyes shut.

And then I saw it.

A dark countenance, with wild, white-rimmed eyes of darkest brown, the black pupils merging with the brown irises so that it was like staring into a bottomless well. The black hair was tight-curled, and the curls writhed and wriggled like maggots. The brow was pronounced, overhanging those terrible eyes like a cliff, and the beautifully sculptured nose flared into wide, distended nostrils above the full-lipped mouth. I wanted to look away but I could not; I wanted to close my eyes but they were already closed.

And as I watched something happened to the nose . . . It began to extend, to flow towards me, and as it did so it changed shape, the wide tip narrowing and elongating as if it was made

of clay beneath the hands of a sculptor. On, on it came, and I
knew its intent was full of evil and malice. It was not a nose
now, it was a snout, and the flesh was covered in warty lumps
. . . I'd seen a snout like that, I knew what it was, and I heard
myself moan in terror.

The snout was huge now, right up against my face, and the
creature began to open its mouth, slowly, slowly at first, then
with a great snapping crack.

And the crocodile's jaws gaped at me as its deadly rows of
sharp, inward-leaning teeth began to close.

I was on the floor, my head in the filth. I gave a great yell and
began to struggle up, trying to stare in every direction at once,
but Captain Zeke's strong hands were on my shoulders holding
me down, and his warm human presence was all around me.
'You're all right,' he panted, 'it's stopped.'

I rounded on him. 'You saw it? That–that *thing* that came
out of the face?'

I knew from his expression he hadn't. 'I saw nothing,
Gabe. But I heard it, that wailing.'

I had heard no wailing.

I got to my knees, leaning heavily on my hands. 'We must
get away from this place,' I muttered.

'We will, but first we must search it.'

There was no gainsaying him.

With reluctance so profound that it almost paralysed me, I
staggered to my feet.

The space we were in was tiny – perhaps three paces by two
– and the deck above bore down hard just above our heads
while the deck beneath our feet sloped upwards. Captain Zeke
could just about stand upright, but he was considerably shorter
than me. I was fighting a growing sense of claustrophobia,
having to tell myself very forcefully that the ceiling was *not*
steadily coming closer.

Captain Zeke was moving slowly around the perimeter in
one direction, and I did the same in the other. Each of us
held up our lantern, feeling with the free hand all around the
oak walls, across the boards of the floor, around each beam
and rib. We were perhaps a pace apart, about to meet and

complete our inspection, when I heard him draw in a sharp breath.

'Gabe,' he said in a hoarse whisper.

I went to stand beside him, adding my light to his.

The body was tiny. Trying to gauge its height, I reckoned about four foot, perhaps less. It was skinny, almost skeletal, the flesh desiccated and yellowish. I thought in the first horrified moment that it was that of a child.

But then, leaning in closer and holding my lantern right beside the face, I saw the yawning mouth. There were gaps where teeth had been lost, and those that remained were worn down with long use. Whoever this man was, he had died in advanced old age.

The body had been pinned to the rib by means of an iron spike through the neck.

Captain Zeke cleared his throat and said very quietly, 'Is that how he was killed?'

'No,' I said instantly. 'The spike was driven into the wood quite recently.' I pointed to where a splinter of oak had been split away as the spike went in. 'That looks fresh.'

Captain Zeke nodded. 'That's something,' he muttered.

In any case, I reflected, life had left this man a long, long time ago.

The body was clad in some sort of flowing robe that clung to its bony protuberances. The fabric was pale and perhaps had once been white, and it was torn and, in places, little more than tatters of cloth. There was the remains of a headdress – a turban of some sort – that seemed to consist of a long strip of the same cloth, intricately wound. Delicately raising an edge, I could make out sparse tufts of tightly curled hair, black streaked with grey. I ran my hand down over the shoulder and chest, the concave belly and the hips . . .

The pelvic girdle stood out stark, interrupting the fall of the ragged garment. With an exclamation, I pushed the cloth aside and held the light right up to where the legs bifurcated from the pubis.

'It's a woman,' I said.

Captain Zeke and I stacked the biggest pieces of wood back in place, much as they'd been when we made our discovery, and made our way as swiftly as we could back through the dark spaces of the lowest deck and up towards the light. Emerging on the open deck, both of us stopped and simply stood there in the daylight, breathing in the clean air. Never had it smelled so sweet.

A handful of the men had quietly come to stand around us. One of them said, 'Well?'

I waited for Captain Zeke to speak. He didn't. He glanced at me, and I thought he gave a faint nod as if to say, carry on.

'Not ghosts, lads,' I said with all the certainty I could muster, telling myself firmly that the ghastly vision I'd seen was no more than the aftermath of the blow to my head. 'There has indeed been a presence down there on the lowest deck' – there was a muffled exclamation and I saw at least two sailors cross themselves – 'but it was a human presence: unbeknownst to you, you've had men secretly living aboard.'

Somebody began a protest: 'But the blue men! I *saw* them, and you can't tell me—' But someone else quickly stopped it with a curse and what sounded like a surreptitious blow.

'There's evidence that people were down there,' I went on, raising my voice in case anyone else felt like interrupting, 'and it's clear that they've been helping themselves to food and water, and that they used a barrel for their waste. Ghosts don't eat and drink, lads, and they don't piss and shit either.'

Now the muttering came from more than one part of the group of men who encircled us. Before speculation could grow, Captain Zeke spoke.

'Enough,' he growled. He didn't raise his voice; he didn't have to, for his crew fell silent and attentive at that one word. 'Doctor Taverner is right,' he said. 'Whatever has been on board with us was made of flesh and blood. They've gone now, whoever they were.'

There was a stunned silence. Then a tall man with a sleeve of tattoos and a scar on his chin said, 'How did they get off without us seeing them?'

Captain Zeke shrugged. 'The more important question, Willum, is how did they get on board? And where?'

A spate of chatter broke out – excited, nervous, alarmed – and it occurred to me that it was only the present, extraordinary circumstances that had made the men forget their discipline and start talking among themselves when their captain had just told them not to. Looking round at the faces, I realized that my matter-of-fact explanation, my insistence that the *Falco* was not haunted but had given a bunch of men a free passage across the Atlantic, hadn't really convinced them at all.

I felt a sudden wave of vertigo, and for a moment thought I was going to be sick. Risking a swift look out across the water, I saw that it was still calm. Not the old trouble, then, I told myself firmly. I'd just had a blow to the head – putting up my hand, my exploring fingers felt a lump like an egg on the back of my skull – and no doubt that was the cause of my symptoms.

But, whatever the reason, I had to go. If I stayed I risked throwing up in front of Captain Zeke's crew, and that might make them think I might not believe my solid, rational explanation any more than they did.

'I must search out the coroner,' I said quietly to Captain Zeke, drawing him a few paces away from the group of sailors. He nodded, turned to issue orders – he too must have realized that standing around speculating wasn't good for discipline or morale – and then rejoined me.

'You look awful,' he said bluntly.

'I *feel* awful.'

'That was a hard knock you took, down there.'

'Yes.'

'The coroner?' he said, turning the word into a question.

'You and I just discovered a body. Your ship is in Plymouth harbour, which falls within the coroner's jurisdiction. Before you tell me it's very far from a recent death' – for he had opened his mouth to speak – '*I* must tell *you* that it makes no difference.'

I could sense the anger building up in him. 'So I must endure some skinny, dried-up, busy-bodying local damned official poking his long nose into every corner of *my* ship?'

'Yes,' I said firmly, with a private smile at how far Captain Zeke's imaginary coroner differed from reality. 'First thing in the morning. Don't let anyone go near that hidden space in the meantime.'

He gave a sudden guffaw. 'You think anyone'd go *near* even
if I threatened the lash if they didn't? Goodbye, Gabe. See you
tomorrow.'

Then he turned and stomped back towards his cabin.

I made my stumbling way back to the inn where I'd left Hal,
mounted up and headed out of the town. The thought of the
long ride home was too depressing – my head was pounding
now and the nausea threatened to return – so I concentrated on
remembering the quickest way to Theophilus Davey's residence,
at Withybere. 'Between the village and Warleigh Point,' I
muttered to myself, the precise form of words Theo had used
when he first told me where he lived. We had become good
friends since then, despite the fact that there were secrets
between us; dark matters that Theo suspected and the truth of
which he would never discover.

He was married to a fair and comely woman called Elaine
and they had three lively children. I would be disturbing them
in the evening, in what ought to have been family time, but
there was no help for it. I hoped they would understand that I
wasn't going to make it all the way back to Rosewyke without
a rest, and in any case it was my duty to inform Theo that there
was a body on board the *Falco*.

I reached Theo's house. I slid off Hal's back and fell over. I
picked myself up, made sure I had secured his reins to the ring
in the wall, then tapped on the door.

It opened, spilling out light, warmth, the sound of voices –
someone was singing, an adult, female voice with lighter children's
voices joining in – and the smell of food. Catching sight of me,
Theo bit back the greeting and took hold of my arm, taking my
weight and helping me inside.

'My horse . . .' I said. 'I've left Hal outside, he's—'

'*Peter!*' Theo yelled. A voice called back and Theo said, 'See
to the doctor's horse.'

I relaxed a little.

'In here.' Theo was helping me through the open door that
led to the family's quarters, supporting me as together we
climbed up the stairs, crossed a wide landing and went into
the parlour. The fire was lit and he lowered me down onto a

settle. Staring at me, his face full of concern, he said gruffly, 'What in God's name has happened to you?'

'I was on my old ship and I hit my head.'

'Your ship?' He looked deeply perplexed.

I managed a smile. 'It's all right, Theo, I'm not going back to sea. I had a message. My former captain, Ezekiel Colt, said that—' But I didn't think I could manage the details, not just then. 'He wanted me to investigate something, and in the course of so doing, we came across a body in a secret space behind one of the bulkheads.'

'One of the crew?' Theo was watching me, his bright blue eyes narrowed in concentration.

I shook my head, which made me moan in pain. 'No. Definitely not. It's not a recent death, but—'

'But it's my business anyway,' he finished for me.

'I told the captain we'd be back there first thing in the morning,' I said, leaning my head against the settle's hard wooden back and closing my eyes. 'The spot where we found it has been secured and Captain Colt will make sure nobody tampers with it.'

'Good,' Theo said.

I opened my eyes and sat up straight. 'Now, if I could trouble you for a drink, and perhaps a piece of bread' – I wasn't hungry, but I knew I wouldn't get home unless I ate something – 'I'll be on my way.'

'Don't be an arse, Gabe,' Theo said. 'You are not fit to ride further tonight. I shall fetch Elaine, and she will tend to your injury, and then there will be good food and a warm bed for you.'

'But Celia—'

'We shall send word to your delightful sister that you had to call here late on a matter of some urgency – which is no more than the truth – and that we prevailed upon you to dine with us and stay the night.' He grinned. 'I won't mention the smack on the head unless you do.'

It was probably a measure of how hard I'd hit myself that I gave in so readily. Theo brought paper, quill and ink, and I wrote out a brief note. Theo summoned one of the stable lads and he rode off to deliver it. I think I might have slipped into a brief sleep round about then, and when I woke up, Elaine was beside me. She was pressing something very cold to the lump on my head, and her touch was as gentle as down.

'I'm sorry,' I muttered.

'No need,' she replied. 'Will you eat? You should,' she added reprovingly.

'Yes, then.'

She brought a bowl of savoury-smelling stew and some pieces of bread, and I managed about half.

Then Theo returned, and between them he and his wife helped me to bed. I can't remember when a soft mattress, warm blankets and a blessedly cool pillow under my sore head ever felt so good. I was afraid I would dream – there had been horrors enough that evening – but, after a sudden vivid image of a crocodile that shot me back to wakefulness just as I was slipping into sleep, I didn't. I slept deeply and was aware of nothing until I heard a boy's voice saying brightly, 'Doctor Gabriel, you snore even louder than *Daddy*!' and, opening my eyes, I saw that it was morning and realized with great relief that my headache had gone.

In a modest but scrupulously clean lodging house set a few streets back from the Plymouth quayside, a dark-haired man in a cloak of costly blue wool let himself into a room on the uppermost floor. Two other men were already inside, one standing beside the small window and staring down into the busy street, the other lying sick and gaunt-faced on one of the narrow beds, propped up by pillows.

The newcomer took off his cloak and flung it across another of the three beds with a furious gesture. 'Those women!' he spat out. 'They are brazen whores, and they will not leave a man alone!'

The man by the window smiled to himself. He too was dark-eyed, but his once-black hair was largely white. He was almost into his seventh decade but looked older, for his face was lean and deeply lined, his skin sallow. 'You must act as if they do not exist,' he murmured.

The man on the bed – roughly the same age as the man by the window – added, 'You are too handsome, my friend.

The women like a good-looking man, it makes their job more enjoyable.' He began to chuckle, and the laughter turned swiftly into a violent fit of coughing.

Ignoring them both, the newcomer said starkly, 'The men have fled. I have not been able to pick up a trace of them.' Then, ruthlessly cutting across the angry response of his companions, his dark eyes narrowing to glittering slits, he added, 'But all is not lost.' He paused. 'They have left *her* on the ship.'

The white-haired man gasped, crossing himself rapidly several times. The sick man, nodding slowly, a cruel smile twisting his mouth, said softly, 'And wherever *she* is, they will not be far away.'

THREE

Theo and I were back on the quayside bright and early. We stood at the foot of the gangplank and I called up to the sailor standing on deck. Even as I did so, Captain Zeke appeared at his side and beckoned us to come aboard.

'Captain Zeke, this is Theophilus Davey, Coroner. Theo, Captain Ezekiel Colt.'

I watched as they shook hands, noticing how carefully they were eyeing each other up. Then, with a grin, Captain Zeke said, 'You're not how I imagined you, Master Coroner,' which Theo greeted with an enigmatic smile.

The crew seemed to have melted away. Other than a lad working on a sail up in the bows, I didn't spot anybody, although there were sounds of activity from various parts of the ship. 'A peaceful night?' I said quietly to Captain Zeke.

'Peaceful enough,' he said gruffly.

We made our way down through the lower decks until once again we stood in the cold galley. Then we progressed through the maze of large holds and small storage spaces until we reached the stack of wood against the furthest bulkhead. Captain Zeke and I moved it aside and the opening was revealed. Captain Zeke looked at Theo, at the narrow little aperture and back at Theo. 'I'll manage,' Theo said.

Theo Davey is by no means a small man.

Captain Zeke went first, Theo followed and I pushed him from the rear. It was bad enough for me, and Theo is much broader than I. But he made no complaint, and presently all three of us were in the secret space, Captain Zeke standing upright, Theo and I crouching.

'You had men hiding in *here*?' Theo demanded; I'd given him a brief account of yesterday's discovery as we rode over.

'So we believe,' Captain Zeke replied. He nodded towards the barrel, whose cover was now firmly in place and, to an extent, lessening the terrible stench. 'That seems to prove it; that and the food remains scattered on the floor.'

Theo nodded. 'The body?'

Captain Zeke led him to it. All three of us carried lanterns, and we held them up.

Theo stood for some time without speaking, staring at the little body, lifting the folds of cloth, peering into the face with its wide-open mouth. He inspected the spike, then, turning to me, said, 'Not the means of death, I'll warrant.'

'No,' I agreed.

Eventually he stepped back, absently wiping his hands against the skirt of his long robe. Not that the gesture was necessary, for the corpse was desiccated and not a drop of bodily fluid remained anywhere upon or within it.

Captain Zeke and I waited, and I sensed the captain's barely suppressed anger at having to yield authority to another man on board his own ship. But suppress it he did; I decided that something about Theo – perhaps the uncomplaining way he'd squeezed his large frame through that small entry; perhaps his quiet air of knowing precisely what he was about – must have impressed my former captain. And *that* didn't happen very often.

Eventually Theo sighed and said, 'Seen enough, Gabe?'

'I have.'

'Very well. Captain Colt, I have given orders to my men to come and fetch the corpse and they are already on their way. They will take it down and bring it to my offices, where Doctor Taverner will examine it?' Again he turned to me.

'Of course,' I agreed. I could have added that I'd have fought off any man who tried to take my place.

Theo was staring round the small space. 'I sense there is more here than meets the eye,' he muttered. So he was picking it up too, I thought.

'I plan to have this area cleared out,' Captain Zeke said. 'Provided there is no objection?'

Theo smiled at him. 'It is your ship, Captain Colt,' he said courteously. 'I would, however, be very grateful if you would share with me any discoveries you make?' He turned it into a question, which I thought was wise.

'I will,' Captain Zeke said. He was staring at the barrel of waste. 'First job will be to empty that fu— that blasted thing.'

'How will you do that?' Theo asked.

Captain Zeke smiled grimly. 'I shall summon every man still on board, taking on extra hands if I need to, as I am sure I shall, until I have a human chain stretching from here to the upper deck. Each man will have a bucket, and the buckets will be passed up and down the line until the barrel is empty, when it will be turned on its side and removed in the same manner in which it must have gone in.'

Theo, already backing away, crouched down and began to wriggle out through the hole in the bulkhead. 'Let me know if you find anything,' his voice floated back.

'Other than an awful lot of shit?' Captain Zeke murmured. But I didn't think Theo could have heard.

Theo and I had been back at his residence for not much over an hour when a cart pulled up outside. We had used the time for Theo to ask me a series of perceptive questions about my time on the *Falco* and, perhaps more pertinently, about her captain and her crew.

'I recognize barely more than a handful of men among the ship's company,' I'd told him, 'for it's seven years since I was of their number, and a ship's crew does not remain constant.'

I had, however, told him rather more about Ezekiel Colt.

Now we stood side by side out in the road, staring down at the small shape lying beneath a dirty blanket on the planks of the cart. Theo's man Jarman Hodge jumped down from the bench seat across the front, handing the reins to one of the two lads he'd taken with him.

'Grim place, that hidden hold, or locker, or whatever it was,' he said. He didn't elaborate. The lads had slid the corpse off the back of the cart and now stood holding it between them, still draped in the blanket. 'Where do you want it?'

'Down in the cellar,' Theo replied. He didn't need to ask me, for I had worked down there before, many times. Quite often we'd had to move decaying bodies up the road to the crypt of another house that Theo rented for the purpose, for his family lived adjacent to his work place and it was not fair to force them to endure the smell.

Not that this was going to be a factor now . . .

The two lads carried the body as easily as if it had been a bag of bones, which in effect it was. With a nod, Jarman Hodge got back up on the cart and, clicking to the horse, turned into the yard. I followed the lads down to the cellar, watching as they laid their burden down upon the trestle table set ready. Theo had taught them well for, young though they were, they treated the corpse gently and respectfully, and, when they were done, stepped back and stood for a moment or two with bowed heads.

'Thank you, lads,' Theo said. 'You may go now.'

We listened to the pound of their retreating footsteps on the steps and along the passage above. We heard a brief exchange of voices, the slam of a door, then silence fell.

Theo padded round the cellar, lighting torches and a couple more lanterns. As the soft golden light waxed and Theo came to stand opposite, I stepped up to the trestle table and folded back the blanket.

Then I began my examination of the body.

Once more I was struck by the incongruity of the child-sized body and the ancient face. I stared down into the deep-set eyes. The lids were almost closed, but there was a tiny gap between them and it seemed for an instant that the flames of the torch in the wall behind my head glinted on some reflective surface; as if a living, sentient being still dwelt in the little corpse. Suppressing my horror, I looked more closely, leaning right in over the body, and realized my mistake. It had been an illusion – it must have been – because the eye sockets were as dry as everything else about the corpse.

I had only just begun my task, and it was far too early to start imagining things.

I straightened up, closed my eyes and took a couple of breaths. Then, the practical, logical man of science back in control, I bent to my task and began a careful head-to-toe evaluation.

Out of consideration for my companion, I voiced my findings as I went along.

'The head is covered in a long strip of fabric, which from

its inner folds is revealed to be white, although its outer surfaces are a beige-grey shade and stiff with very old dirt.' I paused, holding the unwound cloth between my hands. 'I think this is cotton,' I said, turning to Theo. I handed the cloth to him and he folded it and laid it on the empty trestle table behind him. 'The hair is short, wiry in texture and tightly curled, and mostly grey, although in places still black.' I ran my hands all over the skull, slowly, letting my fingers examine the bumps and hollows. 'No obvious injury to the skull.'

I moved my hands to the ears. 'Ears small and well-shaped, the lobes pierced and with a tiny shell earring in each one.' I smoothed my hand over the forehead and the brow ridges, then checked what I'd just felt against my own head. 'The brow ridges are quite prominent, more typical of a man than a woman.'

'But you told me this is a woman?' Theo said.

'Yes, I did.'

I was wondering if I could have made a mistake; if the absence of external genitalia that I'd noted on board the *Falco* was perhaps the result of mutilation. I wanted to check but restrained the impulse. All in good time.

I made myself return to my steady top-to-toe examination.

'The nose is well-shaped and broad at the base, the nostrils generously flared. The mouth is wide and the lips are deep.' I moved on down to the neck. 'The body was pinned to the rib by an iron stake through the throat, and the resulting wound is large and gaping, giving us a glimpse of the body's interior and verifying the assumption of total desiccation.' I looked briefly up at Theo. 'It's a very long time since this corpse held blood, or indeed any other bodily fluid.'

Then I reached down to the ragged garment and gently folded it back. The ancient crone lay there before us, and instantly I felt a sense of sacrilege and wanted more than anything to cover her up again.

I fought it off.

'The breasts are small and quite flat. The skin over the chest and abdomen is well preserved, and I presume that the internal organs are still present.' I bent down to examine the pubis and pudenda, gently parting the legs, and Theo discreetly turned his back. 'The woman has borne at least one child.' I put her back as she had been, swiftly going on to examine the legs and feet. Then I gathered up the discarded robe and carefully covered her up again. 'You can look now,' I said quietly.

I heard Theo let out the breath he'd been holding. He wasn't finding this any easier than I was.

I picked up her arms and laid them across her breast, crossed at the wrist. Her hands, I noted, were long-fingered, the nails well kept.

'Whoever she was, she didn't do manual work,' Theo remarked, leaning over to look.

'No, you're right.' I ought to have noticed that myself.

'What's that stuff under her nails?' Theo pointed.

I picked up a lantern, holding it right over the crossed hands. 'I don't know. Pass me my instrument roll, please.'

I selected a long, fine-pointed probe and ran its tip beneath the index and middle finger on the right hand, then wrapped both probe and retrieved matter in a cleanish scrap of loose cloth I'd just torn off the woman's garment and tucked it back in the leather roll.

'Any ideas?' Theo asked.

I was pretty sure it was blood, but somehow now was not the moment to say so.

'I'll look at it when I'm back in my study and let you know,' I said tersely.

We stood either side of the corpse, staring down at it. At her. Then Theo said – and there was a note of impatience in his voice – 'Well? What have you got to tell me?'

I came out of my reverie. I'm not sure where I'd been, but it took me a moment or two to return to Theo's cellar. 'Definitely a woman, and she was at an advanced age when she died.'

'How old?'

'Oh—' The reply that had almost shot out of me was that she'd been well over a hundred years old, but it was incredible, for surely nobody lived to be a hundred. 'Eighty, ninety,' I muttered.

'And how did she die?'

'I can't see any obvious cause,' I admitted. 'No injury, no signs of disease on the bones or the skin. Old age perhaps, or some sickness that leaves no external evidence.' I ran my eyes over the little corpse again. 'She's perfect,' I murmured. 'Her limbs are straight and true, her skull is elegantly shaped, and the bones of her face suggest she was very beautiful.'

Theo nodded. 'Yes, it's strange, but when I look at her I seem to see two different images. One is as she now is, the other appears to show how she must have been in the prime of life. Although I only see that image very fleetingly,' he added, as if that made it perfectly reasonable. 'It's probably just—'

'Just your imagination,' I finished for him. 'Yes, Theo. I know.'

I met his eyes. There was no need to tell him I'd seen it too.

'So what was she doing on Captain Colt's ship?' Theo asked, his tone brusque as if to say, *Enough of this fanciful nonsense, we must return to the matter in hand.*

'I have no idea,' I replied. 'It seems reasonable to conclude she was brought on board by whoever was stowing away down in that hellish little space, for the spike had been driven into the beam only recently and it is really too much of a coincidence not to link her presence with the uninvited passengers.' I paused. 'As to why they brought her, I can't say. Yet,' I added optimistically.

Theo didn't answer. He was still looking at the ancient woman, one hand absently hovering just over her own hands as if he wanted to touch her but didn't dare. 'I . . . it's odd that—' he began.

'What?'

He shook his head and abruptly moved his hand away, staring at it as if he'd been surprised to see what it had been doing. 'I was just thinking that she inspires something like respect, or rather awe, in me, and I suspect in you too?' I nodded. 'Yet whoever took her onto the *Falco* treated her with incredible brutality: they hung her on the wall with a spike through her throat.'

'She was dead, Theo,' I pointed out. 'She's been dead for years. Decades. Perhaps more. Once a body has dried out like this, it's almost impossible to say, but it could easily be a century or more since this woman walked the earth.'

'So?' he said belligerently.

I sighed. 'So they didn't really treat her brutally, did they? She was dead, far beyond feeling pain or distress, and—'

'It's no way to treat a woman, even if she *is* dead!' Theo burst out. Then he gave a sort of gasp, as if he'd just heard what he'd said. He looked at me and I knew what he was thinking: all at once he'd had enough, and he was desperate to get out of the cellar and what was in it.

'We have finished here, Theo,' I said softly. I saw him slump slightly in relief. 'Let's leave her in peace and return to the sunshine.'

We extinguished the flares and the lanterns, then climbed the steps and emerged into the house. Theo went ahead and he didn't stop but went on, out through the front door and onto the road outside. He stood quite still, taking deep breaths as if he'd been starved of air.

He turned to me. 'There was a smell down there,' he said. 'Did you notice it? Not a bad body smell, but more like . . .' He shrugged. 'I don't know. Incense? Perfume?'

I had indeed noticed it, and it seemed to me that it was what I'd briefly smelt down in the hold, just before the stench from the barrel full of waste had annihilated it. 'Yes,' I said briefly.

'Any idea what it was?'

'No.' That was not true, for I had several ideas which I intended to test against the little piece of cloth I'd torn from the woman's robe. My selection of that particular scrap hadn't been as random as it had probably seemed, for I had noticed that the elusive scent was quite powerful in that spot.

I wondered now why I hadn't told Theo what I'd done and planned to do, and opened my mouth to do so. But from somewhere within my consciousness a voice said softly, *No*. So I didn't.

Theo was looking more like his usual self and now, turning to me with a smile, he said, 'Well, I suppose I should wait a while to see if anyone comes to claim her, and if not, see about getting her buried. I don't suppose there's much chance of finding out who she is.'

'No,' I agreed. 'But I think you're right not to bury her straight away.'

Theo was eyeing me closely. 'You think they meant to take

her with them?' he said quietly. 'You surmise they had to leave the *Falco* in a hurry, and now will try to reclaim her?'

I shrugged. 'It had crossed my mind.' I hesitated, then added, 'I can't help thinking she was very important to them, which is totally illogical because I don't know who she was and have even less idea as to the identity of the men.'

Theo had clearly had enough of vague fanciful matters for one morning. 'I must return to my desk,' he said firmly, 'where a score of other matters awaits my attention. May I offer you refreshment before you leave, Gabe?'

'No, Theo, I too must get on with my day,' I replied. I turned towards the yard, where I knew Hal would have been made ready for me. 'Please thank Elaine for looking after me, and for her hospitality. I'll let you know if I make any discoveries.'

He was already walking back into the house and didn't turn round, merely raising a hand in farewell.

Hal and I were well on our way home and I wanted nothing more than to be back at Rosewyke; back in the wonderful normality of my daily round. My head was throbbing now, and I thought longingly of a light meal comprising the best that Sallie's kitchen could offer, followed by a sleep in the serene solitude of my bedchamber.

But as I neared the place where I would turn for home, I turned instead towards the village, Tavy St Luke's. To the priest's house beside the church, in fact, for I knew I wouldn't rest unless I spoke to Jonathan Carew. The vicar of St Luke's is a good friend. Certain recent events had brought us to a new understanding, and I had utter confidence that he would give me the time I needed.

I found him in his little house, and as soon as I had tethered Hal to the hitching post and replied to Jonathan's greeting he led me into his study, sat me down and handed me a very decent measure of brandy.

'You look as if you need that,' he remarked. I nodded my appreciation. 'What has happened?'

'I hit my head,' I said.

He studied me, eyes intent. 'That is not the true cause of your distress,' he observed.

So I told him.

I was amazed at what poured out of me: faithful repetitions of what Captain Zeke's crew said they'd seen; a description of the atmosphere of fear and danger on board the *Falco*; my own reaction to what I saw, heard and, most crucially, sensed; what we had discovered down in the furthest corner of the lowest deck.

What I'd felt, and what I was sure Theo had felt too, as we stood in the cellar with that ancient corpse.

'I don't believe in ghosts and hauntings,' I said when at long last I found I'd run out of words.

'So how do you explain what you have just told me?' Jonathan asked quietly.

'Others believe they have experienced the inexplicable, and I have simply picked up their fear,' I said firmly and a little too loudly.

Jonathan smiled. 'I see.'

'You're not telling me *you* believe in ghosts!'

I should have remembered who I was speaking to; it was a careless, thoughtless, stupid remark to make to a priest.

But he sat perfectly still as if considering the matter for some moments before saying, 'It depends, of course, on what you mean by ghosts. If you are asking if I believe some evil spirit lives aboard this ship and manifests itself as a man with blue skin, then I have to say no. If you mean, however, do I believe there is a whole realm that exists beyond what we habitually see, hear, smell and feel in the tangible world, then yes I do.' He gave me a sharp look. 'Of *course* I do, Gabriel.'

FOUR

J onathan insisted on seeing me on my way back to Rosewyke. He sensed I was far from my usual robust state of health, and he assumed responsibility for making sure I was all right.

We walked side by side, and I led Hal. For some time neither of us spoke, and then Jonathan said, 'Would you like me to come to the coroner's house to view the body from the ship?'

'Yes, I would be very interested to have your observations, and—'

He laughed. 'I wouldn't be there as a natural scientist, Gabriel, but as man of faith. Different eyes, I believe.'

'Whatever eyes you look with, Jonathan, I would welcome it.' I hesitated, and, noticing, he indicated for me to continue. 'What I think would be really helpful, however, would be if you were to visit the *Falco*. Perhaps if you were to say a prayer, or even hold a short service, Captain Colt and his crew would undoubtedly find that a comfort and a reassurance.'

'Are you asking me to perform an exorcism?' he asked bluntly.

Was I? I didn't know. 'Would you?'

He sighed. 'Yes. But I am not sure you understand what is meant by the word. Exorcism, in brief, is the means by which an evil spirit is forced to abandon its possession of a person. Remember how Jesus told the evil spirits to abandon the madman they were possessing, and they were driven out and into a herd of pigs, which fled over a cliff edge and were drowned.'

I nodded, for it was a well-known parable. I'd always felt sorry for the pigs – I like pigs – but I knew better than to say so.

'It is also possible to command malicious spirits to abandon an object, or a place, although I have never experienced such a process myself,' he went on. 'Strictly speaking, a priest requires permission from those to whom he answers, or that was the case under the old religion; I would need to ask my bishop before performing the abbreviated version of the rite that I would be using . . .' He frowned, deep in thought. Then he said, 'Please ask Captain Colt if he wishes me to go on board his ship. If he says he does, then I will hold a service of purification asking God to bless the ship and her crew.' He paused, still clearly thinking hard. 'First, however, I wish to see the body that now rests beneath Theophilus Davey's house, for I suspect that, now it has been removed from the ship, the manifestations will have ceased.'

'So you're saying—'

'Gabriel, I'm not sure *what* I'm saying,' he said with an edge of impatience. 'I need to think and, far more importantly, spend some time in silent prayer in my church in the hope that I may receive understanding and guidance.'

'I'm sorry, Jonathan, I realize this is quite a burden to lay upon you.'

He shook his head, smiling. 'It is what I am here for. Now, mount up and go home, Gabriel,' he urged, 'eat, rest, and tomorrow come and call for me early in the morning, when we shall proceed to the coroner's house so that I may experience this strange matter for myself.'

I did as he bade me, and he nodded in approval. He watched me as I rode off, then turned back towards the village.

With the last of my strength – I couldn't believe how very drained I was feeling – I let Hal take me back to Rosewyke, where I put him in Tock's capable but slow hands before putting myself in those of my housekeeper. Sallie tutted and fussed – 'You look all in, Doctor!' – and while I sat at the kitchen table wolfing down bread, butter, a thick slice of ham and a mug of ale, she went up to my room and turned back the bed for me.

I only paused to take off my boots before flinging myself down and closing my eyes. I was aware of a flashing succession of images: a tiny, very beautiful woman with skin like ebony . . . a crocodile whose mouth gaped wide enough to gulp down the entire world . . . a terrified man with an iron spike in one hand and a hammer in the other . . . the beautiful woman again, now soothing me, singing to me, her long-fingered hand smoothing my aching head as she murmured *sleep, forget* . . . and then I was deeply, dreamlessly asleep.

*   *   *

I woke to evening light, and my sister sitting on the edge of my bed.

'I thought you were never going to wake up!' Celia said brightly. 'Sallie said you had hit your head so I've been to see Judyth, Judyth Penwarden' – as if there was any other Judyth, I thought – 'and she said you were to take this.' She thrust a small packet at me which, on unfolding it, proved to contain powdered herbs. 'She says it's strong, and it'll make you sleep, so perhaps you'd better save it until bedtime?' *Since you've been asleep all afternoon*, she seemed to add silently.

'I shall. It was very kind of her to send it, and of you to go and acquire it,' I said, swinging my legs round and standing up.

Celia smiled prettily. 'Not at all. So, come on, Gabe! Tell me all about it.' We crossed to the door, and I found to my relief that I was steady on my feet. 'You've been back to the *Falco* in response to that note your old captain sent yesterday, and I want to know what he wanted and how it was, being back at sea.'

'I wasn't at sea, for the *Falco* is in Plymouth harbour, and I'm not sure I should tell you the reason for the summons, for it really isn't at all suitable for—'

'For a young woman's delicate ears? Rot,' my sister said bluntly. We were out in the long passage that runs along the back of the house now, making for the stairs, and she paused to fix me with a very hard look. I read her thoughts as if she'd spoken them aloud, and I understood.

My sister is not a delicate young woman. She fought and overcame a terrible event in the recent past, and in doing so discovered that she was a great deal stronger than she and everyone else believed she was. She is, in short, a survivor. She is also quick thinking, intelligent, imaginative and perceptive, and just then I couldn't think of anyone with whom I'd rather discuss what had happened on the *Falco*, and what had happened afterwards.

Delicious aromas of good beef cooked in red wine were wafting up from below: Sallie was about to serve our dinner.

'Let's eat,' I said as we crossed the hall, 'then we'll retire to the library with a decanter of brandy and I'll tell you all about it.'

She looked at me suspiciously. 'Promise?'
'Promise.'
She grinned and led the way into the dining room.

After an excellent meal – Sallie appeared to believe that acquiring a lump on my head the day before meant I was in urgent need of feeding up, and my platter had been heaped with good food – Celia and I were now in the library, in our comfortable chairs either side of a merrily-burning fire, candlelight setting off a soft gleam in the fine oak panelling, fine crystal goblets of very good brandy in our hands.

'Now, Gabe, honour your promise, if you please,' Celia said in the sort of voice that isn't to be argued with.

So for the third time I told my tale. It wasn't the curt, business-like account I'd given to Theo, nor was it the alarmed story of ghosts and hauntings which Jonathan had heard. I tried to make it matter-of-fact, although that wasn't easy when I came to the many inexplicable things that had been encountered. It took some time, but my sister sat in silence, nodding occasionally, and didn't say a word until I had finished.

Then she took a thoughtful sip of brandy and carefully replaced her glass on the small table beside her.

'You have had quite a time on board your old ship,' she said. 'The vestiges of the crew, scared half out of their wits and whispering to each other of blue men and bad atmospheres. A crawl into a filthy space where the stench all but made you choke. An unnaturally tiny female body nailed savagely to a beam.'

'A rib,' I corrected. 'Beams run the other way.'

'And, as if all of that were not enough,' she continued, not acknowledging the interjection by even so much as a nod, 'a blow to the head that briefly rendered you insensate.'

'The injury was not serious and already I—'

She put up her hand and I stopped. 'Please, Gabe. I'm working out a thought and it won't help if you keep interrupting.'

I grunted but didn't go on with my objection.

Eventually she turned her bright eyes to me and said, 'I may be wrong, but from what you say, not one of you – Captain Zeke, Theo, Jonathan, you yourself – has asked the question that shouts out for an answer. Well, to me it does.'

'*What*?' I demanded. I was trying hard not to be irritated that my little sister had come up with something everyone else had overlooked.

She smiled swiftly, as if knowing full well what I was thinking. 'If we are to take it that the presence on board the *Falco* was human and not supernatural, which I'm assuming we are, then we need to ask who the illicit passengers were, and why they were there.'

She was absolutely right.

'We only discovered the signs of their presence late yesterday,' I said. 'It's very likely that Captain Zeke is already making enquiries.'

She nodded. 'Fair enough, and that is something you can ask when next you speak to him. But, Gabe, what is to stop you and I from speculating a little? From asking ourselves where the fugitives might have crept on board and why they wanted to get to England.' She frowned. 'Or, possibly, why they needed to get away from wherever they were,' she added softly, although I barely heard.

I was trying to remember what Captain Zeke told me of the details of the *Falco*'s voyage. Leaping up – making my damaged head throb violently – I went to the bookshelves beside the big table in the window and ran my hand along the rolled-up maps and charts until I found the one I wanted. I spread it out on the table and Celia came to stand beside me.

'The Caribbean,' she said, nodding. 'So that's where they've been.' Then: 'Was the *Falco* engaged in the triangular trade?'

And a different note had entered her voice as she spoke those words.

Celia is a rarity among young women, for she is interested in all manner of matters not usually regarded as suitable for or relevant to her kind. In addition she is thoughtful and knowledgeable, having been extremely well-educated by our formidable grandmother Graice Oldreive, and she has a retentive mind. She is very like our grandmother in her character, for she holds strong opinions and it is very hard to make her change her mind once she disapproves of something. One of the things she disapproves of is the slave trade: the fact that the great and the powerful of our nation see nothing immoral in capturing men, women and children from their home lands and selling them in order to fund the purchasing of goods to be sold back in England astounded her when she first learned of it, and has continued to do so ever since.

Bearing that in mind it was a relief to be able to say, 'The *Falco* is not a slaver, Celia.'

She raised her eyes from the map and stared hard at me. 'I have your word?'

'Yes.'

The *Falco* is too small, I could have added, and not built with the cargo space for a hundred or more human beings, even crammed in so tightly together that they can barely turn over and stacked in layers so the ones on top are forced to urinate and defecate on those below.

I kept quiet, for Celia's anger burned brightly and painfully enough without my adding fuel.

'So where precisely did Captain Zeke go and what was he doing?' she asked.

I pointed out the *Falco*'s course. 'The islands of Dominica and Trinidad, then Maracaibo – that's in Venezuela – and on to Panama.' I ran my finger over the map, hovering at the places Captain Zeke had mentioned. 'Guatemala, then they sailed up the coast of the Yucatan peninsula – here – and on towards Cuba, passing it on its southern side. Then Hispaniola, and from there, eventually, out into the Atlantic and home.'

'And what were they doing?' she insisted.

I hesitated. 'Looking out for English interests,' I said.

She gave a short laugh. 'By which I suppose you mean robbing – oh, I'm sorry, *relieving* the ships of other nations, specifically the Spanish, of their cargos.'

'Cargos which they had no right to in the first place,' I pointed out.

'Oh, *that's* all right, then.' Her coruscating tone came straight from Grannie Oldreive, as did the high moral stance. I thought it best not to reply.

'The *Falco* would have made port regularly?' she demanded after a few moments' calming down.

'Yes.'

'So, in theory, the men could have slipped on board anywhere

from here' – she put her forefinger on Dominica – 'to here?'
Now she pointed to Hispaniola.

I thought about it, recalling how Captain Zeke had described
the voyage. 'In theory, yes, but it's unlikely to have been before
Hispaniola because they were hit by a devil of a storm the first
time they set out for the Atlantic and were driven right back to
the western end of the island, where they found shelter and
waited until the bad weather had passed before taking on fresh
supplies, making what repairs they could and trying again, that
time successfully.'

She was frowning. 'So why couldn't they have been down
there hidden away before the storm?'

I remembered Captain Zeke's vivid description of the storm's
power. Of baling out the ship, of frantically trying to stay afloat,
of the growing fear of death taking them all. And I heard again
his ominous words: *there was something unnatural about that
storm.*

I felt a long, slow shudder go right up my back.

My sister was waiting impatiently for an answer. 'Because
the ship barely survived,' I said shortly, 'and anyone trying
to stay alive down there in that tiny, hidden space would be
dead.' Two, maybe three men, I thought, tossed around like
fleas in a blanket, no idea of which way was up, no point of
reference at all in that awful darkness, confined by enclosing
walls, low ceiling and sloping floor, and as if all of that wasn't
bad enough, a half-man-sized barrel full of liquid waste intent
on crushing them at every roll, pitch and shudder of the tortured
ship.

No. The fugitives could only have slipped aboard after the
storm, which meant Hispaniola: the western end of the island,
to which the ferocious winds had blown the helpless *Falco*.

Celia had turned her attention back to the map, apparently
willing to take my word for it. 'Here, then.' She tapped the
western end of the long, thin island. 'So, what were they doing
there, and why did they want to get to England?' A thought
struck her, and she said, 'Gabe, what are the penalties for hiding
on board a ship?'

'I can't think that it often happens, but if it did, and if the
people hiding were discovered, then death, I imagine,' I replied.

'Likely to be straight away, as soon as they've been dragged out from their hiding place.'

'And there would be no alternative?'

'Oh – perhaps the illicit passengers might be put to work in payment for their passage, but I doubt it. The more humane captains might hang them, or possibly shove them over the side.' I'd once heard a rumour of that having happened in the eastern Mediterranean.

'Without even the vestiges of a trial?' she asked coolly.

'They'd already be guilty because of where they were,' I pointed out. 'Their reasons for being there are irrelevant.'

'I see.' She nodded.

'What are you thinking?' I asked when she didn't speak.

She turned to me. 'Isn't it obvious? The men who stowed away on the *Falco* must have known how terrible the voyage would be and how unlikely it was that they would survive it, hidden away down in the dark depths of the ship, even without a storm trying to sink them. Furthermore, they must also have been aware what would happen if they were discovered. Dying on the way was far more likely than reaching port and managing to get safely ashore in England, yet they took the risk.' She paused, looking at me expectantly.

'So whatever drove them to do what they did, it must have outweighed the ghastly prospects of the voyage itself, or of being discovered and put to death,' I said.

And, with a small smile, she said, 'Precisely.'

FIVE

The lump on the back of my skull was throbbing in time to my heart by the time I went to bed and it would be hard to sleep, so I availed myself of Judyth's powdered herbs. The preparation worked like a charm, and I fell deeply into unconsciousness as if I'd been hit all over again.

I didn't even dream, or not that I recalled.

I awoke because someone was shaking my shoulder and calling out my name. 'Doctor Taverner!' said a man's voice from close beside me. 'Doctor!' came shrilly and repeatedly from the foot of the bed, and, 'Gabe! *Gabe!* Wake up, it's late!' from somewhere just behind whoever was shaking me.

I rolled onto my back and opened my eyes.

Jarman Hodge stood over me, with Celia beside him. Sallie stood at the end of the bed holding a large jug of steaming water.

'*What?*' I bellowed, making them all take a swift step backwards. I shouldn't have shouted, but I'd been dragged from profound sleep, I was disorientated and feeling embarrassed at still lying in my bed when the angle of the sun shining brightly through the window told me it was already mid-morning.

I sat up, realizing as I did so that my sore head wasn't sore any more. 'I took Mistress Penwarden's sleeping draught,' I said in explanation. 'It was rather more potent than I anticipated.' That was all I was going to say on the matter, and to demonstrate the fact – and to remind these people just whose house this was and who was in charge here – I turned to Jarman Hodge and said, 'What brings you to Rosewyke, Jarman?'

He had retreated a further step and now, looking decidedly sheepish at having just been shaking me, he stood up very straight and said in his most detached and formal tone, 'Message from the coroner, Doctor. He says to tell you the body's gone.'

'The body . . .' It took me a moment to catch up. 'The body in his cellar? The one from the *Falco*?'

'That'd be the one, sir.'

'*Gone?*'

'Gone.'

I looked round at the three faces: Jarman's expression was impassive (which is his usual demeanour), Celia looked as if she had a dozen questions to ask, which I was quite sure she did; Sallie's eyes were round with fascinated horror.

'Leave me,' I said to them, with the imperious tone of an autocratic monarch. 'Is that water for me, Sallie?' She nodded, holding it out as if to demonstrate its reality. 'Then please wait for me downstairs, Jarman, and I will return with you to Master Davey's house as soon as I have washed and dressed.'

Sallie insisted on giving me a hot roll spread with bread and honey to eat as I rode, and Celia hissed as I strode out of the door, 'You *must* tell me what you find out, Gabe!' I thanked Sallie, muttered 'Of course,' to my sister, hurrying out to the yard to find Jarman Hodge mounted and Samuel, my outdoor servant, holding Hal. Hoping that the sense of unreality would soon wear off and I'd catch up with myself, we clattered out of the yard.

'We didn't hear a thing,' Theo said with a scowl.

We were standing either side of the trestle where the little corpse had lain. The table was bare, and the length of cloth I'd removed from the head had also disappeared.

'How secure is your house?'

'The front door and the one out to the yard are locked and bolted at night. I do it myself.'

'I'm sure you do. What about the windows?'

He hesitated. 'The one in the scullery's ill-fitting and the frame is rotten – I keep meaning to have it seen to, Elaine complains of the draught – and it's possible to open it from the outside.'

'Show me?'

He led me up the steps and turned to his right, down the passage leading back through the house. He opened the yard door – it was as stout as the front door, and there was a lock with a huge iron key as well as bolts top and bottom – and

took me down a passage along the side of the building. He
stopped, pointing up at a little glazed rectangle some five or
six feet off the ground.

I reached out and pushed it. It held for a moment, so I pushed
harder and it flew open.

I turned to stare at Theo. '*This* window?' I asked disbelievingly.
It really was very small.

'It's the only possible access. I know, Gabe, but there is no
alternative!'

He was right, for the windows of the upper chambers were
far above our heads.

Both of us turned back to the scullery window.

It measured perhaps a foot by a foot and a half.

I could have got my head and perhaps one shoulder into the
aperture, although whether I'd have extracted myself again was
doubtful. Theo probably wouldn't even have managed the
shoulder.

'A child?' he suggested.

I nodded. 'Your Carolus could slip through there, although
we'd have to give him a leg-up.' Carolus is ten years old.

'Then we'll assume the lad had an accomplice. So he runs
through the house, light on his feet, nips down into the cellar
and picks up the corpse.'

'First replacing the headdress,' I put in.

'Yes, yes,' Theo said impatiently. 'Then he passes the body
to whoever's waiting the other side of the window and follows
it out.'

'How would he reach the window on the inside without
someone to lift him up?' I demanded.

'Easy. There's a stone sink runs along beneath it, he'd have
stood on that.'

Without a word we turned and strode round to the door, and
Theo went ahead to the room from which the little window
opened. There was the stone sink, and, just as he had said, it
made a convenient step for someone intent on climbing out.

If anything, the aperture looked even tighter from this side.

'Could it be done?' I murmured.

Theo's answer was to step through the door into the passage
and holler, '*Carolus!*'

The boy appeared far too rapidly for him to have been upstairs with his mother, bent over his school books, where he was meant to be; he had evidently been standing just inside the door that separated Theo's workplace from his family living quarters, and the lad was too young to disguise the fact.

'Father?' he said, looking up at Theo with the same bright blue eyes, his wearing an expression of exaggerated innocence.

Theo gave him a long, assessing look, then said, 'Do you think you could climb through that window if Doctor Taverner goes round to the other side to catch you?'

The boy's face lit up. '*Really?* I'm really to do it?'

'You are.'

Not giving his father time to change his mind and rescind this unlikely order, Carolus jumped up onto the sink, took a firm grip on the window ledge and hauled himself up, coming to rest with his head and shoulders through the gap and his chest resting on the sill. 'Gabe!' Theo shouted in alarm, and, equally taken aback at how quickly the boy had responded, I raced outside and positioned myself below the window. Carolus grinned down at me.

'It's all right, Doctor, I don't really need you,' he whispered. Then in an even softer voice: 'I've done this heaps of times before.'

I'd suspected as much. 'I won't tell,' I whispered back.

I watched, ready to leap forward and catch him as he insinuated the rest of his lean body through the window. But he was right, he didn't need me. Keeping firm hold of the window frame, somehow he wriggled himself round so that he was feet first, then extended his arms until his feet were only ten or twelve inches off the ground and let go. He landed easily, brushed some fragments of rotting wood from his hands and gave me a grin.

'Well done,' I said as we went back into the house.

'Have I been helpful?' he said eagerly.

'Very,' I replied. 'Your father and I had a bet as to whether it was possible,' I said. For clearly he wanted an explanation, and I was reluctant to tell him we feared someone had gained access to the sleeping household.

He smiled in satisfaction. 'I don't think *you* could have done

it, Doctor Taverner,' he said politely. 'And as for my father . . .'
He rolled his eyes.

I suppressed a grin.

'Thank you, Carolus,' Theo said. 'Now, back to your books,
if you please. And *close the door*,' he added pointedly as the
boy sprinted away.

'He managed it easily,' I said when Theo and I were alone.

Theo stared at me, clearly expecting more. Not wanting to
betray his son's confidence, I merely said, 'I think you should
get that window fixed as a matter of some urgency. If one person
managed to get into the house that way, others could too.'

Theo nodded. 'Yes, I've already sent one of the men to fetch
the carpenter. Look what I found while you were outside.'

Relieved that Carolus's secret was safe, I bent over the sink
to where he was pointing. Scattered at its base were the same
flakes of rotten wood I'd just seen on Carolus's hands.

'Could your son's exit not have made them?' I asked.

'Carolus went *out* through the window. I'd wager, wouldn't
you, that these resulted from someone coming *in*.'

We went back through to Theo's office, and he threw himself
down in his chair. 'Think it was the uninvited passengers from
the *Falco*, come to reclaim what they left behind on the ship?'

'Who else?' I replied. 'For one thing, only a handful of people
knew the corpse was here. For another, who else could possibly
want to steal it?'

'Well, if nothing else, it proves they were human and not the
ghosts conjured up by the ship's company,' Theo muttered.

'Oh, they were human all right,' I said. 'We were discussing
them last night, Celia and I, and—'

'What did Celia think?' Theo interrupted. He has a high
opinion of my sister, which is no surprise since his choice of
wife indicates a preference for strong, intelligent women.

'We studied a map showing the *Falco*'s recent voyage and
came to the conclusion that the fugitives must have slipped on
board before the ship left her last port of call, which was at the
western end of Hispaniola. I'd planned to return to the ship this
morning, in fact, to see what Captain Zeke thinks of the idea.'

'Good, good, don't let me stop you,' Theo said. He sighed
gustily. 'I have a desk loaded with matters awaiting my

attention' – he waved an arm over the stacks of papers and files – 'and now the ancient corpse of a very old woman has been stolen from my cellar and I have absolutely no idea who she was, who stole her and what in the good Lord's name they propose to do with her.' He gave me a rueful smile. 'If you discover anything the least bit helpful, Gabe, please don't hesitate to share it with me.'

He came out to the yard to see me on my way; I guessed it was a means by which to postpone tackling those stacks of paper for a little longer.

But I was not to make it to Plymouth that day, for as I mounted Hal and turned his head to the open gates, there came the sound of a horse being ridden hard towards us. Theo pushed past me and stood in the road, and the horseman – it was a young man of perhaps fifteen or sixteen – pulled his sweating mount to a halt.

'Body's been found,' he panted, pushing a lock of damp hair out of his eyes. His face screwed up in an expression of distaste, fear, I wasn't sure. Looking into the yard, he saw me and instantly looked relieved. 'That the doctor?'

'It is,' Theo and I said together.

The young man crossed himself, muttering a prayer of thanks. 'We need him and all,' he said. 'Will you come with me, now, straight away?'

Theo's stable lad, observing from the rear of the yard, was already busy. By the time Theo had hurried back inside to fetch his cloak and his cap, his thick-set mare was ready. He gave some brief orders to the stable lad to prepare the horse and cart and follow after us, then he mounted up and the young man put heels to his horse and set off back the way he had come. He set a fast pace – something had clearly upset him – and Theo had to tell him to slow down, for the cart coming along behind us needed to keep us in sight so as to know where to go. In silence, – I didn't feel like talking, and clearly Theo didn't either – we rode on.

We kept up a reasonable pace for the best part of four or five miles, the cart jolting along behind us with the stable lad at the reins, heading roughly north east and passing the turning for Tavy

St Luke and Rosewyke, away to the left. Then abruptly the young
man slowed, taking a lane that led off to the west and that, I was
fairly sure, headed down towards the river. We were near to
Buckland, where my friend the retired doctor Josiah Thorn lives,
and as we descended to the riverside, I wondered if we were close
to his habitual fishing place beneath the old willow trees.

Now the boy was following a narrow track down by the
water, and presently it rose once more, leading up to a small
promontory that jutted out over a bend on the river; the water
was undercutting it, and in time it would collapse under the
constant pressure. A tall, graceful beech tree stood a few paces
back from the edge, and beneath it lay the body.

There had been some attempt to dig a grave. It was flat on
its back in a scrape of hollowed-out earth, with what looked
like a few handfuls of soil covering its feet and legs. All three
of us dismounted and I handed Hal's reins to the young man.
He kept his distance – presumably he'd already had sight
enough of what awaited us – but Theo and I advanced until
we stood over the body.

It was that of a man, quite young, with a shock of black,
curly hair and a scrappy beard. The eyes – wide open – were
very dark brown. The nose was wide and quite flat and the lips
were full. The mouth gaped hugely as if in a silent scream.

The body was naked. The man – perhaps he was more accurately a boy, but I was uncertain of judging age when it came
to people of mixed blood – was big-framed but very skinny,
his ribs standing out sharply under the taut skin and the bones
of his pelvis jutting like two hills either side of the shrunken
belly. His legs were long, and as I brushed away the earth to
examine his feet – bare, like the rest of him, large and wide across
the spreading toes – I noticed something. It tallied with another
factor I'd already observed, and I looked up, immediately above
me, and that seemed to make it certain.

I returned to his head and neck, feeling the ground beneath
him and then widening my search into a broad circle all around
the place where he lay.

'What are you looking for?' Theo asked very quietly.

'Blood.'

He muttered an oath, then bent down to help me, working

in the opposite direction until between us we had completed a circle with a radius of roughly four or five feet, its centre by the body's feet, our spread hands patting the earth and the grass as if one of us had lost a precious jewel.

Theo straightened up. 'I didn't find any. It hasn't rained for a few days, and the ground is quite dry, so it'd be easy to find blood if it were there.'

I nodded. 'No, I didn't either.' But I hadn't expected to.

I returned to the corpse.

What had they done to him? Well, I knew, or thought I did; the more pertinent question was *why* they'd done it, and I had a horrible suspicion that I might know the answer to that too.

Theo was watching me. 'Share your thoughts, Gabe.'

I turned to glance at him. 'They are deeply unpleasant ones,' I warned. I was trying to spare him; all the time I kept my conclusions to myself, Theo could go on believing it was an ordinary, sunny October day, that we might be standing by a recently-deceased boy but he'd died of natural causes, all was reasonably well with the world and we'd all go home that evening to a good dinner and a cozy evening by our hearths.

'Tell me,' Theo said, and now his voice had changed and carried the weight of his authority and his ancient office.

'He was suspended by his ankles from the branch just above us,' I said. 'Here is where the rope cut into his flesh' – I bent down, Theo did too, and I showed him the red grooves just above the feet – 'and up there you can see the end of the rope, still tied around the branch.' Theo followed the line of my arm and pointing finger. 'Then someone took a very sharp knife and made two very deep cuts either side of his throat, opening the big tubes that carry blood to the brain.' I reached down and gently opened up the cut on the right side, pushing its sides apart so that it gaped up at us. Theo made a faint retching noise, but he controlled himself. 'I doubt there is much blood left in this poor boy's body,' I went on. 'If the heart was still beating when the cuts were made, its action would have pumped out blood like a fountain. Then when it stopped, whatever remained would have simply drained from the corpse.'

'It's barbarous,' Theo said, and I heard the suppressed fury in his voice, that one man – more than one man, probably –

could be capable of this. 'Why? They had rope and a tree, so why not hang him?'

Hanging could be as terrible, I thought but didn't say, for unless there was a good long drop and a sharp jerk at the end of it, slow strangulation was the likely result.

'He'd not have felt much beyond the first great exsanguination,' I said gently. 'He'd have passed out, and been unconscious when his soul fled his body.'

Theo nodded. Then again he said, 'But why this method?'

I hesitated, weighing my words. 'Some religions specify that all meat consumed must be drained of its blood as the animal is slaughtered,' I said eventually. 'This is the method by which I believe the required result is achieved.'

'They treated him like an *animal*.' Theo's outrage was flowing off him like steam. Then, as a yet more horrifying thought struck him, he said, 'Dear Christ, Gabe, you don't think they—'

I stopped him before he could finish. 'No, Theo, I don't think they had any plans to eat him.' His relief was palpable, and it seemed a shame to stop it. 'But I do, however, believe they had a use for his blood.'

He had paled again. 'His blood?'

'It's not here.' I indicated the circle of ground we had just examined. 'We can be fairly sure this is where he was killed, for we have the evidence of the rope marks on his ankles and the other end of the rope, still tied around the branch. His blood ought to be here, right beneath where he was suspended, but it isn't. The obvious conclusion, it seems to me, is that as they cut into his neck they held vessels of some sort in precisely the right place to catch the blood as it spurted or dripped out of him.'

'Like the Holy Grail, which received the blood of our blessed saviour as he hung on the cross,' Theo murmured.

'Yes.' I waited a moment, out of respect for the image he had just summoned. It seemed right, somehow, to invoke the presence of Jesus in this place of ghastly death. Then I said, 'I believe I know what they wanted it for.'

Theo sighed. 'Go on, then.'

'Blood is the liquor of life,' I said, thinking it out even as I spoke. 'It has power, and in some religions it is venerated both in itself and as a symbol for vitality and strength.' I paused,

then said, 'You were about to ask just now if they were planned
to eat him, and I said no. But as I just said, however, they had
something in mind for his blood.'

'They— they were going to drink it?' Once again, I thought
Theo might be about to throw up.

'Possibly, yes. I have heard tell of ceremonies where that is
done. There are other uses, however.'

'In God's name, what?' he demanded.

'In magic rituals,' I said softly. Then, for Theo was staring
at me as if I'd taken leave of my senses, 'If I'm not mistaken,
this man is one of the fugitives from the ship.'

'But how can you—'

'The *Falco* has been in the Caribbean, Theo, where many
have similar features. Life is harsh there,' I hurried on, eager
to put my thoughts into words, 'and the islands and their peoples
have a deep, dark, ancient heart. I know only a very little of
what is done in the name of religion; of what rituals and ceremonies are performed away from the curious eyes of strangers.
I have spoken with men and women who are revered in those
lands, and I have been told much that I find hard to believe.' I
paused as one or two specific memories sprang to mind. 'I have
extensive notes back in my study at Rosewyke, and I will return
there when we have finished here and see what I can find. For
now, I suggest we bear the body over to your cart, cover him
up as best we can and take him back to your cellar.'

Theo nodded. Walking back along the path, he called to the
stable lad, who came running up, although the young man
who had escorted us there kept his distance. The stable lad
blanched a bit at the sight of the body, but gathered his courage
and did as Theo commanded, and between the three of us we
laid our burden on the flat bed of the cart and Theo draped a
length of sacking over it.

One of the corpse's hands was sticking out from beneath the
sacking, and the stable lad picked it up and tucked it out of
sight. I was just thinking it was brave of him when he uttered
a soft exclamation.

'What is it?' Theo demanded.

The lad pointed a shaking finger. 'Why is his skin all blue?'

*   *   *

In the high room at the top of the Plymouth lodging house, the youngest of the three men was pacing to and fro, to the clear annoyance of the sick man in the bed. He said tetchily, 'Sit down. You tire me out with your restlessness.'

The younger man shot him an angry look, then swiftly wiped it off his face. He went to perch on the crude bench beneath the window beside the white-haired man.

'So she has gone,' said the sick man. He gave the younger man a glance of grudging admiration. 'You use your eyes and ears well.' Then, raising an eyebrow, 'They have her?'

'Undoubtedly,' said the white-haired man. 'They depend upon her' – he shuddered and crossed himself – 'and it can only have been dire necessity that forced them to leave her behind when they fled from the ship.'

'Their dependency on that evil *thing* is their own fault!' the sick man cried. 'They turned away from the truth, and evil inevitably followed! They—' But his words were choked off by a fierce bout of coughing. The white-haired man silently passed him a mug of water. He sipped, nodded, and wiped the spittle from his chin with a clean cloth.

'But they did turn away,' the white-haired man said softly, 'and they were faced with the consequences, and in their terror they fled, and we had no choice but to follow.' He glanced down at the sick man, a faint frown creasing his brow. 'And you are not well, and we do nothing to ease your distress.'

'I don't need ease!' the sick man protested furiously, coughing again. The others could hear the phlegm rattling and bubbling in his chest and the whistle of his breath. The white-haired man waited, glancing briefly at his younger companion. 'And don't you dare plot with him behind my back,' the sick man went on as soon as he could speak. 'We must only have dealings with the locals when there is no choice, and nobody – *nobody* – is to come close.' He stared hard at them. 'Understood?'

And slowly both men nodded.

The sick man closed his eyes. Presently he began to snore.

The younger man turned expectantly to the man beside him. Reverting to their own language – the sick man insisted that they used only the mother tongue of this alien land, even when there was nobody around to overhear – the white-haired man said very quietly, 'I have accounted for one of them, although regretfully I did not learn anything from him. We have some difficult decisions to make, my friend.' He shot a glance towards the bed. 'He is in command, and our sworn duty is to obey. But . . .' He left the sentence unfinished.

The younger man nodded. 'But we have come so far, and our mission must not be put in jeopardy,' he murmured.

'It will not be,' came the soft reply.

'Then what should we do?' the younger man pressed. 'We are in the wrong place. They have her now' – the white-haired man made a brief gesture with one hand, as if defending himself from the very mention of the thing – 'and will not be lodging in the town.'

The older man nodded. 'And it is far to go each day even on horseback, from here to the places where we must search.'

His companion did not reply straight away. Then he said, 'Of the two men who went aboard the ship, the big man who rides the black horse is a doctor, and the other one – the broad man – is an official into whose care the dead are given.'

Again the white-haired man nodded. 'We must—'

But with a snort and a bout of coughing, the man in the bed woke up.

SIX

I went back to Rosewyke.

The body was on its way to Theo's cellar, Theo riding escort and the young man who had come to fetch us riding on the cart along with the stable lad, whose fear was manageable with another living, breathing human being sitting beside him. The young man's horse trotted along behind the cart, having displayed only a brief initial reluctance at being so close to a corpse.

I had decided that there was no need to carry out my inspection of the corpse straight away, for I was already almost certain how the man had died. Three things were calling me home: I knew there would by now be patients needing me, some of them urgently; I was itchy with impatience to be alone in my study and spreading out on my desk every single note I'd ever made on the subject of dark magic; and, perhaps most imperative of all, I hadn't eaten since the hot roll Sallie had thrust into my hand several hours ago and I was ravenous.

Theo and I parted company at the turning for Tavy St Luke, and I watched for a few moments as he rode on towards home, the cart bumping along behind him. I glanced down at the village, and the church standing serene beside the green, tempted to pause and spend a few moments in silent prayer. It had been that sort of day, and I could have done with Jonathan's company, even briefly. But I nudged my knee into Hal's side, turning him towards Rosewyke, and he set off eagerly. Perhaps he was as hungry as I was.

It was twilight when I rode into the yard. Samuel took Hal from me, and I could hear Tock inside the stables, already busy making up a feed. I wished Samuel a brief good evening, then went inside.

'Is my sister at home?' I asked Sallie as she came to greet me. 'No, Doctor, she is dining with her sewing circle and will not be home until the morrow,' my housekeeper replied, in the sort of tone which said plainly, *surely you haven't forgotten*?

'Of course,' I said. 'Any callers, Sallie?'

'Three, but none of them needed you tonight and I said you'd see them in the morning.' She rattled off the details.

'Very well. I have work I must get on with and so please bring me some supper. A large supper,' I added, 'and a draught of your excellent ale.'

Up in the study, a fire was laid ready and I put a flame to it. The clear skies we'd enjoyed all day had continued as darkness fell, and it was going to be a cold night with a heavy frost. As the cheerful noise of burning wood broke the silence, I went to the shelves and the chests where I keep the journals of my days at sea and selected the first of the relevant volumes. I'd spent a great deal of time in the Caribbean over the years, and there were several notebooks to go through.

I had eaten my supper and worked my way through most of the jug of ale by the time I found what I was looking for. It was in my journal for the year 1595 – the year Francis Drake died – and the *Falco* had been in port on a small island between Hispaniola and Cuba, stuck there for more than a fortnight while repairs were made to a hole in her hull. With little to occupy me on board, I had taken an excursion up into the hinterland and encountered a man who claimed he could walk through the veil separating the living from the dead and commune with the ancestors.

He was old; or, at least, his body was old. He was shrunken, skinny, his limbs were skeletal and his dark skin was dried and wrinkled, hanging on his frame like a loose shirt. His wiry hair was white and his face was scored with wrinkles so deep they looked like crevasses.

His eyes, however, were bright, shining and alert; the eyes of someone in the first full power of manhood.

I sat in my study by a Devon river and read through what I had written, and I was carried back through time and across the wide Atlantic to the place where I had sat and listened to an ancient man who, while he spoke, cast a spell on me and made me believe everything he told me.

He had been taken from his West African homeland when

he was a boy, brutally treated by the slave traders from the neighbouring tribe and made to march to the Gulf of Guinea, where he'd been loaded onto a ship with more than a hundred others. They had been transported across the sea and those who had survived – a little over half, he said – were sold on Hispaniola and put to work on the Spanish-owned plantations.

They had been torn from everything they knew and brought nothing of their former lives with them. Nothing material, that is; what did come with them, and what could not be removed from them by physical means, were their mystical, deep-rooted beliefs.

They believed in a supreme god: unknown, unknowable; too awesomely powerful for weak, humble men and women even to contemplate trying to approach. Underneath the omnipotent one were the spirits who controlled the affairs of the world and they were called the Loa; there were many of them and each had their own sphere of influence. Prayers were made to the relevant Loa, and offerings made of the vegetables and fruits preferred by that spirit on the spirit's favourite day of the week and in the place of preference, in the hope that the Loa would look into the matter in question – perhaps to do with business, or love, or family concerns, justice, health – and decide in favour of the supplicant.

I'd made a note here: *Not dissimilar to the former practice of praying to the relevant saint: St Anthony when you'd mislaid a precious object; St Roch when someone you loved was sick; St Jude when you'd tried everything else and were really desperate.*

It was as well, I thought now, that my notebooks were not accessible to anyone but myself and, I supposed, my household, although Celia was the only member of it whom I could imagine having the desire to look. Read by unsympathetic eyes, my words might well translate as heresy. I decided it might be wise to remove them, so I tore out the relevant part of the page and put it on the fire.

Such is the mood of the times in which we live.

Feeling shaken, I refilled my mug and took a draught of ale. Then I went back to my journal.

The old man had told me much about his healing methods

and I'd made page after page of notes. I hadn't understood all he said; we'd been speaking a basic form of Spanish, but he included many words I didn't recognize and which I suspected were as likely to be from his own language, whatever it was. But I concluded that he believed a man to be made up of three distinct parts: first, the physical body; second, whatever force it is that animates flesh, sinew, bone and blood; and lastly, what I translated as personality, or awareness, and that gives us the understanding of who and what we are; the soul, perhaps. Chillingly, the old man told me that a practitioner such as himself had the ability to separate this third element from the living human being and store it away in an earthenware vessel. Leaning closer to me, he had whispered that it was possible to extract this – the essence of a person's character and willpower – and he hinted that it could then be used to bend the person to the practitioner's will.

It was chilling stuff.

I had asked him how it was possible to perform this extraction, and he had spoken of substances which I knew were highly toxic: matter extracted from a species of toad, and a powerful poison found in marine organisms such as the puffer fish. He also told me of something used by his brothers in the Yucatan – I hadn't understood precisely what he meant by *brothers*, and concluded he referred to fellow priests, or practitioners of magic, or whatever term he used to describe himself – and which he called *flesh of the gods*. I'd gathered from the description that it was a sort of mushroom, and gave rise to startling visual and auditory hallucinations, and I'd wondered if it was by ingestion of these that he was able to wander through into the world of the ancestors.

I stood up to stretch, easing the cramp in my left shoulder. I crossed to the hearth, poking up the fire and adding fuel. I would be sitting there at my desk for some time yet.

The ancient sorcerer had described many more medicinal plants, not a few of which I had experimented with myself. I have always believed that the healing practices of other cultures should be investigated, even if the first reaction is quite often incredulity and disgust. I was following in worthy footsteps, for the king of Spain's personal physician, Francisco Hernández, went to Mexico with the Conquistadors and wrote extensively on a substance called *ololiuqui,* which he claimed was derived from the morning glory plant. Whether or not he used it in a preparation for his king, I do not know: he suggested it was a cure for flatulence, venereal diseases and in addition good at controlling pain, all of which qualities might or might not have been relevant to the king of Spain, but he also reported that it produced visions. I have always wondered if he spoke from personal experience.

I went on through my journal, presently finding a section where I had recounted various mutterings I'd overheard among the crew. They'd been bored, wanting to sail away from the island, suffering from the extreme heat and humidity, with little to do and too much time to relieve their boredom with tall tales and scary legends. One of the sailors had been told of a ritual in which a dead man had been brought back to life and, by magic, made to carry out the wishes of the sorcerer who had reanimated him. Another sailor echoed this, saying that he'd been told of something called *vodou,* and of people being reanimated as a punishment; 'When by rights and all that's holy and Christian,' he'd added indignantly, 'they oughta have been left peaceful in their graves!' Yet another had been treated to a highly imaginative tale of a newly-dead corpse having the blood drained out of it, in the belief that the precious liquor was the very stuff of life and contained the dead man's power, and how the blood once absorbed into the body of someone still alive would endow them with the qualities of the dead man.

I sat back in my chair.

It was fully dark outside now, and probably had been for some time. The fire was no more than embers. Suddenly very much in need of warmth, and even more of light, I leapt up and threw on more wood. The beer was long gone, so I went down and fetched the brandy bottle. I forgot to bring a glass, so I drank from my beer mug.

I had remembered aright. There it was, in my own handwriting: my passage of notes on the stories told to the *Falco*'s gullible crew while they waited, overheated, homesick and more than ready to entertain anything to relieve the monotony of the long days, for the repairs to the ship to be completed so that they could sail away and forget all about that wretched little island.

I'd written the stories down to amuse myself, for I too was bored, and if anyone had asked me if I'd believed them I'd have said 'No, most certainly I do not, for I am not wide-eyed and ignorant like the crew but a man of science and discernment.'

But a recently-dead body was even now awaiting me in Theo's cellar, and it would be receiving my attention the next morning. Although I told myself I must be wrong, that I was permitting the late hour, the darkness, my solitude and my fatigue to sway me, still I could not shake off the unpleasant suspicion that what I'd always taken to be a sailor's tall travellers' tale might have rather more than a grain of truth in it.

I took Flynn out for the usual breath of air before we both turned in. I stood by the gates at the end of the track that leads up to my house, deep in thought. Flynn was wuffing and snuffling at some rodent in the hedge, and I was about to call him away and head back inside when suddenly I knew someone – some presence – was watching me.

I stood quite still, listening. Flynn came to stand beside me, and as I put my hand on the back of his neck I felt the hairs rise up. He is a brave dog, unafraid of any danger that he can see to attack, but just then he was frightened.

I hated to admit it but so was I.

In that moment, with all that I had recently read and experienced vivid in my mind, I was quite sure that if I searched I would find nothing, for whatever was out there had no tangible form.

I slept poorly. I couldn't get warm and I had a series of very colourful dreams, in one of which someone had removed all my blood, which was why I was so cold. It was a relief to wake up from that one.

I set out after an early breakfast, leaving word for Celia with Sallie not to expect me until late. Ruthlessly I drove all thoughts of bloodless corpses and reanimated dead bodies from my mind and forced myself to give the morning's three patients my full attention. Fortunately for me – even more for them – not one of them was seriously ill: one required a change of dressing on a stitched and healing wound; one needed more cough syrup, which I had brought with me; one suspected what would be a very welcome pregnancy, and I referred her to Judyth Penwarden, who would no doubt be able to tell for certain after only the briefest of consultations.

Then I set Hal's head for Withybere, and what awaited me in Theo's cellar.

He greeted me distractedly, his thick light brown hair standing up from where he'd repeatedly run his hands through it; clearly he was not having a great morning. I inclined my head towards the cellar, and he nodded. 'Yes, yes, get on with it!' he snapped, then immediately apologized: 'Sorry, Gabe, too much to do and Jarman Hodge has gone off on some investigation of his own.' He muttered an oath; several oaths, in fact. 'He was here when we brought the corpse in yesterday and when I told him where it had been found, he said "Buckland, you say? Near to Buckland Abbey?" as if it meant something, although for the life of me I can't see what, and now the bloody man's not *here* when I need him, and—'

His complaint was rapidly turning into a rant and he wasn't really talking to me any more. I left him to it and headed down the steps into the cool cellar.

The body was on the trestle where the tiny corpse from the *Falco* had been until someone came in the night and took it. It lay beneath a length of worn but clean linen which covered it from head to toe. I folded back the top third and began my inspection.

I was alone this time, so there was no need to speak my findings aloud. Slowly I began the examination, looking again at the two cuts in the sides of the neck, and reflecting now that they had been done with skill and efficiency.

Which led straight away to an interesting thought . . .

I didn't hurry. Slowly and carefully I studied the head, feeling all over the beautifully-shaped skull, running my fingers deep in the thick curly hair to feel the bone beneath the skin. The hair, I noticed, was extremely dry, and strands broke off right down close to the scalp as I lightly touched them. Then I went on to the chest, the belly, the thighs and legs. I observed what I'd noticed already, that while the youth was tall, deep-chested and broad in the shoulder, he was very skinny, and now I judged by the condition of the body that it was a very long time since this young man had eaten properly. His skin was dry and scaly.

With a soft exclamation I went back to the face, this time gently parting the soft, full lips. His teeth had been very good – white, large and even – but now at least three were missing, and the gums were purplish and spongy.

Whatever food scraps he had managed to purloin from the *Falco*'s stores, lemons, limes and fresh vegetables hadn't featured in his diet, for he'd had scurvy.

We had known about the debilitating and frequently fatal sickness that struck down sailors ever since ships had begun the long voyages that saw them at sea for weeks, and sometimes months, at a time. Sailors were no use when they were weak and exhausted, when their teeth fell out and agonizing pain in their joints stopped them working, and the least knock marked their flesh with huge, painful bruises. Many cures had been advocated, and it was John Hawkins's son, Admiral Richard Hawkins, who had introduced back in 1593 the rule that every man on board the Queen's ships be given orange or lemon juice each day. Nobody knew why the remedy worked, only that it did.

And the young man lying dead before me hadn't seen an orange or a lemon in months.

I went on with my inspection.

His hands, feet, joints and his long, elegant limbs showed signs of hard physical labour. I peered more closely at his hands, and the lad who'd brought the cart was quite right: the skin definitely had a blue stain. I reached for a lantern, holding it close to first the right arm and then the left. On both sides the colour that had penetrated his dark skin reached right up above the elbows, on the right side almost to the shoulder. Reaching beneath him, my arms supporting his shoulders and hips, gently I turned him over to repeat the examination on his back.

Between his ribs on the left hand side I discovered a hole.

It was almost circular and about the diameter of my thumb-nail. The flesh around the hole's perimeter was raw and had bled a little. This young man's breast had been unmarked, which meant that the projectile that had entered him from the rear was still inside him.

I went to my roll of instruments and selected a long, thin probe. I inserted the tip into the hole, exerting just enough pressure to let it follow the projectile. The track that it had made angled upwards, I noted. Then the tip of the instrument struck something hard.

I removed the probe, then stood in thought for a few moments. Returning to my instruments, I removed a tool originally designed to extract arrowheads and whose purpose was to enlarge the track made by the arrow's entry so as to facilitate extraction. It has two jaws which sit together as you insert it into the body and which, by adjusting the handles, can be opened out once in place.

I put the jaws into the wound and, once I felt the ends strike the hard object I'd found with the probe, gently opened them. The flesh parted and, peering into the enlarged hole, I saw what had caused it. Holding the jaws open with my left hand, I reached for my long-nosed tweezers. After quite a lot of fumbling and a deal of cursing – it was as well my patient was dead and insensate to pain – I got a firm grip on the object and very carefully withdrew it from the wound.

It was a musket ball.

Whatever had stopped its progress through the young man's chest cavity cannot have been hard, for the lead ball was still roughly round and, had it hit a rib, it would have been grossly misshapen.

I wiped it and studied it. I thought I knew what had happened: someone had fired a musket at him and the ball had hit him in the back. Whoever fired the weapon was some distance away, since musket balls fired at close range tend to blast right through the body and leave an exit wound the size of my two clenched fists put together. Whoever had fired had been shorter than the victim, or, more probably, firing from below; the young man might, for example, have been trying to escape by climbing up a low rise.

The musket ball had found his heart.

'It was still there inside him when they strung him up,' I said softly. 'By accident or design, the men who did this to him kept his body stoppered up like a bottle with very valuable contents until they had him upside down and were holding their cups under his severed blood vessels ready to catch his blood.'

I have had a great deal of experience with penetrating wounds. I have seen a man pierced by a huge splinter of wood powered into him as a cannon ball hit the ship; a man whose life I could have saved had I been there to staunch the wound as the splinter was removed, and had it not been torn out of him by a well-intentioned shipmate long before I reached him. In every ship I subsequently served on I drummed it into the crew every time we went into action: *don't remove anything from wounds until I tell you to do so.*

I turned the young man over again. I stared down into his face. He looked peaceful, and I told myself this indicated he had died swiftly and had not known much about it. I knew full well there was nothing in a calm expression to prove any such thing, but something about the man had roused deep pity. If he really had been one of the fugitives who had endured that terrible voyage down in the depths of the *Falco* – and the staining on his hands and arms seemed to place it beyond doubt that this lad had been one of the 'blue men' – how poignant it was that he had survived it only to end his life a matter of days afterwards.

I drew the cloth up over him again, covering him to the chin. For a moment I rested my hand on his forehead. 'I am sorry,' I said quietly. 'I will do what I can to discover who you are, and why you came here, and then we will bury you and prayers will be said for you.'

Then I pulled the cloth up over his head and left him.

I went into Theo's office. He was looking slightly less harassed, and waved a hand for me to tell him my findings. 'He died from a musket ball that hit him in the heart,' I said. 'It looks to me as if they killed him quickly – catching him by surprise, probably, for there are no signs that he tried to fight them off

– and then immediately hung him up and opened the vessels in his throat to drain him of his blood.'

'Jesus Christ,' Theo muttered. *'Why?'*

I thought back to what I'd been reading the previous night, but decided it was too soon to share it with Theo. I needed to sit alone and think; to let the connections form, break and re-form, and I knew nothing would even begin to clarify until I could do so.

'I don't know,' I said shortly. 'Yet. I'm off to see Captain Zeke,' I went on before Theo could ask me anything else.

'Very well. Report to me as soon as you have any information.'

I nodded my assent, then hurried away.

I found the same uneasy mood on the *Falco*, but now unease had been joined by resentment and a very obvious dissatisfaction. It was hardly surprising, since the crew were still engaged on the awful task of emptying out the barrel in the hiding place. I stood on the upper deck beside Captain Zeke, listening to the regular sound of bucket-loads of unmentionable waste matter being hurled into the sea. The men had been ordered to throw their noisome burdens over the *Falco*'s bows, on the port side, so the filthy puddle polluting the clear blue-green sea and slowly dissipating was mostly concealed from the crowds on the quayside.

'They hate it,' Captain Zeke said unnecessarily, nodding towards his surly crew.

'I'm not surprised.'

He grinned briefly. 'I didn't mean the task itself, although in truth they're none too happy about that either. I meant they hate having to go down there, where the fugitives hid. To begin with, I ordered the chain of men to change their positions only every couple of hours, but it wasn't working.' He didn't elaborate. 'Now they're shifting around like a troupe of country dancers.' He hawked and spat over the side, the gesture eloquent of his disgust.

'They're still seeing blue men?' I asked.

He nodded. 'Aye.'

I hadn't come merely to ask him where the fugitives might

have boarded his ship: there was something I had to tell him, and I judged now was the moment. 'A body has been found,' I said, keeping my voice low. There were sailors busy nearby, and what I had to say was for the ship's captain to hear first.

He spun round, his light eyes staring penetratingly at me. 'Go on.'

'It's that of a young man, tall, very thin, dark-skinned. He was hung from the ankles from a tree up at Buckland, and his body was drained of blood.'

'And why are you telling me this?'

'Because his hands and his arms were stained blue.'

Captain Zeke didn't speak for some moments. Then he said heavily, 'There was more than one man down there – there *had* to be.'

I thought I understood. He was desperate for answers: how and where the fugitives had managed to board the *Falco*, why they had done so, how they'd managed to stay alive for the duration of the crossing of the Atlantic and how they'd left the ship without being spotted. If there had only been the one man who had crept on board and he was now dead and beyond explaining, Captain Zeke was never going to find out.

'I think so too,' I said. 'I'm thinking that his death was the result of a fight among them – the group of fugitives. They'd have been in a bad way, if the dead youth is anything to go by. He hadn't eaten a proper meal in a long time.'

'You expect me to feel sorry for him?' Captain Zeke snapped.

'He endured the unendurable. He knew the risks, yet went ahead anyway. He must have had an incredibly powerful reason, and he made it all the way to England only to be murdered soon after he achieved his aim. So yes, I do.'

I'd spoken more harshly than I'd intended, but then it was I who had stood over that pathetic body. And Ezekiel Colt wasn't my captain any more.

He lowered his furious eyes and muttered something that might have been an apology, although I doubted it.

'I came to ask you something as well as bring you news of the body,' I said after a moment.

'What?'

'Whether you have any idea where your uninvited passengers might have come on board.'

'Not before Hispaniola,' he said, with an alacrity that suggested he'd thought long and hard on the matter. 'You've seen the tiny space where they hid, Gabe. We'd have been hauling corpses out of it if they'd been down there during the storm.'

I nodded. 'That's what I thought. So, would it have been possible? For them to get onto the *Falco* without being observed?'

He gave me a withering look. 'Of course it was possible,' he said. 'They were *there*, weren't they? Down in my sodding hold, helping themselves to my supplies, pissing and shitting in that *fucking* barrel that *still* isn't empty!' The last words came out in a furious shout of frustration.

'Stupid question,' I muttered. 'Sorry.'

He gave a curt nod. 'As to how they managed it, I can't say. You know what it's like alongside, Gabe, when you're taking on supplies before sailing. All manner of men and even a few women come pushing and shoving their way onto the deck and you don't usually do a head count to make sure they all go ashore again. Great God, who in their right mind would *want* to sneak down to the lowest, darkest, smallest hold and hide there while we buck and wriggle our way across the Atlantic?' He shook his head. 'It's beyond me, the whole damned, blasted mess.'

I felt very sorry for him. 'I spoke to a good friend of mine who is my parish priest,' I said. 'He has offered to come on board and perform a service of cleansing, if you think it would help.'

Captain Zeke turned to me. I thought his eyes looked slightly moist, but it was probably nothing more than the stiff breeze off the water. 'You did that? Went to this priest friend and asked for his help?'

'Yes.'

He slapped me across the shoulders, hard. 'You're a good man.'

I was feeling decidedly embarrassed now. 'Well, the *Falco*

was my last ship,' I muttered. 'I'll always wish her well, *and* her crew.'

'Tell him yes, and thank him,' Captain Zeke said. He must be feeling better, I thought, since his utterances were coming out like orders again, just as they usually did.

I turned to go, hiding my smile. 'I will. Good day, Captain, and I will be back soon.'

I called in on Jonathan on the way home and told him Captain Zeke would be pleased to accept his offer. 'He even said to thank you,' I added.

Jonathan smiled. 'And that is a rarity?'

'You have no idea how favoured you are.'

'I shall go as soon as time permits,' he said.

'May I accompany you?'

His smile widened. 'Yes, Gabriel. Otherwise I shall have to tramp up and down the Plymouth quays until I happen upon the right ship.'

Then, at last, I was riding up the track to Rosewyke. Once again I seemed to have let the day go by without remembering to eat, and I looked forward to asking Sallie to serve up something tasty that with any luck Celia and I could share.

Samuel took my horse, and I paused in the yard to wash the worst of the day's accumulated filth off my hands. Inside, I added hot water to my list of requirements from Sallie, and she thrust a full jug at me: 'There you are, Doctor, if you don't mind taking it up yourself, only I must get on with your dinner.'

I stripped, washed, dressed in clean linen and had a short but welcome sleep. Then I went downstairs to find Celia waiting for me and dinner almost ready.

I didn't want to talk about bodies, or sickness, or fugitives, and my intelligent, perspicacious sister realized it and instead entertained me with a lively and very funny account of the brother of a matchmaking friend of hers who, persuaded by his well-meaning but unobservant sister that Celia was in need of a new husband, had been trying to woo her.

Having dismissed him and his suit in a few short but

devastating sentences – I hoped she'd been kinder and less abrupt when she'd spoken to the poor man than she was when she related the exchange to me – she sat back for a while in a reflective silence, absently twirling her crystal wine glass. Then she said casually, 'Isn't it time we invited Jonathan to dine with us again?'

SEVEN

I was very busy the following morning, with four existing patients to review and three new ones to call upon. I returned to Rosewyke at noon, determined not to let another day go by without so much as a morsel of food to sustain me between breakfast and dinner, to find Sallie in the yard waiting for me.

'Oh, *there* you are, Doctor!' she said with a hint of reproof, as if my absence had been due to some boyish lark rather than the pursuance of my duty. 'I was on the point of sending Tock to look for you!'

I glanced across at Tock, whose mouth had fallen open in horror at the very thought of such a mission. Tock works hard, is loyal and has been with my family since he was a boy, but even we who are fond of him would not credit him with anything in the way of initiative, and I was at a loss to think how Sallie thought he might have gone about searching for me in the wide area of countryside in which my patients reside.

'Don't worry, Tock,' I said, 'I'm here now.'

He gave me a lopsided, toothy grin and melted away before anyone could ask another impossible task of him.

'What is it, Sallie?' I asked.

'A message from Plymouth, Doctor.' She screwed up her eyes, presumably to aid her memory, and rattled off, 'Captain Colt of the *Falco* requests your urgent presence because something has turned up at the bottom of the barrel.' She opened her eyes again. 'Now don't go asking me which barrel, or what's been discovered, because I'm sure I have no idea,' she went on primly, spoiling the effect by adding in a whisper, 'I don't suppose *you* could make a suggestion or two, Doctor?'

I knew which barrel, although out of respect for her sensitivities I wasn't going to share the knowledge with her. As to what had been found . . . it could be virtually anything, but the pressing nature of the summons suggested it wasn't a horn button or a chicken bone.

'No, Sallie,' I said. 'Now, if you will kindly cut me some bread and cheese, I will set off again and eat as I go.'

The disgruntled crew of the *Falco* must have overcome their abhorrence, for they had completed the ghastly task and the barrel now stood on the open deck. As Captain Zeke led me towards to it, I deduced from the lack of smell that it had not only been emptied but also swilled out.

'There's nothing in it now,' Captain Zeke said. There were several muttered comments from the men, standing around in a loose semicircle, generally to the effect that the barrel's empty state was entirely due to them and nobody had been nearly grateful enough.

'All right, all right,' growled one of the senior officers – a tough-looking individual with half of one ear missing who went by the name of Sebastian Waldington – 'you'll get your reward later, lads,' and he nodded towards the large cask of rum that sat on top of the stack of supplies.

'This way, Gabe,' Captain Zeke said curtly. He strode on past the barrel, the assembled crew parting to let us pass, towards the aft, where something lay on the deck covered in sacking.

I stared down at it. I still hoped very much that what lay beneath the sacking would be nothing more than a dead dog but I had little faith that the hope was going to be fulfilled.

I sensed the men moving to re-form their semicircle, this time with a new focus. Captain Zeke nodded to one of them – it was Willum, the tall, scarred man with the tattoos – and he reached down and twitched the sacking aside.

Instantly a powerful stench of putrefaction rose up.

The body lay on its left side and was tightly curled in a foetal position, knees up to the chin, arms wrapped around the thighs. The skull bore vestiges of long hair, some of it braided into a thin plait. Much of the flesh had rotted from the face, giving the illusion that the lips had been drawn back in a howl. A few teeth remained, long, brown and fang-like. The short spine was curved like a bow, and the limbs were stumpy.

'It's not a child, is it?' someone said. Turning, I saw that Sebastian Waldington stood beside me.

'No. Look at the teeth.' As I pointed he leaned closer, and

gave an exclamation of disgust as he accidentally inhaled the stink. 'This was an adult,' I went on. 'A man, I think, but I need to examine the corpse more closely.' I looked enquiringly at Captain Zeke, who nodded.

I crouched down over the body. 'This was found in the barrel?' It was all but unbelievable.

'It was,' Sebastian Waldington affirmed. 'Willum, tell the doctor.'

I looked up at the tattooed man, then straightened up so that we were face to face. He was even taller than me. 'If you please, Willum,' I prompted.

He seemed to be in a daze, and it took him a moment or two to focus on me. He looked . . . puzzled, was the word that sprang to mind. He opened his mouth a couple of times as if trying to form the words, then shook his head violently, tried again and said, 'It was bad down there. Towards the end, we had to change the order of the chain every few minutes, since not one of us could bear to be delving down into that barrel for long.' He shuddered. 'It wasn't just the smell, it was something else.' He shuddered again, his whole body briefly convulsing. 'It was like someone was trying to hold us back. Some of the lads said they could hear moaning, or keening. And some of us saw things,' he added, dropping his voice so that I barely heard him.

He, I understood in a moment of clarity, had been one of the latter. 'What did you see, Willum?' I asked softly.

He turned, meeting my eyes. His were wide with remembered horror. 'A face. It was a woman, and I thought at first she was beautiful, but then she wasn't, she was old, unbelievably old, and then the middle of her face changed and it came poking out towards me, and she had a crocodile's snout where her nose ought to be and then it—' He stopped abruptly.

There was no need for him to go on. I knew what he had seen, for I'd seen it too. I touched his upper arm, hard with muscle. 'It wasn't real, Willum,' I said firmly.

He shot me an incredulous glance. 'Looked real to me,' he muttered.

'There is some substance down there in that far hold that acts on the mind, producing auditory and visual hallucinations,'

I said. Seeing that he didn't understand, I added, 'Visions, and imaginary sounds.'

He went on staring at me and I sensed I hadn't begun to convince him.

'This substance gives off a scent, a perfume,' I went on, 'and—'

There was a harsh, disbelieving laugh from the man standing next to Willum. 'A *scent*?' he said scathingly. 'Doctor, have you any idea what we were breathing in down there? Right from the start it was bad enough, but by the time we were nearing the bottom of the barrel it was all but intolerable. D'you think we'd have been able to smell *perfume*?'

I nodded, acceding the point. 'No, I'm sure you couldn't,' I replied. 'All the same, it was having its effect on you. It was an awful task,' I pressed on before anyone could argue with me, 'and I admire the resolution with which you stuck to it.' They'd had no choice, of course, since it had been the captain himself who gave the order, but it did no harm to show some appreciation. 'But there was something in the air, whether you could detect it or not. I noticed it when the hiding place was first discovered.' Remembering the piece of cloth I'd saved from the first little corpse's garment, I resolved to examine it as soon as I was back at Rosewyke. I tried to recall what I had done with it, hoping I'd put it away somewhere safe.

Beside me, Captain Zeke emerged abruptly from whatever had been absorbing him. 'You'll be wanting these remains taken to the coroner's house,' he said. 'Willum, cover the corpse again, and you, you and you' – he pointed to the three sailors closest to Willum – 'help him get it off my ship.'

The four men leapt to obey, and in a very short time they had the corpse covered, on a length of plank and on its way.

There were always carters touting for business on the quay. Willum collared one, the corpse was loaded on to the cart and, having fetched my horse, I went ahead to alert Theo. He was as amazed as I had been to learn that a body had been found in the barrel.

He looked at me dubiously. 'Have they cleaned it?' he demanded.

I hesitated. 'It's possibly had a bucket of sea water sluiced over it.'

He stood up. 'Then we'll not have it here,' he said very firmly. 'Get the carter to go to the empty house.'

Earlier in the year, Theo had formalized his arrangement to use the crypt of an uninhabited house up the road, and now he paid rent for the privilege. He had been heard to complain at the money he was obliged to part with, but the advantage of not having stinking, putrefying corpses underneath the house where he and his family lived would, I reckoned, have been worth twice what he was paying.

Theo and I helped the carter to unload the corpse, still on its plank, and we put it down in the yard behind the empty house while I paid off the carter. As we heard him in the lane outside whistling to his horse and setting off back to Plymouth, Theo was already at the pump, filling up the pail that stood beside it. I removed the sacking, and we took it in turns to throw pail after pail of water over the body until most of what had covered it inside the barrel had been washed away. Despite our efforts, however, it still stank of shit, and now the stench of rotting flesh was adding to the effect.

Theo sighed. 'We'd better get him down into the crypt.'

He stayed with me, honourable man and good friend that he is, while I performed my examination. I am accustomed to bad smells, and I usually find that becoming deeply absorbed in whatever task has ordained my close proximity to a stinking body helps me to overcome the natural repugnance. Theo, however, did not have a medical man's resilience, and as I worked I frequently heard him dry-retching. But he did not complain.

Presently I stopped. There was more to do, but I reckoned I had found the cause of death, which was what Theo needed to hear. I would tell him, I thought, and he could make his escape.

'Come up into the fresh air,' I said, leading the way up the steps. We emerged into the yard, and Theo took some deep breaths.

'Well?' he asked. He still looked pale.

'The body is that of a man, advanced in years and probably

over sixty,' I began. 'There are clear signs of ill-usage: he has been worked extremely hard, and I found what looked like the scars of the lash on his back.'

'A sailor?'

'Probably, yes.' If I was right about his age, and his teeth and the state of his bones suggested I was, then he could have been at sea for getting on for half a century. Boys of twelve or even younger were commonly recruited for ships' crews.

'And what killed him?' What small colour that had returned to his face drained away again as he added, 'He wasn't shoved alive into that barrel, was he?'

'No.' I was reasonably confident of what had killed him, and in any case it was hard to imagine his companions selecting that particularly awful death for one of their number. 'He was sick. I believe he died of his illness.'

Theo muttered a prayer. 'Thank God,' he breathed. 'What was it, then, this sickness?'

'Have you heard of scurvy?'

'Er – I *think* so.'

Briefly I described the symptoms. 'It's thought to be caused by some element lacking in the diet,' I went on, 'partly because a sharp increase in its incidence cropped up around the time ships began to be at sea on the world's great oceans – and thus denied access to fresh food – for longer and longer stretches.'

'Can it be cured?'

'Yes, provided a sufferer is not too far gone. More importantly it can be prevented, by dosing the crew with a daily intake of the right medicine.' I smiled.

'No doubt foul-tasting and stinking like that corpse?'

'Not in the least. Relatively pleasant, in fact: oranges, lemons or lime, either the fruit or the juice.'

Theo thought for a moment. 'And this man wasn't given any,' he said.

'He'd almost certainly been sick even before they set out, so I would imagine the scurvy affected him swiftly and very gravely,' I said. 'He was malnourished and his body was worn out.'

'So why was he in the barrel?' Theo asked, then, before I could speak, he answered his own question. 'Because after he'd died he begun to rot, and the stink was bad enough down there already, so they put him in with the – with the waste.'

'Yes,' I agreed. 'There was, I suppose, little option.' For his companions couldn't have done what men at sea normally do, and put his body over the side, without being discovered. They probably hadn't seen the sea and the sky and breathed the clean air for days, if not weeks, by the time the old man died, shut up as they were in their self-imposed incarceration deep within the ship.

'Poor bugger,' Theo murmured.

We were both briefly silent, as if in recognition of the old man's suffering. Then I said, 'Theo, the lad in your cellar had scurvy too.'

He nodded. 'Stands to reason. If they'd been part of the same group, they'd have shared the same conditions.'

'True. Unlike the man in the crypt, however, the younger man would have recovered.'

'Had someone not fired a musket ball into his heart and then drained him of his life's blood,' Theo said heavily. Then, turning away and heading for the gate, he added, 'We need to get to the bottom of this, Gabe. It is monstrous.'

I returned to the crypt to finish my examination, but I found nothing of note except for the fact that, like the lad who had been exsanguinated, this corpse too had blue hands and fore-arms. Then I covered the old man's body with the sacking and left him.

I rode home via the village, calling in to see Jonathan. He was not in his house and, noticing the hour, I guessed he was in church. I would have liked very much to go and hear even-song, but I had work to do. I left a note for him asking if he could come with me to the *Falco* during the afternoon of the next day to perform his cleansing ceremony, then left.

Celia noticed my distraction and, as soon as we had eaten, said she was retiring to her room to finish a piece of embroidery. I bade her goodnight, then went straight to my study.

I found the fragment of cloth precisely where I'd remembered I'd put it, tucked away in the leather roll in which I keep my

instruments. I took it out, spread a piece of clean parchment
on my desk and smoothed out the cloth on top of it.

I held the light right over it and stared at it. Whatever
substance had stained the white cloth was golden in colour,
darkening to brown where the concentration was most intense.
I had detected the perfume as soon as I had taken it out of the
instrument roll, and now, leaning over it, I breathed it in deeply.

And immediately wished I hadn't been so incautious, for my
senses were swimming, there were stabs of pain in my head,
bright white flashes of light popped before my eyes and,
just for a heartbeat, I had an image of the woman's face with
the crocodile snout.

I leaned back in my chair, my eyes closed, while these powerful
symptoms slowly faded away.

Then I drew forward my notebook, dipped my quill in the
inkhorn and began on my observations. In summary, these
were that the substance was slightly tacky to the touch; that
there seemed to be slight crystallization at the edges of the
largest area of staining; that the perfume was a little like
incense but also smelt of leaves, or possibly grass; plant or
vegetable matter of some sort.

I went over to my books, drawing out a volume describing
the use of herbs in healing. I found nothing bearing any simi-
larity to whatever had soaked into that piece of cloth. I knew
I needed the advice of someone better versed than I in traditional
remedies, and with a flood of pleasure that quite surprised me,
acknowledged that I had the perfect excuse for riding over to
visit Judyth Penwarden.

She lives in a tidy little house near the village of Blaxton, where
the ferry crosses the Tavy, and as I arrived early the next morning
I caught her about to leave it; I had only just raised the heavy,
angel-shaped door knocker when the door flew open and there
she was.

Her dark hair was smoothly bound up beneath an immaculate
white cap, over which she had drawn up the deep hood of her
heavy cloak. The day was bright but very cold with a hard frost
and she had clearly dressed for it, for her gown was of thick
wool and she had wound a long scarf round her throat. Her

light eyes looking up at me held the habitual hint of amusement, as if she was well aware of some interesting fact that I could only guess at.

'Doctor Gabriel!' she greeted me with a smile. 'What brings you to my door so early on a chilly October morning?'

'Not too early, I hope?'

'No indeed, for as you see my day has already begun and I am on my way out.'

'Have you time to spare for a brief consultation?'

Now her smile widened and she laughed. 'I am a midwife, Doctor. Can it be you have confounded nature and God's laws and find yourself carrying a child?'

I was not sure whether she intended her remark to have the potently sexual undertones that I picked up; given how attractive I found her, these could well have existed only in my own head. 'Er—' I began.

She took pity on me, taking hold of my arm and ushering me inside, closing the door firmly behind me. 'I apologize, Doctor,' she said. 'The jest was in poor taste. What did you wish to talk to me about?'

Now she was business-like, sweeping off her cloak and hanging it on a hook, then indicating one of the pair of chairs beside the hearth and sitting herself down in the other one. Straight-backed, she fixed me with her extraordinary eyes – silvery-grey with barely a hint of blue, and so rare as to be remarkable in a woman with her dark-toned skin and black hair – and I gathered my thoughts to prepare my answer.

Before I explained my presence, however, there was something else.

'First, thank you for the draught you prescribed for me.'

'It worked?'

'Of course it did, for you are a woman of great skill.'

I thought she blushed faintly, but it might have been wishful thinking. 'Your head no longer pains you?'

'No.'

She nodded, then said expectantly, 'Well?'

I told her about the crew of the *Falco* and the deep fear that had affected them on the voyage home, briefly describing what had been found in the hidden hold and the strange vision

I had seen down there. I described the perfume, powerful enough to be detectable amid the stench, and described to her how I had torn off a strip of the garment in which the tiny body had been clad because it was marked with a strong-smelling substance which I could not identify. I took the piece of cloth from inside my tunic, unwrapped it and held it out to her. 'Take care,' I warned, 'for it is potent.'

She nodded. She stared at the little patch of gold, picked at it very gently with a fingernail and then held it about a foot from her nose and took a tentative sniff.

'*Oh!*' She blinked rapidly a few times. 'It is indeed,' she murmured. She raised it to her eyes, and I noticed that she held her breath. Then she put it down on her lap, smoothing it with long fingers.

I waited.

'You said you could not identify this?'

'I did.'

Slowly she shook her head. 'Neither can I, and . . . please do not take this as an insult, Doctor, but my failure is more inexplicable than yours, for I have spent my life in the study of herbs and potions and it is many years since I have been confounded in this way.'

'The *Falco* had lately been in the Caribbean,' I said, breaking a silence that had lasted for some time.

She grinned briefly. 'Ah.'

'I should have said that at the outset,' I observed.

'Yes, you should.'

'What *can* you tell me?'

She thought for a few moments, then said, 'Some elements of this smell I do know: lemon, or possibly lime; basil; hemp. I also detect an aroma that is reminiscent of incense. There is also a strong underlying fragrance which I do not recognize. Together these would appear to have combined to make the strong, enduring perfume . . .' Tentatively she lifted the fragment and sniffed it again. 'But there is some sort of fine powder here, Doctor, which I believe is ground-up seeds.' She shook her head. 'I have no idea what it consists of, nor can I explain the effect it has when the aroma is inhaled.' She held the cloth out to me, and I wrapped it up again and put it away.

'So what do I do now?' I muttered, more to myself than to Judyth.

But she responded anyway. 'Well, do not despair, for one thing,' she said brightly. 'The majority of what I know of plant medicine was taught to me by a remarkable teacher who knows far, far more than you and I put together' – again that sudden undercurrent of sexuality – 'will ever know.'

'And will this man agree to speak to me?' I asked. Distracted by the sparkle in her eyes, I was finding it difficult to keep my attention on the matter in hand.

'Yes, I have no doubt of it. But why do you assume my teacher is male?'

Then, of course, I understood.

'My apologies,' I said sincerely. 'I ought to have realized, for I know the woman.' I paused. 'Don't tell her, will you?'

'That you referred to her as male? No, for it would rule out any possibility of her coming to your aid now or ever again. But I will tell her of your difficulty, and ask her to call upon you.'

'Thank you.'

I had taken up enough of her time and I rose to leave. She saw me to the door, and we wished each other a rather stiff good day.

I rode away suppressing the turbulence within me, set off both by having just been talking to Judyth Penwarden but equally by the prospect of an imminent visit from our local wise woman, Black Carlotta.

I had met her on several occasions, most frequently when my patients were adding to their chances of surviving what ailed them, as they no doubt would have explained it, by consulting a practitioner of the old ways alongside one of the new. To her credit she never disparaged what I was able to do, and her attitude towards me was largely that of a fellow healer, tinged with a pinch of patronizing pity. I had to admit that I admired her, and the depth of her wisdom was profound.

Nevertheless, knowing that she would soon be knocking on my door was not altogether comfortable.

EIGHT

Jonathan Carew stood hunched within the dark confines of the hidden hold, his bible open in his hands, his eyes closed in concentration. Captain Zeke and I were either side of him, and Sebastian Waldington crouched just inside the entrance passage. Willum and a small group of crew members had assembled in the adjacent hold. Not one of them was prepared to come any closer.

The hiding place was clean now, and with the barrel gone it seemed less claustrophobic. The smell of body waste had been scrubbed away, although strangely I could still detect the scent that had permeated the garment of the tiny corpse. It was powerful indeed, I reflected, to persist even after the crew's thorough scrubbing . . .

Jonathan's strong voice rang out in the confined space. The purification service had begun up on the open deck and he had kept it simple, beginning with prayers and then asking God's blessing on a place that had become befouled and on those who dwelt within it. We had then descended to the lowest regions of the ship, and Jonathan had insisted on crawling into the dark, malign little hold where the fugitives had lived. It was not dark now, for he had commanded the lighting of many lanterns. Now the little space was both light and becoming uncomfortably hot.

I listened to my friend's words as he threw his spiritual power behind his plea to God to have mercy on whatever troubled soul had dwelt here, to ease its pain and give it rest so that the malice and the fear it had created might dissipate and disappear. There were murmurs of *amen* from both within the space and from the adjacent hold, and I saw Captain Zeke cross himself at least twice.

Now Jonathan raised his bible and, his voice waxing in strength, he read the beautiful words of the twenty-third psalm. 'Yea, though I should walk through the valley of the shadow of death,' he declaimed, 'I will fear no evil; for thou are with me: thy rod and thy staff, they comfort me.' He paused, and it seemed to me as I listened to him, transfixed by the words even though they were so familiar, that his voice had turned into something visible, and that it bore its message – God's message – through the dense air of that secret space and out into its walls, ceiling and floor, permeating the very fabric of the ship with a forceful combination of the rejection of the residual malignity, the promise of God's loving protection and a powerful sense of hope.

Suddenly the light seemed brighter and, turning to my companions, I saw that both Captain Zeke and his officer were smiling.

Jonathan led us in the Lord's Prayer, blessed the ship and its company again and then, after a brief silence, gently closed his bible. He stood for a moment with his eyes closed, then, opening them, said to Captain Zeke, 'I believe, Captain, that whatever held sway here has gone.'

Captain Zeke thumped him on the back, too overcome to say anything, and, standing back, indicated for Jonathan to lead the way out through the entrance. When we were all in the next hold, I heard Sebastian Waldington give orders for the gap in the bulkhead to be thoroughly re-sealed.

Captain Zeke demonstrated his gratitude in tangible form, having ordered a feast in the wardroom, several bottles of very fine wine and a cask of French brandy. Jonathan ate and drank sparingly, and I sensed he was finding it hard to respond adequately to the thanks of the captain and his officers. Not that they would have noticed, for they did not know him like I did.

As the brandy was produced yet again and I saw Jonathan refuse, I met his eyes and read the appeal in them.

'Captain,' I said, getting to my feet, 'his reverence has many calls upon his time, and I think he—'

'Of course!' Captain Zeke too stood up, so abruptly that his chair fell over. Turning to Jonathan, he gave him a low bow, thanked him yet again and apologized for keeping him so long. Jonathan and I were escorted off the ship, someone was despatched to fetch our horses, there were yet more expressions of appreciation and exclamations of relief at the *Falco*'s deliverance, then at last we were on our way.

We were out beyond the town walls and in open country before Jonathan spoke. I had attributed his silence to fatigue, for he had not spared himself and I was sure there must be an emotional as well as a physical toll. But his words were not at all what I expected.

'You were right to ask me to do that, Gabriel,' he said, 'for there was indeed something present on the ship.'

'You detected it?' He nodded. 'You saw, or heard, something?'

He paused, frowning, then said, 'I have never experienced anything quite like it; for of a sudden I found I was picking up two conflicting forces.'

'Two forces – do you mean the howling and wailing that some of the crew reported and the visions seen by others?' Including me, I might have added.

But Jonathan shook his head. 'No, not that.' He paused again. 'There were warring powers down there, Gabriel, or I believe it to be so. One was powerfully aggressive, evil, malign; it had its origins far away and a long time ago, for it carried the darkness and the cold damp of the deep earth, and it was transfused with ancient power. It—' He stopped abruptly, and I saw from his expression that whatever he had perceived had affected him deeply. 'But I will not speak of what it did.' He was quiet for a short time, and slowly the profound distress in his face eased. Then, his brow creasing in bemusement, he said, 'The other power, very much to my amazement, seemed to be a protective spirit.'

'*Protective?*'

'I understand your perplexity, Gabriel, for it is unexpected, to say the least.'

I struggled to understand. 'So the fugitives brought two contrary forces with them, one that was evil and the other benign?' Yet I had felt nothing but malignancy when I'd stood in the stinking dark in that ghastly hole. 'How could that be? What—'

But Jonathan raised his hand, as if physically stopping my

words. 'I don't know, and therefore I cannot answer your questions,' he said. 'As I just said, I have not encountered such a conflict before. I am at a loss to explain it.'

We rode on in silence. Then, as we reached the spot where my road led to Rosewyke and his to Tavy St Luke, he relented and, with a smile said, 'I need time to think on this, Gabriel. I suspect there is an answer – there almost always is – and I hope that it is one that prayer and quiet contemplation will reveal to me.'

'You'll tell me if it does?'

His smile broadened. 'How could I not?'

'Come and dine with us very soon,' I said on an impulse, recalling Celia's words of the night before last. 'Not so that I can badger you to explain the inexplicable,' I added, 'but because it's too long since you visited us.'

He gave me a small bow. 'On those terms, I accept, and thank you.'

He tipped his cap to me, and rode off down into the village.

Although it was not yet late, Celia and I had eaten our supper and she had gone upstairs to her own rooms. I was restless, however, and I got up from my chair by the fire to wander through the house. The kitchen was immaculate – I have never known my diligent housekeeper to leave it in any other state at the end of the day – and, her work done, Sallie had also retired. I let myself out through the yard door and took Flynn for a run. We did not venture far, for although the night was beautiful – the skies were clear, affording a magnificent view of the stars – frost was forming and it was very cold. All was quiet as we came back through the yard, and only a softly-flickering light showed from the stable block. I heard the restless movements of one of the horses, and Samuel's calm voice speaking quiet words of reassurance.

Flynn preceded me into the house, his claws clicking on the floorboards as he headed for the kitchen and the old blanket by the hearth where he sleeps. I was on the point of locking and barring the heavy old front door when someone tapped on the other side.

It probably happens a dozen times a year that a man, or

sometimes a woman, comes to summon me late at night because of some domestic emergency. With a sigh of resignation, I opened the door again, trying to alter my expression to benign interest rather than a man longing for his bed.

A small but erect figure stood on the step, dressed in black and with an elaborately-folded headdress. Strands of pure white hair framed the face, which showed all the signs of advanced age and years spent out of doors yet out of which a pair of clear, bright eyes stared up at me.

I flung the door wide and said, 'Mistress Carlotta, I did not hope to see you so soon.' For it had only been that morning that Judyth had volunteered to seek her out, although in truth it seemed longer.

She narrowed her eyes. 'I'm intrigued to know what this scented substance is you've found. Going to ask me in?'

'Of course.' I stood back, and she advanced into the hall. I hurried to go past her – she was slowly circling the wide space, looking around with a faint smile – and added, 'Come through into the library. The fire is still hot, and we shall be able to talk without disturbing my housekeeper, whose room is off the kitchen.'

There was something about Black Carlotta that made me feel I ought to explain myself.

She sat down in Celia's accustomed chair and accepted the glass of brandy I offered. Almost straight away, she cast off the heavy cloak she wore, as well as the woollen shawl beneath it, closely wrapped around her. I was surprised, for the fire was not giving out very much heat and I'd been about to put on more wood.

She raised her eyebrows, clearly having perceived my thoughts. 'I'm not used to warm houses, Doctor.' There was a hint of superiority in her expression, as if she was contemptuous of weak mortals who had to huddle within walls by a well-stoked fire in order to survive. I had no idea where, and how, she herself lived; rumour had it that she habitually made her bed under some convenient hedge, but I did not believe that. She was clean, for one thing, and in addition, she was a healer, a provider of remedies and simples, and therefore must surely have at least a workroom somewhere.

'Finished?' she said caustically.

I refused to meet the challenge, instead giving her a smile. 'If you are comfortable here, and can tolerate the heat' – she flashed a grin at the remark – 'I shall fetch the piece of cloth stained with the substance in question.'

She didn't answer, save for a nod, so I hurried off upstairs.

Celia peered out from the passage leading to her rooms as I headed back along the gallery towards the stairs. 'Who's that?' she hissed. I might have known she'd both have heard the arrival of the visitor and not be satisfied until she'd found out who had come calling.

'It's a mysterious wise woman known as Black Carlotta,' I whispered back.

Her eyes widened. 'Oooh, I've heard tell of her! Is she as terrifying as they say?'

'She is only a little terrifying, and I am going to make sure not to antagonize her.'

'Gabe, don't joke about such matters.'

My courageous sister actually looked quite frightened.

I went over and gave her a quick, tight hug. 'Come and meet her and see for yourself,' I said impulsively.

'Oh no! I'm not dressed, I'm in my nightgown and robe!'

'She won't mind.'

Celia gave a grimace. 'It's not her I'm thinking about.' But she had glanced at me, seen the challenge in my expression and was already tightening her sash and smoothing her long, loose hair. 'Very well, then!'

'Mistress Carlotta, may I present my sister Celia?' I said as we returned to the library.

Black Carlotta eyed Celia with intent, sharp-focused eyes, and Celia returned the look. 'So you are Celia Palfrey,' Black Carlotta said. She had used Celia's married name, so she clearly knew of my sister's marriage and, presumably, was also aware that she had been widowed. She was still staring hard at Celia, but I saw a softening in her expression. She pointed to the chair on the opposite side of the hearth – my chair, in fact – and said, 'Sit down and have some of your brother's brandy.'

I saw Celia's face brighten with amusement at our visitor's casual assumption of the hostess role. Turning to Black Carlotta,

I caught an intense, complex expression on her face as she looked at Celia: severe, yet at the same time full of compassion and not a little admiration.

I knew, then, that somehow she was aware of exactly what had happened a year and a half ago; how Jeromy Palfrey had met his death, and the roles my sister and I had played.[1] I further knew that, far from condemning us, she admired our actions and would undoubtedly have done the same herself.

She met my eyes and gave an all but imperceptible nod.

And that was that.

I held out the fragment of material I'd torn from the tiny corpse's robes. 'There is the unknown substance,' I said, pointing to the stain.

She took the fabric in her hands and for some time simply stared down at it. Then she gently scraped a fingernail across it, rolling whatever small amount of matter she had collected between her forefinger and thumb. She smelled it and then put it up to her mouth, touching it to the inside of her lower lip, waiting for some moments and then touching it with the tip of her tongue. She sat back in the chair with her eyes closed for quite a long time, not speaking, not moving and, to judge from the slow and shallow rise and fall of her chest, scarcely breathing. Finally she gathered herself, crushed the material between her hands with some force and, as a powerful cloud of that strange, unknown perfume filled the room, put the fabric right up to her face and breathed in deeply.

I heard Celia make a sound between a gasp and a sob, and, tearing myself away from my intense, anxious attention on Black Carlotta, went to kneel beside my sister.

'What's she *doing*?' Celia whispered. For now Black Carlotta sat bolt upright, eyes tightly closed, a grimace on her face, rocking from side to side and twisting her head convulsively to and fro as if trying to escape some malign influence. 'Is she all right?'

'I don't know,' I said.

Black Carlotta, I was fairly sure, was in the grip of a powerful trance. I was feeling unsteady and slightly nauseous, and Celia

1 See *A Rustle of Silk*

had paled. We were only receiving the edge of the potent but invisible cloud that Black Carlotta had just released from the length of material; she had breathed in a far larger dose.

'Should we do something to help her?' Celia asked, already half out of her chair.

'*No!*' It was one thing for Black Carlotta to absorb the full potency of an unknown substance, for she knew what she was doing and had had a lifetime's experience with the power of herbs and plants, and probably had a degree of immunity to the most perilous substances. The potential effect on Celia was unknowable and I was not going to let her risk it.

'But *look* at her!' Celia persisted, struggling against my hands on her shoulders holding her down. 'Gabe, she's in trouble!'

'She's deep in a vision, Celia,' I said urgently. 'We can do nothing for her just now, for her mind is telling her she is seeing things that aren't really here, hearing sounds that exist only within her head.'

'But—'

'We must watch her, make sure she does not jump up and do anything that might harm her, then, when she returns to us, keep her warm and give her more brandy,' I said very firmly. 'She will be herself again once the effects wear off.'

Celia gave me a shrewd glance. 'You sound as if you speak from experience.'

Remembering with a shudder the secret hiding place and the image of the crocodile-snouted woman, I muttered, 'I do.'

I settled on the arm of Celia's chair and put my arm round her, and she leaned against me. We waited, and presently Black Carlotta's eyes fluttered open and she gazed at us. She smiled, giving Celia a look of great tenderness. 'You've a good heart,' she said, her voice a little hoarse. 'I heard what you said, but your brother was right, weren't nothing you could do for me. But I thank you for the thought.'

'I was – we were worried,' Celia said. Then she got up and put a very generous slug of brandy in Black Carlotta's glass. 'I think you have earned that,' she remarked.

There was silence for some time. Black Carlotta folded the piece of cloth into a tight wad and handed it back to me, and I covered it up and put it back inside my instrument roll. It was probably my imagination, but I felt as if the air in the room was clearer once I had done so.

Black Carlotta sat sipping her brandy, her shawl wrapped around her, and at last she said, 'You've got a rare old substance there, Doctor. Not from these parts, I reckon.'

'No. I believe it originated in the Caribbean. One of the islands, or possibly the wide lands of the Spanish Main.'

I had wondered if those terms would have any meaning for a countrywoman such as Black Carlotta but yet again I had underestimated her, for she nodded and said, 'There's powerful magic weavers over there in those dark places, so I understand. They walk with their ancestors, they know how to penetrate the veil and they are not afraid to let the force that runs throughout the living world assist them in their journeys in the spirit realm.'

I very much wanted to ask her how she knew of the practices of men and women thousands of miles away, but I held back for fear of sounding as if I doubted her. Celia, however, had no such inhibitions. Leaning forward, her face eager, she said, 'Have you *been* there?'

It was not, I supposed, out of the question, for all that it seemed unlikely, for Black Carlotta's long life had been lived close to a great sea port from which voyages across the Atlantic were no rare occurrence. But she shook her head, smiling, and said, 'No, lass, I haven't. Others have, however, and they reported their findings. Some, the bravest of them, risked much by smuggling out samples of the powerful potions made in the lands around the deep blue sea.' She paused, her eyes focused on something neither Celia or I could see. Then, snapping back to the present moment, she looked at me and said, 'I'm not telling you *how* I know, for to do so would betray another's confidences, and in any case such matters are not for outsiders and, strictly speaking, I shouldn't even be here speaking to you of them.' Darkness briefly crossed her face. Then, picking up the thread of what she had been saying, she went on. 'The substance you just showed me, Doctor, has unbelievable power. There is only a small amount on that bit of cloth and it's not fresh, but all the same it took me on such a journey—' Once again, she seemed to be back in whatever place of dread she'd been transported to. 'I had both the sights and the sounds of that other world,' she muttered, 'and so very real they were . . .'

I thought as I watched her that she wasn't yet fully back with Celia and me in the warm, cozy library, with the glowing remains of the fire and the shutters closed against the night; so powerful had the vision been that she was still partly in its grip. I almost felt I was wandering there with her . . .

Then Celia's clear, brisk voice broke the spell. 'Do you know what this stuff is made of, madam?'

Black Carlotta smiled at the title, and gave Celia her full attention. 'I believe I do, yes. There is a base of oils derived from several plants, and it is this mixture that produces the strong smell. It is quite pleasant, I find.'

'Yes,' Celia agreed. 'I caught a hint of something that reminded me of incense, and there was also a sharp, tangy element.'

Black Carlotta nodded. 'You discern well,' she murmured, and Celia looked pleased. 'These oils may have some effect – I am sure they do – but they are not the main active ingredient. That is found in the fine powder that you have probably observed, Doctor, within the stains on the cloth?' She fixed her eyes on me.

'Indeed I have,' I agreed. 'You know what it is?'

'Possibly,' she replied. 'I once knew a Spanish man who had voyaged in the lands that border the deep blue sea to the south, where in the low-lying, hot, steamy river lands there grows a particular tree that produces a bean. This man was fleeing for his life, for he had seen things he should not have seen, and both the civil and the church authorities were eager that he should not speak of them. He came to England, reasoning that the home of his nation's enemy might offer him safe refuge, although in the end it did not.' The sadness of old grief crossed her face. 'He told me what the ground-up beans could do; how the powder derived from them, when mixed with tobacco and smoked, or blended with the ashes of certain tree barks and leaves and eaten, gave rise to the most powerful mind travels. The trances are enduring, and those who undertake them do so for the well-being of their people. They are brave, those men and women, for the effects upon their own bodies and minds are damaging.'

I sensed there was more she could reveal. I knew, too, that she wasn't going to.

'I have no idea how you came by that piece of cloth, Doctor,' she said, rising to her feet. 'But be warned: whoever made the preparation that stained it is not to be trifled with, for they are powerful and they are dangerous.'

Celia too was standing now, holding out an arm towards Black Carlotta, but the old woman, smiling, waved the proffered assistance aside. 'I'm all right, lass,' she said.

'You're not leaving?' Celia said in amazement. 'But it's dark and it's *very* cold outside!' The faint note of reproof made her sound briefly just like our mother, and I smiled.

'I am,' Black Carlotta said, gathering up her cloak and arranging it around her. 'I need to be on my way,' she added, and it was clear from her tone that she wasn't to be argued with.

Celia and I saw her to the door, and we wished her good night. Just as I was about to close the door, she turned back and said, 'Remember what I told you, Doctor. Don't go thinking your book learning and your fine education will protect you against the dark forces from an older world because they won't.'

With a curt nod she was gone, disappearing into the night as if she had been no more than a figment of our imagination.

As I firmly closed the door, Celia let out a long breath and said, '*Well!*'

Recalling that someone – Samuel, probably – had still been up when I'd returned to the house earlier, I went out to the yard to check whether he was still awake and had heard our nocturnal visitor.

He was standing in the open door to the stables, Tock just behind him. Seeing me approach, he said, 'Your horse has settled, Doctor. It wasn't anything serious.'

'Oh, good,' I said. 'We've had a caller, but she's gone now.'

'Right,' Samuel said. 'Thought I heard the front door shut.'

We exchanged a remark about the clear sky – Samuel opined that there would be a sharp frost before dawn – and Tock nodded vigorous agreement. But in the very act of doing so, he suddenly stopped, spun round to stare over at the gate and, eyes wide, emitted a strange sort of bark and muttered something.

And suddenly I'd had enough. Enough of enigmas, enough of dead men with blue hands who gave no clue as to their mysterious pasts, enough of sensing hidden eyes watching me with malevolent intent. I picked up the muck fork that Tock or Samuel had leant against the wall. It was a hefty implement, stout ash handle, four long, curved tines sharp from endlessly being scraped across the stone-slabbed floor of the stables.

I ran to the gate and yelled out into the night, 'Be gone! Get away from this house! If you have business with me, seek me out openly and stop spying from the shadows, you cowardly fucking bastard!' I paused for breath. 'If I catch you here again it won't be this muck fork I ram through you but my sword!'

My furious blood began to cool, my heart to stop its hammering. I lowered my improvised weapon, took one last look across the dark, peaceful countryside, then closed and barred the gate and walked back towards the stables.

Samuel was looking at me worriedly. Tock's eyes showed white all round the iris, his mouth was open and his arms were raised before him, hands clenched into big fists like a pair of anvils.

I touched him gently on the shoulder and said, 'I am sorry, Tock, if I alarmed you. I thought I heard someone out there, and I've sensed recently that I'm being watched.'

Tock shook his head as violently as just now he'd been nodding it. He muttered something, but I don't find him too easy to comprehend at the best of times – among which this most certainly didn't rank – so I turned to Samuel for interpretation.

Samuel too was calming Tock, a great deal more effectively than I was. 'It's all right, lad' – Tock is older than me, but his mental development was arrested around the age of six or so – 'nothing to worry about,' he murmured, his hand gently smoothing Tock's broad back as if he was a spooked horse.

Tock said something, a long string of syllables among which I picked up only a few words, one of which was *fox*.

Nodding, Samuel said calmly, 'Right, lad, I'll tell the doctor,

you go and find your bed. Off you go.' He turned Tock and
gave him a firm push towards the stable door.

'He says he was looking out because he heard the fox again,'
Samuel said in a low voice once Tock was within. 'He likes
foxes, see. Anyway, he's also frightened because we've both
seen a man, or maybe more than one man, hanging around
recently and—'

'You should have told me, Samuel!' I said in a suppressed
shout.

Samuel gave me an assessing look. 'Been a question of stopping you long enough to say more than *good day*,' he muttered.
He was right; it seemed to me that I'd been in a tearing hurry
for days. 'I should have done, Doctor, and I'm sorry,' he added.
'I hope there's no harm done.'

'Tell me now,' I said.

'Not much to tell, in truth. Two, three days back, Tock comes
and tells me he's seen footprints down by the river, and they
don't belong to any of the folk who usually go down there.'

'He can tell?' I was surprised.

Samuel nodded. 'He may not have many wits but he keeps
his eyes open and there isn't much he misses,' he said. 'Anyhow,
I thought no more of it – it's not Rosewyke land down there
and folks have a right to walk the waterside track if they so
choose, although most prefer to take the high path, even if it's
further, and keep their feet dry – only then Tock sees a man
watching the house from over there' – he pointed to the thicket
of fruit trees and currant bushes that stand between the south
west corner of the house and the ground that slopes steeply
down to the river – 'and he calls out to me, and I see the fellow
too, then he notices we've spotted him and he's not there any
more.'

'What – you mean he stepped back behind a tree trunk, or
ducked down out of sight?'

Samuel shrugged. 'Maybe. Like I say, he wasn't there any
more.'

It almost sounded as if Samuel was suggesting the man had
vanished. But that would be impossible. Wouldn't it?

'What did he look like?' I said briskly, trying to drag the
conversation back from the realms of superstition and fantasy.

'Medium height, not fat, dark clothing, wore a hood. Dark,' Samuel repeated. 'He was dark. That was my impression, anyhow, for what it's worth.'

I thanked him, told him to keep his eyes open and report any further sightings, then at last went into the house.

NINE

I called in on Theo Davey the next morning. By the time I reached his house it was almost noon, for I had paid what I'd expected to be a brief call on a vast old woman suffering from dropsy and, having found her purple in the face and struggling for breath, I'd stayed with her until her niece could be summoned and while the digitalis I administered took effect.

'I was on the point of coming to find you,' Theo greeted me. His wide desk looked tidier than usual and he had an air of purpose about him. 'A body gone missing, one down in my cellar, and another in the crypt up the road, and we're no nearer identifying them and finding out who, if anyone, was responsible for their deaths than we were at the start. Any progress to report?'

'Some,' I said, 'although more in the way of developing a theory than hard facts.'

'Well, I'll have it anyway,' Theo said with a sigh. 'Sit, and tell me.' He glared up at me as I pulled up a chair. 'Facts first, if you please.'

I thought swiftly. 'Both the body found at Buckland and the one in the barrel had blue staining to the hands and arms, and so we can conclude that the two were companions before they were together on board the *Falco*, and, according to logic and to Captain Colt, almost certainly slipped onto the ship at her last port of call in Hispaniola. We should also assume that the little female body we found in the secret hold was taken there by the fugitives, that for some reason they left her behind when they fled from the ship and that it was they who took her from your cellar. Which means,' I went on as my thoughts clarified, 'that there is at least one more fugitive still at large. The man lying beneath us couldn't have got through that little window because he's too big.'

'At least one more,' Theo repeated. 'You're suggesting there may be more of them?' he demanded sharply.

'How can I say?' I snapped back.

He waved a hand in apology. 'Fair enough, you can't. But why are they here, Gabe? What made them crawl into that hellish space and endure a long sea voyage, knowing that discovery would probably mean death even if the very conditions they were enduring didn't kill them first?'

'Those conditions did just that to the man in the barrel,' I pointed out.

'Yes, indeed they did,' Theo agreed. 'So, any ideas? Does this theory of yours attempt to explain why a group of native inhabitants of a Caribbean island suddenly take it into their heads to sneak on board an English warship, accompanied by the dried-out corpse of a long-dead old woman, and hide in a stinking hole until they manage to sneak off it again once they reach Plymouth?'

A group of native inhabitants . . . His words set off a thought, and I barely heard what he said after he'd uttered them. 'The man in your cellar is African, or at least partly, although I suspect he also has Spanish blood.'

'African? So, you're saying he's a slave? That maybe all of them are, or were, and they're on the run?' His face lit with excitement. 'They were trying to get back to Africa!' he exclaimed, 'and for some reason imagined that was where the *Falco* was bound!'

'It's possible, I suppose,' I said, but even to myself I didn't sound convinced.

'It is!' Theo insisted.

'I see two objections.' It was important to stop Theo racing too far off down this path, for I didn't believe it to be the right one. 'First, why would anybody assume an English ship setting out across the Atlantic after a long voyage would be heading anywhere but home? Second, surely even an escaped slave desperate to return home would appreciate that it was the very place least likely to offer sanctuary, for the chances would be very high of being recaptured and shipped straight back again.'

'You're assuming the fugitives were thinking rationally,' Theo said. 'If they were desperate, fleeing the wrath of the masters they'd escaped from, would they be capable of such logic?'

'I don't know,' I admitted.

'What about the corpse in the barrel?' Theo said. 'Was that man African?'

'Sorry, Theo, but not enough of him remained for his race to be determined. You must have seen as much for yourself.'

Theo ignored that. 'But you said he'd been lashed,' he persisted. 'We assumed that meant he'd been a sailor, but slaves are lashed too, are they not?'

'Undoubtedly,' I agreed.

'So that might mean he—'

'Theo, I'm sorry but you're not going to persuade me to say any more than that the fugitives definitely included one man of African blood,' I said firmly.

He gave me an irritated look, which presently turned into a grin. 'Well, it was worth a try,' he muttered.

'And it may yet prove that you're right, and they *were* all escaped slaves,' I said.

He nodded. 'So we wait until the rest of the band show themselves?'

I shrugged. 'If they do.'

It wasn't an optimistic note on which to conclude the discussion, and I wasn't the least surprised when he dismissed me with no more than a muttered 'Keep me informed.'

Back at Rosewyke, I found that a sketchy noon meal of bread and ham had been laid out on a tray for me, and the kitchen was fragrant with cooking smells. Sallie and Celia were both hard at work, and Celia, a vast white apron tied over her gown and a scarf covering her hair, greeted me with a beaming smile and said, 'A note was delivered from Jonathan soon after you left this morning, Gabe, and he is coming to dinner this evening!'

'Is he bringing half the village with him?' I asked, returning her smile and indicating the extensive food preparations that were going on.

'Don't be silly, of course he isn't,' she said reprovingly. 'But you know as well as I do that he doesn't feed himself properly' – I wasn't at all sure that I did – 'and, like all men living alone, probably exists on meagre scraps and the simplest of meals.'

'Miss Celia is quite right,' Sallie put in, 'and tonight we'll be demonstrating the best that this house can offer!'

'I'm sure he will appreciate it,' I said, picking up my tray and backing out of the kitchen.

'Where are you off to, Gabe?' my sister called after me.

'To eat my meal,' I replied.

She tutted with impatience. 'Obviously, but I meant later, this afternoon.'

'I have a patient to see' – my large old lady needed more heart medication – 'and then I thought I'd take Flynn out for a long walk.' I very much needed some time alone in which to try to make sense of all I'd been reading and hearing recently.

'Well, don't you *dare* be late back,' Celia said. 'I really cannot have our guest arriving and you still sweaty and muddy and stinking of wet dog.'

'I'll be washed, dressed in my best and standing ready in the hall,' I promised.

She gave me a look that suggested she would believe that when it happened, then went back inside the kitchen and slammed the door.

I sat with my old woman, whose name was Jane Percival, for some time. Her niece had already left. 'She has her own family, she can't be expected to bother herself with me,' Mistress Percival said wistfully, and I forbore to point out that she too was her niece's family.

I watched her as, hospitable in the traditional way, she struggled up to fetch me a mug of ale. The fluid had accumulated in her legs and feet, and I suspected that the little slippers she had forced on over the gross swellings were for my benefit.

'Thank you for bringing me more of my drops, Doctor,' she panted as she fell back into her chair. 'They help so much when my heart begins its hammering and its pounding.'

'I'm glad,' I said. I wished there was more I could do to ease her discomfort. 'Have you tried putting your feet up?' I asked.

She gave me a scandalized look. 'Putting my *feet* up? What, on a stool or something?'

'Yes. You could put a cushion on it, to pad it out and make it more comfortable.'

'But- but people might see my ankles!'

'People?' I echoed gently, and she accepted the point with

a wry smile. 'And what would it matter if they did? In any case,' I went on before she could answer that, 'we could arrange a light cover over your legs and feet, and in this way modesty would be preserved.'

Still she looked dubious. 'But a lady always sits up, Doctor. Spine straight, feet on the floor, hands folded in the lap. So I was taught.'

I imagined her as a little girl, some strict parent or nursemaid drilling into her the rules of ladylike behaviour.

'I think, don't you,' I replied, 'that it is time you made up your own mind.'

A delighted smile spread across her face, and I saw in the fat old woman the pretty girl she had once been. 'Now that I am old and it no longer matters, you mean?'

I grinned. 'Exactly. Now, why don't we try it?'

Without waiting for approval, I searched around and found a low stool, some two and a half feet wide and a foot or so deep, and a soft feather cushion. There was a shawl hanging from a hook on the back of the door, and I gathered that up too. With some difficulty my old lady and I between us got her legs up onto the stool, and I arranged the shawl over them. It was an intimate act, and I sensed her reluctance to have my help, but wisely she must have told herself that I was her doctor and I didn't count.

I gave her a short time to accustom herself to the new position, then said, 'How does it feel?'

She turned to me, her face full of wonder. 'Better! Doctor, it really does feel better! The terrible throbbing has lessened already, and the pain is definitely reduced!'

She was staring at me as if I'd performed a miracle, and I thought I ought to disabuse her of the notion. 'The swelling is due to fluid, accumulating at the lowest point,' I said. 'The fluid has nowhere else to go, and it stretches the skin and is the cause of the discomfort. By elevating your feet and lower legs, the accumulation is eased.' I could see by her face that she didn't understand. 'Imagine you have half-filled a bottle with water,' I went on. 'When you hold the bottle upright or stand it on a table, the water fills the lower half. Yes?'

She rolled her eyes. 'Yes. Of course.'

'Now imagine that you turn the bottle on its side, but not to such an extent that the water runs out. Now what happens?'

'The water lies all along the lower side,' she replied.

'Exactly! And there's not so much of it at the bottom of the bottle.'

She began to nod, slowly at first then enthusiastically. 'And my poor old legs are the bottle?'

'They are.'

'Well, now!' She was looking delighted. 'Who would have thought that such a simple trick could give such relief?' Her face fell and hurriedly she added, 'Not that I'm calling you simple, Doctor Taverner, and I do hope you didn't think I was, and please don't think me ungrateful, for I—'

Her hands were waving in distress, and gently I took hold of them and lowered them into her lap, stilling them. 'It's all right, Mistress Percival,' I assured her. 'I'm glad to have helped.'

Flynn and I walked for miles. My mind was teeming with thoughts, from the poignancy of a fat old lady all on her own worrying about people seeing her ankles through how to determine the racial origins of a rotting corpse to the use of plant substances so potent that they took the consumer into the terrifying world of the spirits.

I managed to remember that I was expected home, and in good enough time to tidy myself before the evening, and Flynn and I arrived back in the yard as the sun was setting. I gave Flynn a wipe-down and set food out for him; Tock had rushed out to do these tasks for me, but I thanked him and said I'd do them myself. Flynn had given me his undemanding company for the greater part of the afternoon, and it was a way of saying thank you.

Then it was my turn, and I slipped into the kitchen for a large jug of hot water to take up to my room. Sallie was sitting in front of the fire – I suspected I'd interrupted her in a doze – and she went to get up, only I told her to stay where she was. From the wonderful aromas wafting through the house, she'd been working hard and deserved a rest.

'Mistress Celia is having a nap,' she told me. She shot me a sly glance. 'She's excited about the vicar coming this evening. It's brought a flush to her cheeks, and she's looking most comely.' She raised her eyebrows in an arch look, which I pretended not to see.

Celia and I stood together in the library, staring out through the window that overlooked the track up to the house. I turned to glance at her, taken aback at how lovely she looked. Her fair hair shone bright in the candlelight, and she was wearing it in some new style which was very becoming. She had lost a lot of weight during the traumatic events of a year and a half ago, but Sallie's good cooking – and perhaps also the pleasant tenor of our life together at Rosewyke – had fleshed her out again, and now her full bosom, small waist and long legs made her a fine woman. She was dressed in a gown of jade green silk, its low neck made modest by a generous lace-edged frill, and she wore a pair of long jade earrings.

'You look very fine,' I said. 'Is that a new gown?'

'Thank you. Yes.'

I was going to make some remark to the effect that Jonathan would be flattered to know the gorgeous gown's inaugural outing was on the evening he came to dinner, but I sensed Celia was nervous, and I kept my mouth shut.

But I couldn't resist a mild tease. 'This is a new shirt,' I said, drawing out a length of linen from beneath the collar of my tunic. 'Do I look fine too?'

'It's *not* new, Gabe, and well you know it, for haven't I been telling you for weeks, if not months, that your wardrobe is in urgent need of attention? You have a position to keep up, you know, and it's bad enough that you wear your hair to your collar and still insist on keeping that gold ring in your ear, although heaven knows why, without you making it worse by dressing in worn-out garments that have seen far too many washdays and— *Oh!*'

She had spotted Jonathan, riding up the track. Thanking him silently for his timely arrival that had cut short my sister's well-intentioned but too oft-repeated lecture, I took her arm and we went out into the hall to welcome him.

I had promised Jonathan that I would refrain from badgering him to explain the inexplicable, but in fact it did not even occur to me to do so. From the start, the three of us seemed to create a mood of easy happiness, for we were pleased to be together: it was as simple as that. Jonathan entertained us with some lively accounts of recent happenings in the village and, as always when he spoke of his flock and his precious little jewel of a church, his love and devotion were very apparent. I in my turn described some of the more humorous anecdotes of my doctor's life, including the recent occasion when a batty old woman, believing me to be a villain intent on robbing her, ravishing her or both, contrived to shut me in her stable and bar the door with a hefty plank. Her son arrived home and let me out, his face scarlet with embarrassment and muttering that his mother wasn't really herself and had difficulty distinguishing the real world from the lurid happenings within her own head. On seeing me upon my release, the old girl acted not only as if she hadn't just shut me up in her stinky stable but hadn't even met me, which was harsh considering how long I'd been treating her for a particularly noisome and persistent catarrhal infection.

Celia was a delight, frequently laughing with genuine amusement, pink in the face and her eyes sparkling. She too contributed much to the steady flow of talk, and her devastating word pictures of some of the more repressive and domineering women of her acquaintance reminded me of just how perceptively she views the world.

The food was a triumph. Samuel had recently slaughtered a pig, and the roast leg of pork was cooked to perfection and accompanied by a spiced fruit sauce that was both savoury and sweet. Apples with cinnamon and currants, carrots, cabbage; brawn; black pudding; a pie containing beef, kidneys and onion; preserved fruits served with cubes of marzipan; a slab of gingerbread; a tart filled with a custard concoction of Sallie's own invention and flavoured with rosewater. I had buffed up my precious Venetian wineglasses, and the French wine with which we filled them was a fine accompaniment to the food.

We had been at table for long enough for us to have sampled a little of every dish and think about which to return to for a second, larger helping when I thought I heard hoof-beats from outside. I waited, silently hoping I was not about to receive an urgent summons from the husband or father of some desperately ill person. Nothing happened at first, and I began to relax. But then I heard Sallie's voice out in the hall, remonstrating, saying firmly and repeatedly that the doctor was entertaining this evening and did he *really* have to be disturbed?

I stood up, meeting Celia's eyes. 'Oh, Gabe, must you?' she said quietly.

I put my hand briefly on her shoulder. 'I don't know yet. I'll go and see who it is.'

I strode out into the hall. Sallie was standing in the open doorway, as if by her solid physical presence she could bar the intruder and prevent him from spoiling our evening.

But I had already recognized the young man who stood on the step: he was one of Theo's, the lad who had driven the cart that brought the Buckland body back to Theo's house.

I went to stand beside my housekeeper. 'Thank you, Sallie, I will speak to him,' I said.

She gave me one swift look and then nodded and melted away.

'What is it?' I asked the young man.

'Coroner says you're to come,' he said. 'There's a badly wounded man been brought in and Mistress Davey is tending him, but she says he's bleeding badly and she needs you.'

'Very well.' My bag stood always ready close to the door and my heavy cloak hung above it. I was about to return to the parlour to make my excuses to Celia and our guest, but they were already coming into the hall.

'What has happened?' Jonathan asked. I told him, flinging on my cloak as I did so. He nodded. 'Does the wounded man require my services?'

'Not yet, vicar,' the lad said. 'He's conscious, muttering-like. I don't reckon he's dying.'

'I ought to go home . . .' Jonathan murmured.

It was perfectly clear, both from his expression and Celia's, that neither of them wanted this and he'd only made the remark for form's sake.

'Please don't,' I said. 'There is a great deal of lovingly-prepared food on the table, and it would be a pity to waste it. Besides,' I added quietly, leaning close to him, 'Celia has been looking forward to this evening, for she loves to entertain.'

Jonathan gave me a considering look, as if he was assessing whether there was a deeper meaning beneath the words. 'Very well,' he said. Turning to Celia, he added, 'If you are quite sure?'

'I am,' Celia said firmly. She took his arm and they returned to the parlour, Celia calling out almost as an afterthought, 'Try not to be too long, Gabe.'

I had the definite feeling that I'd been dismissed.

TEN

They had put the wounded man in the room that served as Theo's outer office, where his officers filter out the queries that can be dealt with by one of their number from those requiring the more weighty judgements of the coroner. Chairs and tables had been shoved back against the walls and someone had fetched a straw-filled mattress, covered with a length of sheet. The white linen was heavily bloodstained.

Theo's wife knelt beside the patient. Theo, hovering behind her, was holding a bowl of water that had turned red. Jarman Hodge perched on a stool in the corner. Elaine raised her head to look at me as I entered the room.

'I am relieved to see you, Doctor Taverner,' she said.

I threw off my cloak and knelt down beside her. 'What has happened?'

'He has been savaged by a dog,' she replied, 'and—'

'Two dogs,' the patient interrupted, 'if not more. Great brutes they were, spikes on their collars and teeth like a dragon's. *Aaargh!*' He moaned, either in horror at the memory or simply in pain.

I studied him. He was around thirty years old, his skin deeply tanned and his hair black and tight-curled. His eyes were blue. His frame was broad and stocky, but there was very little flesh on him. He was clad in a thin shirt beneath a stained, dirty tunic, breeches that ended at the knee and an inadequate pair of light shoes.

His left leg, from the shin to halfway between the knee and the thigh, was slashed with a series of deep wounds from which the blood was slowly leaking.

'The blood flow has lessened since we sent the lad to fetch you,' Elaine said, 'so I do hope we have not interrupted your evening for nothing.' She pressed a clean pad of linen to the worst of the wounds, and again the man groaned in pain.

'No, you did right,' I assured her. Looking the man in the face, I said, 'Mistress Davey has done a fine job in cleaning out the wounds, and some of them will heal on their own. Some, however, will need stitching.'

The man spat out a colourful oath, then, shooting a look at Elaine, muttered an apology which she received with a gracious nod.

I looked up at Theo. 'You have more water set to heat?'

'Yes. Want me to fetch it?'

'Yes.' I reached in my bag and drew out a preparation that Judyth had given me and which she said was good for washing open wounds. She had also mentioned the use of raw garlic, which by some strange miracle seemed to reduce the production of inflammation and pus. 'And would you peel a few cloves of garlic?'

'*Garlic?*' he mouthed, his face a study of incredulity. I nodded.

Elaine was the perfect assistant, holding the lantern steady as I bathed the wounds, and Theo lent his strength as I stitched up the two deepest slashes, holding the man still as he writhed beneath my hands. The lavender and rosemary scent of Judyth's preparation and the sharp smell of garlic steadily permeated the room, going some way, although not far enough, to combat the stench of the patient's long-unwashed body.

Then at last the work was completed, and fresh bandages covered the man's left leg from his groin to his ankle.

He stared up at me, his face pale beneath the dark skin. I knew full well what he'd suffered while I stitched him up and I said, 'I am sorry to have caused you such pain. It was necessary.'

'Yes,' he murmured. He looked exhausted, and I saw the signs of long torment and strain around his eyes and mouth.

I straightened up and looked at Elaine, now standing close to Theo; he had his arm round her, giving silent comfort. She too looked pale; it is not easy to watch with equanimity as someone stitches torn flesh.

'Is it possible for the patient to stay here tonight?' I asked. 'He needs rest, and I will give him a draught so that he will sleep, and begin to heal, and it would be better if—'

'Of course,' Theo interrupted, and Elaine nodded her agreement.

I knelt down beside the man once more. 'You need to sleep,' I said. 'I will make a drink for you that will help.'

He whispered, 'I can't pay you, Doctor.'

'Don't worry,' I replied. Then, for the despair I sensed flowing out of him was growing fast, I tried to lighten the mood: 'I'll add a coin or two to the next rich man's bill I present.'

He managed a feeble smile; he was a brave man.

Elaine fetched a mug of hot water and I mixed a sleeping potion. I helped the man raise his head and he took a few sips. Then, as the drink cooled, he finished it.

'I will stay with him for a while,' I said to Theo. Elaine had bade me good night and disappeared upstairs, but Theo was still hovering in the doorway. Jarman Hodge had also vanished, although I suspected he wasn't far away. 'Go to your wife, Theo.'

'Very well.' He looked relieved, but then he said, 'Call me before you go.'

I sat down on the floor beside my patient. He was restless still, the straw of the mattress rustling as he turned this way and that.

'Is the pain still severe?' I asked. I had put a drop or two of poppy in the potion, so his discomfort should have been easing.

'It's not so bad,' he admitted. 'But—' He shut his mouth like a trap.

'But you are very anxious about something, or someone,' I finished for him. He shot me a glance, and I realized I'd guessed right. A worrying possibility struck me: 'Was someone with you?' I asked. 'Were they too attacked by the dogs?' I had a vision of a man lying in a ditch, his throat torn out; or stumbling about, gravely wounded and desperate for help yet having been overlooked by whoever found the man lying before me.

He shook his head. 'No. I was by myself. We– I thought to slip in, unseen, and it seemed better to go alone. Besides, it's no task for an old man, and the wall was high . . .' He gave a great yawn, his eyelids fluttering. He was on the edge of sleep, about to give in to it, but then he muttered something else.

I leaned over him, trying to make it out.

'. . . wasn't right, what happened,' he was saying, 'not what we expected, but they misunderstood. The messenger said it would be different, or so we thought . . . I saw it, saw the fire and the good food, the fine gentlemen and the pretty ladies, and we were dancing . . . shapes in the firelight, bodies in the flames, and the serpent's dark eyes glittering . . . can't . . . shouldn't have . . .'

The pauses between the meaningless words were getting longer. Presently the man gave a deep sigh, turned on his side and gave himself up to sleep.

I waited for a while, listening to his steady breathing. I put my fingers on his forehead, but he felt warm rather than hot. There was nothing more I could do for him that night.

I stood, picked up the lantern, walked softly out of the room and quietly closed the door. Jarman Hodge materialized from wherever he had been waiting. 'How is he?' he asked.

'Asleep.'

He crossed to the door that opened onto the stairs up to Theo and his family's quarters, tapping on it. 'He'll not want you to leave before speaking to him,' he said, noticing me watching.

'No, he said as much to me.'

We heard footfalls on the stairs, and Theo emerged into the hall, closing the door behind him. 'The patient's asleep,' I repeated before he could ask.

'Good. Come in here.' He led Jarman Hodge and me into his office.

I put the lantern on his desk and the three of us sat down. 'You wanted to talk to me?' I said.

'I did,' Theo said. 'Jarman, go on.'

'Did you notice the man's hands, Doctor Taverner?'

'No, I did not, for the damage was all to his left leg. That was a violent attack,' I went on, angry on behalf of my patient, 'and he will suffer permanent scarring.' Theo and Jarman were both looking expectantly at me, and all at once I understood the import of Jarman's question.

'Blue?' I said.

'Blue,' they echoed together.

Silently I swore at myself for my lack of observation; I who, as a physician, was trained to take in every aspect of a patient.

'You had more urgent matters to attend to,' Theo said charitably. 'But it seems that lying asleep in my front office is another of the *Falco*'s blue ghosts.'

I pictured the man, seeing his features in my mind's eye. His skin and his hair were indicative of mixed blood, but his facial features were those of an Englishman, as were his blue eyes. On the other hand, I had not studied him all that closely; as Theo said, I'd had more important concerns.

'There's still at least one more of them out there,' Theo went on. 'This fellow couldn't have squeezed through the little window at the back of the house any more than the corpse down in the cellar.'

'He said *we*,' I exclaimed, remembering.

'What's that?' Theo demanded.

'When I was talking with him, at one point he said *we* did something or other, but then he changed it quickly to *I*.'

'Will he live?' Theo asked bluntly.

'He ought to, for the bleeding had already slowed down by the time I got to him, thanks to your wife's good work, and that was the immediate danger to life. However, infection may well set in, in which case his prospects are not bright.'

'But it may not?' Theo persisted.

'No. Some people appear to deal better with such injuries, and our man next door may be one of them.' I was also putting my faith in Judyth's quaint garlic remedy, but I didn't say so. I had the feeling that my hopes said more about my feelings for Judyth than the likely efficacy of the treatment.

'We need to talk to him.' Theo rapped the desk in emphasis. 'He's one of the fugitives from the *Falco*, he and his companions endured that awful voyage in that terrible hiding place for some powerfully imperative reason, and now he and at least one other man are at large in my area. I want to know what they're here for and how it's come about that I have had *three* corpses to deal with since they came ashore and one of them is still missing!'

His voice had risen to a shout, and it was a comment on the potency of the sleeping draft I'd administered to the injured man in the room opposite that he didn't wake up and cry out in alarm.

Presently Jarman Hodge stirred in his chair. 'I'm not saying I have the answers to those questions, sir,' he said quietly, 'but I've been working on a theory of my own, and recent events have led me to believe I may not have been wasting my time.'

Theo spun round to face him, eyebrows raised. 'Well?' he snapped.

Jarman paused for a moment, then said, 'I've been absent these past three days, and—'

'Yes, I'd noticed,' Theo remarked.

'—and now I will tell you where I've been.' He looked at me, then back at Theo. 'I rode across the high ground to Start Point, or, to be accurate, Slapton.'

I knew of Start Point, as does every sailor from the south west of England, for it is notorious for shipwrecks. I didn't think I knew anything of interest concerning Slapton, however, although clearly Theo did. Glaring at Jarman, he said, 'And what was your purpose there, or shall I hazard a guess?'

Again he flicked his eyes briefly to me. 'The name does not mean anything to you, Doctor?'

'A long, sandy shore and a small village?'

'Right, and a pleasant place to live, which is probably why a renowned inhabitant of Plymouth has recently purchased a house there.'

'You refer to Sir Richard Hawkins,' Theo said sternly. I detected a warning in his words: *Beware, for he is a powerful man.*

'I'm well aware of whom I speak, sir,' Jarman murmured. 'Son of Sir John Hawkins, sometime mayor of Plymouth, Member of Parliament, vice-admiral in the navy and knighted only last year by King James.'

'I thought he resided in Plymouth?' I said. The house, I'd heard, had been left to him in his father's will, although there had been some sort of dispute between Sir Richard and John Hawkins's second wife. Or so town gossip had it.

'He does,' Theo said. 'The new residence in Slapton is more of a family home.' Impatiently he turned back to Jarman. 'So, Slapton?'

'I had heard tell that Sir Richard has been spending time over in the new house of late, and it seemed logical that anyone having business with him might well try to seek him out there. The house is situated in a quiet spot, protected by a screen of trees and a good three-quarters of a mile from the church, so someone hoping for a few quiet words with Sir Richard might rate his chances of success more highly at Slapton than in Plymouth. Such was my thinking, anyway, although in the event I was wrong – or the talk in the town was wrong – for, apart from a couple of brief visits, Sir Richard has been in the Plymouth house for most of the autumn.'

I looked at Theo, expecting to see him brimming with impatience at this long and apparently irrelevant preamble. But he was watching Jarman intently, his eyes alight with possibilities.

'So I left Slapton as quick as you like and rode back to Plymouth, where I set myself up in an inn with a view of the Hawkins house. I observed Sir Richard's comings and goings, I watched as a stream of visitors stepped up and knocked on his door, I noted his servants going about their daily routine. And then, tonight, I saw what I'd been hoping to see.' He jerked his head towards the room where the injured man lay. 'I saw him, creeping along the wall that runs along between the back yard of the house and the side alley that borders it. I saw him climb over, I heard the dogs go for him and I saw him come flying back out to safety. Not that he found that easy, with his leg torn to rags.'

'Was there anyone with him?' Theo demanded.

'Thought I spotted an older man, watching from further down the alley. He must have fled when I went to the wounded man's aid.'

'And no doubt, had you managed a proper look at him, you'd have observed that he too had blue hands,' Theo murmured.

I said, unable to contain myself, 'But why would a fugitive from the *Falco* want to speak in private with Sir Richard Hawkins? What possible business could he believe he had with a man of his wealth and station?'

Jarman turned to me. 'I'd have thought precisely the same thing myself, Doctor. Makes no sense, really, unless you consider where the hanged man was found.'

We'd cut him down a mere four days ago, but it seemed much longer. He'd received his savage death by the river and close to where my friend Josiah Thorn likes to fish. 'Buckland,' I said slowly, trying to see the significance.

'Yes. Very near to the estate that was the home of another seafaring man.'

'Francis Drake,' Theo said.

I was cross with myself for not having made the connection. I knew full well how the great man had made a highly advantageous marriage and on the proceeds purchased the beautiful house known as Buckland Abbey. I had never been there, and when Buckland was mentioned, my mind had leapt to my old friend the retired doctor.

'I should have realized that,' I said.

'Well, I dare say you're preoccupied with your recent tending of that poor young man's body,' Theo said. 'Each to his own area of expertise, Gabe.'

It was kindly meant, but his remark made me feel worse.

'So one of the fugitives goes to the house where Francis Drake lived,' Theo was saying, 'and . . . and what? Are we suggesting someone in the household shot him in the back and hung him up to drain the blood out of him?'

'Hardly!' I protested.

'Who owns Buckland Abbey now, Jarman?' Theo asked, ignoring my remark. It was interesting, I thought, how Theo was quite confident that Jarman would know.

His confidence was warranted. 'Sir Francis, they say, didn't want the estate to go out of the possession of the Drake family. When he drew up his will back in the 1580s he was required by his marriage settlement to leave Buckland Abbey to his wife, but he didn't sign the document. While he was at sea he added a codicil, by which the bulk of his estate would be left to his brother Thomas, who, unlike Sir Francis, had a son. There was a second son, although I believe he died,' he added, 'and there's also a daughter.'

'So Buckland Abbey is now the residence of Thomas Drake,' I said. It was understandable, I reflected, that Sir Francis would name his brother as his heir, for the two had sailed together on the *Pelican;* she was the sturdy and steadfast ship who was renamed the *Golden Hind* and in which Drake had circumnavigated the world.

Such a voyage must surely have intensified the already strong fraternal bond and the two of them had continued to sail together, Thomas captaining the *Adventure* and part of the group who sailed with Francis on his last voyage . . .

Theo and Jarman were in the middle of quite a heated exchange, and I dragged myself back from my memories and returned my attention to them.

'. . . and you suggest that the fugitives intended to visit both Sir Francis and Sir Richard?' Theo was saying loudly. 'But in God's holy name, *why*?'

'It's more than a suggestion,' Jarman said mildly, 'for I saw the man in the next room climb Sir Richard's back wall with my own eyes, and the spot on the river where the other man was strung up is only half a mile from Buckland Abbey.'

'It doesn't prove he had been there, nor that anyone there is responsible for his death!' Theo protested. 'The mere proximity of the house is scarcely sufficient for me to go charging up there and demand to know if some member of the household shot a runaway from the Caribbean and then drained the blood out of him!'

'Of course it's not, sir,' Jarman said. '*You* can't do anything on such slim evidence.' There was a definite emphasis on the first word.

'But someone else can?' Theo was smiling.

'Oh, I think so,' Jarman said, returning the smile. He glanced at me, then addressed Theo again. 'I plan to ride up to Buckland tomorrow morning, with your leave, sir—'

'Why ask for my leave?' Theo said grumpily. 'You don't usually bother.'

'—and I'd take it as a favour if the doctor here would come with me.'

'I shall be pleased to,' I said. I stood up. 'If we are to have an early start, I will leave you now and return to Rosewyke.'

'Good.' Theo was now also on his feet, and he ushered me out of his office and towards the front door. I paused to check on the injured man, but he was deeply asleep.

I wondered if he would still be there in the morning. Unless Theo locked him in, somehow I doubted it.

Theo and Jarman stood in the road as I rode off, but I was

barely aware of them. My mind was already deeply engaged
in one question: why a group of men had sneaked on board the
Falco in Hispaniola, endured dire peril and unbelievable hardship and finally slipped off again at Plymouth, leaving one of
their number dead and a tiny, dried-out corpse nailed up in their
hiding place, apparently with the purpose of seeking out two
of England's most renowned and admired sea captains.

What was it all about?

The night was very cold and the darkness was profound. Hal
knew his way home and needed no guidance, the countryside
was deeply familiar and held no fears, and I was relaxed, happy
to think I'd soon be asleep in my own bed. It's possible that I
slipped into a half-sleep, soothed by Hal's steady pace. I thought
I heard a sibilant voice, hissing softly as if someone lurking in
the shadows beside the track was speaking to a companion but
not wanting to be overheard.

I came back to full alertness, shaking off the dream, the movement so abrupt that I almost fell out of the saddle. Encouraging
Hal to a trot, then a canter, I hurried for home.

It was very late now. I rode into my own yard and quietly
saw to Hal – Samuel emerged groggy-eyed to help, but I sent
him back to bed – and then went into the house. I glanced
quickly into the parlour, but there was nobody there and all
signs of the meal had been tidied away.

It was a relief. I looked forward to discussing the recent
turn of events with Celia, but just then all I wanted was to go
to bed.

ELEVEN

As Jarman Hodge and I set out the next morning I asked about the wounded man.

'Gone,' Jarman said briefly.

'Ah.'

Buckland Abbey was the largest and most noticeable building for miles around. Its religious origins as a Cistercian house were evident, although the previous owner had begun turning it into a residence fit for a fine gentleman and his family and the Drakes were continuing the process. Nevertheless, the first thing to strike the eye was the vast, buttressed end wall of the chapel; the front façade of the large house next to it still looked like an abbey, to which someone had added a somewhat inharmonious tower.

Jarman Hodge and I took up a vantage point some way away and stared at the place.

Presently he remarked, 'Rising ground over there, Doctor.'

I followed the direction of his pointing arm. There was a low wooded ridge behind the house, and it was easy to imagine a man fleeing for the safety of the trees and not being quite quick enough.

'We'll have a closer look,' I said.

We rode round the imposing grey-stone buildings, careful to stay on the track. Had anybody spotted us – and it was almost certain that someone at Buckland had noted our presence and was keeping an eye – we were simply passers-by.

We rode along the foot of the rise. We came to a place where trees overhung the track; their leaves were falling now and they offered little in the way of concealment, but it was better than nothing.

Drawing rein and dismounting, I said, 'Jarman, would you mind running up that slope?'

He nodded, appreciating straight away why I was asking.

He handed me his horse's reins, then set off up the bank at a lope. I raised an imaginary musket to my shoulder and sighted along what would have been the musket ball's trajectory. Upwards, at the sort of angle taken by the piece of lead in my dead man's chest cavity.

Jarman had only been jogging up the hill, and even so I'd had precious little time to sight and get off a shot, even supposing the weapon had been loaded and cocked ready to be fired.

He was at the top now, looking back enquiringly at me. I beckoned to him.

'It's right for the angle of entry,' I said as he re-joined me. I frowned. 'Could you do it once more, Jarman? This time, running as if you're fleeing for your life?'

He did as I asked, turning and haring away up the slope so swiftly that this time I'd had to have had my musket primed and at my shoulder even as he was setting off in order to have any chance of hitting him.

Jarman trotted back down to me, only slightly out of breath. He kept himself fit, I thought. 'Well?' he asked.

'*I* couldn't have hit a man and found his heart when he was fleeing away up that rise at speed. There was very little time before you were under the trees for one thing, and for another, you were sprinting, and therefore bobbing up and down.'

'Hm.' Jarman thought for a moment, then said, 'Two things. One, the man who owns this house will have a large staff of servants to run it for him and, being a navy man, some of his staff are likely to be former sailors. And sailors in the navy are fighting men, so not a few of them will be proficient with a musket.'

'Yes,' I agreed. 'And two?'

He grinned. 'Two, there's always such a thing as a lucky shot.'

I was struck by an idea . . . I gave Jarman Hal's reins and strode up to the top of the rise, making a way on through the trees. I was already pretty sure I was right, and I broke into a run as the trees thinned and open ground appeared up ahead. The ground fell away before me and there, running along a couple of hundred yards away, was the river. I ran on, right to the top of the long, sloping bank, and through the wisps of mist rising off the water I could make out the promontory where we'd found the body and the tree from which the poor young man had been hung up.

It wasn't conclusive evidence that he'd been shot as he'd fled from Buckland Abbey, but it certainly pointed that way.

I hurried back to Jarman and told him what I'd discovered. 'Hm,' he said. Then silently he jerked his head in the direction of the outbuildings behind the big house. 'Someone's spotted us,' he said quietly.

I turned to look. The gates to the wide cobbled yard stood open, and I saw movement. A young man was walking out of the yard, two older men either side of him. One of them said something to him, and the young man snapped a reply. It appeared that the older man was trying to stop him, for now he put a hand on the lad's arm, but angrily the young man threw it off and we heard the colourful curse from where we stood.

'Think we should melt away, Doctor?' Jarman asked softly.

'No. We have a right to be on this track, which is a public road even if it does pass too close to the house for the Drake family's liking. Besides, you are a coroner's officer in pursuit of lawful enquiries, and I'm-' I stopped, at a loss to explain why being a physician gave me any authority in the present situation.

Jarman grinned. 'You won't need to explain yourself, Doctor T,' he said. 'Everyone knows who *you* are.'

While we waited for the angry youth to come striding up to us, I wondered whether Jarman's remark was a compliment or an insult.

I watched the lad as he covered the last few yards. He was short, broad-shouldered and a little plump, and the fine clothes he wore had an air of disarray, as if he'd been in a hurry when he put them on. He was bare-headed, his reddish brown hair thick and full. His eyes were dark beneath well-marked brows, his nose was long and well-shaped, his red lips still had the fullness of boyhood and it appeared he was attempting, not very success-fully, to grow a beard. He was, I guessed, maybe fifteen or sixteen, and I was pretty sure I knew who he was.

'Master Francis Drake?' I said, stepping forward to meet him.

brother Francis and Richard Hawkins all spent years in the Caribbean, the connection speaks for itself.

I very nearly spoke up.

But something held me back. I was all at once very aware of Jarman Hodge beside me, and while he did nothing so obvious as clear his throat, nudge me or in any other way issue a warning, yet I felt the message emanating as powerfully from him as if he'd spoken the words: *Don't tell him.*

Since it precisely echoed my own sentiment, I kept quiet.

Then, for Sir Thomas was clearly waiting for my answer, I said, 'Proximity, Sir Thomas.'

'And, I would hazard, proficiency with a musket?' he added quietly.

'Perhaps,' I replied.

He thought for a moment. 'It is true that we tend to be a focus for the needy and the desperate, for times are hard and too many are driven to travel the roads and throw themselves on the mercy of the more fortunate. But they know they may obtain relief here, Doctor Taverner!' He opened his eyes wide in an expression of earnest piety. 'The house was once an abbey, and we follow the old practice of doling out food to the hungry. It is rare for there to be any threat from those who depend upon our bounty, for we are very well protected and our defences are strong, and the idea of anyone in my household feeling the need to *shoot* at someone . . .' He smiled, leaving the sentence unfinished as if to underline the absurdity of the very suggestion.

'I see,' I said. 'Thank you, Sir Thomas, for the reassurance.' I stood up, and Jarman instantly did too. 'Now we must be on our way, for—'

But by unfortunate timing, for I was itching to leave and I was sure Jarman felt the same, the boy Francis came rushing back into the hall followed by no less than three servants bearing trays of food and drink.

The servants fussed about pouring the wine – which proved to be delicious – and setting out little bread rolls filled with cheese and ham. I contrived some polite small talk while the wine and the little rolls were consumed, and then at last Jarman and I managed to take our leave.

He stopped dead. 'How do you know?' he said testily, the very words confirming his identity.

'You have a look of your father and your uncle,' I replied. The boy had been named for his famous relative.

'You know my father?' he demanded, disbelief in his voice.

'I have had the pleasure of meeting him.' *And* your uncle, I might have added.

'So if I take you back to the house and march you before him, he will recognize you and give his permission for you to be—'

Beside me I sensed Jarman Hodge's habitual impassivity shift slightly. I was experiencing the same reaction, and I wasn't nearly as good at disguising my feelings.

'Enough,' I said. The single word came out louder than I'd intended, but the lad was getting under my skin. 'This track is not on Buckland Abbey land and we need no man's permission to be on it.'

'But you—'

'Had you had the courtesy and the sense to ask our business, you would have learned that my companion is an officer of the Plymouth coroner, I am a physician, and we are here at the request of the coroner – whose name, for your information, is Master Theophilus Davey – and no-one may stand in our way.'

I was all but shouting now, and found that I had edged closer to the boy and was looming over him. He looked cowed for a moment, stepped back a pace but then gathered himself and stood his ground.

'Then I believe I have the honour of addressing Doctor Gabriel Taverner,' he said, and he gave me a low bow. 'I am afraid I do not know your companion's name?' He turned to Jarman.

'Jarman Hodge,' Jarman said neutrally.

The boy bowed again. 'My apologies, Doctor Taverner, Master Hodge,' he said. 'I will take you to my father straight away. I regret my impulsiveness but this is an out-of-the-way spot, we are a focus of interest for many vagrants, beggars and brigands, and when my father is from home, as he often is, it is my duty to look to the safety of my mother and my sister.' He was swiftly recovering his composure – his arrogance – and, standing very straight, his chest thrown out, he added with feigned nonchalance, 'Of course, I too shall frequently be away myself from now on. At Exeter College, Oxford.'

I tried to suppress my smile and look impressed. Jarman didn't bother.

'Please,' young Francis went on, 'follow me. Someone will see to your horses.'

Someone did; a couple of stable boys came running out as we walked into the yard, taking the reins even as they bowed to the young master; he hadn't deigned to speak to the boys, merely waving a vague hand.

That deeply annoying sense of entitlement is invariably the way of it when sons and daughters are born to privilege.

Thomas Drake received us in the great hall of his magnificent house.

His son had led us from the yard right round to the front of the house and its grand entrance, undoubtedly to make quite sure we took in all the details: the sturdy, forbidding porch, the granite doorway, the heraldic symbols of the Drake family: upraised glove, Drake arms, knight's helmet. The great hall was ornately panelled, there were fluted pillars supporting a decorated frieze and, on the north wall, a vast granite fireplace. All echoes of the building's austere monastic past had been thoroughly obliterated.

The master of the house looked at me through narrowed dark eyes as his son muttered to him, presumably telling him who we were. Before the lad had finished his whispering, his father pushed him aside and strode towards me.

'Gabriel Taverner!' he exclaimed. 'Yes, I knew I recognized the face! You were on the *Mandragora*, under old Ambrose Pemberthy, and my brother summoned you to our ship to take a man's lower leg off because everyone told him a man treated by you stood much the best chance of survival, *and* your methods got him back at his post the fastest!'

'Thank you, Sir Thomas, for remembering me so favourably,' I muttered. 'Did the man survive?'

'Oh, yes.' He glanced at me shrewdly. 'But then I imagine you did not for a moment believe he wouldn't have done.'

'Survival is never a foregone conclusion,' I replied, perhaps there was a note of reproof in my voice, for the man was actually looking slightly discomfited.

He shook it off, giving a broad smile and opening his wide. 'Welcome to my hall!' he said. He spun round to his lurking in his shadow. 'Francis, make yourself useful and about some refreshments, if you please.'

'Yes, sir!' the lad exclaimed, running off as if relieved to leaving his father's powerful presence.

'Now, you are here on the coroner's business?' Sir Thomas said, indicating a trio of settles close to the fireplace and inviting us to sit down.

'Yes. Jarman Hodge here is Theophilus Davey's senior and most experienced agent' – it was true, even if nobody ever mentioned the fact – 'and I am regularly summoned to aid in the coroner's work.'

Sir Thomas nodded sagely. 'Dead bodies, of course.' Then all at once his expression sharpened, and something very slightly threatening entered his genial tone. 'And what brings you to my door?' he asked softly.

'The very same,' I replied. 'A dead body, found on the river bank half a mile away.'

Sir Thomas regarded me steadily. 'And what is the connection to Buckland Abbey?'

'The man was killed by a musket ball.'

'You are certain?'

'I am. I removed it from his body myself. He was shot in the back,' I added.

There was a pause while Sir Thomas considered this. Then, shaking his head as if in regret, he said, 'I am sorry to appear obtuse, Doctor Taverner, but I must ask again: what is the connection to my house?'

The honest answer would be, *because the dead man is one of a group who hid on board an English ship and returned clandestinely to Plymouth. They slipped onto this ship in the Caribbean, almost certainly in Hispaniola, and now one of them has been found dead close to your house while a second has been badly injured trying to climb the back wall of Sir Richard Hawkins's house in Plymouth. And since you, your late*

Our horses were led out to us – they had also been well cared for; it was clear that every task in Sir Thomas Drake's household was performed to a high standard – and we mounted up, spurring our mounts, and hurried away.

'What do you reckon?' I asked Jarman. We were some miles on our way now and we had slowed down a little.

'Sir Thomas Drake himself didn't fire that shot,' Jarman replied.

'I agree,' I said.

'But,' he went on, 'that's not to say someone else in his household wasn't responsible.'

I was about to say I agreed with that, too, when he added, 'And I'd put a small wager that Sir Thomas probably knew all about it.'

Now that *was* a surprise. 'You would? Why?'

Jarman considered the question. Then he grinned. 'Nothing, really. Nothing more than the instinct that's saying loud in my ear that a former pirate made good and living a rich man's life in a grand house, son at Oxford, well-bred lady wife giving him respectability, isn't going to welcome some skinny ghost from his Caribbean past. Is he?'

'No,' I said heavily. 'He isn't.'

We had reached the bifurcation where one track led away to Theo's village and the other on down to Plymouth. Jarman Hodge had clearly been deep in his own thoughts, and I had been reflecting on the man who had been attacked by Richard Hawkins's dogs. Jarman, noticing I had brought Hal to a stop, looked enquiringly at me.

'I'm going to see what I can find out at the Hawkins residence,' I said.

Jarman nodded. 'I'll tell Master Davey,' he said impassively.

Jarman Hodge is a man who never asks unnecessary questions.

As I rode down towards the port, I went through what I knew about Sir Richard Hawkins.

He was a fine example of a thin skin of respectability painted

over a questionable past. His grandfather William Hawkins had
been one of Plymouth's wealthiest merchants, serving two terms
as mayor of Plymouth by his mid-thirties. He abandoned civic
duty to sail to the Guinea coast for pepper and ivory, and to
Brazil for the wood of the trees that produce a highly prized
red dye. There was a Portuguese monopoly on trading with
Africa and South America but William Hawkins simply
pretended it didn't exist, and his insouciance earned him both
fame – or possibly infamy, especially among the Portuguese
– and vast wealth.

William Hawkins's son John lived as a young man in London,
where rumour had it he'd murdered a man by the time he was
twenty-one, returning to lead a trio of ships to the Guinea coast.
This time the cargo was not merely the luxury goods that his
father had traded in but included some nine hundred slaves. He
led his small ships across the Atlantic to Hispaniola, where
there was a constant hunger for slave labour, and was paid in
the sort of goods for which England in her turn was most eager:
gold for the Queen, pearls for the throats of rich men's wives,
and ginger, sugar and hides for those who could afford them.
King Philip of Spain protested vehemently to Queen Elizabeth
at this foreign intrusion on his Caribbean empire, but the Queen
sided with her Sea Beggar and Hawkins's wealth increased
accordingly.

John Hawkins's son Richard endured captivity and
imprisonment at the hands of the Spanish for almost a decade,
subsequently rising through the ranks and becoming an admiral
a year ago; he had also served as mayor. His wife had just
presented him with a son, and, although he had purchased the
house out at Slapton, he lived for most of the time in his late
father's fine house in Plymouth.

It was this house for which I was bound.

I was in the town now, forging a way through the crowds,
the noise and the stench towards the more affluent area
where the Hawkins house was situated. I found an inn and
left Hal in the care of the ostler.

I walked past the front of the house: timbered, with a double
gable, three upper stories of small-paned windows in the jetty,
stout oak door within an elaborately carved stone doorway,

presently very firmly closed. I strolled on, turning down the side alley that bordered the house and coming to the wall surrounding the rear of the property.

The alley was overshadowed and dark, and very narrow. There was nobody about; no sound from either of the streets each end of the alley or from the house or garden. The rear windows, like those at the front and the door, were tightly closed and not a light shone from within.

I looked up at the wall. It was well-made, with only the minimum indentations between the bricks. It rose high above my head and I could not reach the top with outstretched fingers. I searched for something to stand on, for, unless the man who had managed to scale the wall last night was extraordinarily agile or able to fly, he would have needed a stone, or a discarded box, or—

Or a broken barrow.

And an example of the latter was lying on its side at the end of the passage where presumably it had been kicked aside.

I fetched it and positioned it at the foot of the wall. Then, in some trepidation as to whether it would support my weight, I stepped up onto it. There was an ominous creak of strained old wood, but the barrow held together.

Now I could reach the top of the wall. I took a firm grip, then pulled myself up. I scraped with my boots for a toe hold, and soon, panting hard, my heart beating rapidly, I had the upper part of my body across the top of the wall.

The enclosed space before me was some eight or ten paces long, and the width of the house. A door in the back wall of the house opened into it and it was overlooked by a number of windows. There was a low lean-to built into the angle between the wall and the rear of the house, and the presence of some large bones and quite a lot of dog excrement suggested it was a kennel. Fastened into the wall beside it was a large iron ring, probably for tethering the dogs. One dog lay dozing inside the kennel, its nose resting on its huge paws, and the other was standing absolutely still immediately below me, its eyes fixed on me and a very low, rumbling sound reverberating in its deep chest.

'Don't worry, dog, I have no intention of coming down on your side,' I said quietly. The growl intensified.

The house looked deserted, although surely there must be at least one or two servants in residence. I let myself down again and jumped off the barrow. Then I returned to the front of the house and knocked very firmly on the door.

The noise echoed through the house. Nothing happened, so I knocked again, even more forcefully. There was an outbreak of violent barking – the dogs had picked up the sound – running feet, and a voice from within called out, 'Who's there? What do you want?'

'I will not conduct this conversation through an oak door,' I called back.

'You'll bloody well have to,' the voice said – it sounded like that of a youth – 'because I ain't opening it. I've got my orders, see, and I'm not to unbar this door no matter who comes knocking!'

'Is Sir Richard at home?' I demanded.

There was quite a long pause, then the young man said, 'No.'

'He's gone to Slapton, then?' Perhaps sounding as if I knew all about Hawkins and his comings and goings would encourage the servant to trust me . . .

'Might have done,' the voice replied cagily.

'Ah, I'd hoped to catch him before he left,' I went on. 'But there's so much to do, and he'll no doubt be supervising the work.'

'Aye, that he is,' the voice agreed. The ruse seemed to have won him over. 'He left at first light. He hadn't planned to go till the end of the week, but—' Abruptly the brief rush of confidences dried up. 'But then he did,' he finished lamely.

'Well, no matter, I will seek him out there,' I said.

'Want to leave a message?' the voice asked.

'No. Good day.'

I set off back to the inn where I had left Hal, thinking.

One of the *Falco* fugitives had been killed as he ran away from Sir Thomas Drake's house. Another had been savaged by dogs as he jumped down into Sir Richard Hawkins's back yard. Was this no more than men of wealth and property protecting what was theirs?

But then Jarman's remark about Thomas Drake not welcoming

ghosts from his family's disreputable past equally applied to Richard Hawkins.

So what was the truth?

I was in the muddle of streets behind the quayside, almost at the inn, when a woman's voice called out anxiously, 'Are you the doctor?'

I turned to see a slim woman dressed in sombre grey standing in the doorway of one of the tall, narrow houses that lined the street. She wore a large white apron over her gown and her hair was neatly covered by a white cap. She was of early middle age, her face set in lines that suggested a chronic worrier.

'I'm *a* doctor,' I said, walking over to her.

She sighed in relief. 'Oh, good, that's good,' she breathed. 'My neighbour down the street pointed you out to me, and I hope I haven't caused offence by hailing you so rudely, only I'm that desperate, and my daughter's been on at me to do something about it since it's really affecting my other lodgers and I have my living to earn after all, and it's not easy when all said and done when I'm on my own, and—'

'What can I do for you?' I interrupted gently. She did not look unwell; other than the worry lines, in fact, I'd have said she was pretty healthy.

'Well, not *me* exactly,' she said hesitantly, confirming my assessment, 'it's – well, it's *him*.' She jerked her thumb upwards.

'Perhaps I should come in?' I suggested. One of her lodgers was unwell, I guessed, his distress disturbing the others.

'Oh, yes, if you please, Doctor,' the woman said, standing back to let me over the step. 'He's right at the top, I'm afraid.'

I did not have my bag with me but I was willing to look at the patient. If what ailed him was straightforward, I could send the woman to the nearest apothecary for a suitable remedy.

She had gone on ahead and she led the way up three flights of stairs. A narrower flight led off the top landing, and at the top there was a single door.

The woman pointed. 'He's in there,' she whispered. 'They asked for privacy – said they'd be attending to business matters – so I put them up at the top.'

'They?'

'Three of them.' She tutted disapprovingly. 'Leastways, there *were* three. Merchants, they are, although that can cover a multitude of things, eh, Doctor?'

'Indeed it can,' I agreed. I ran up the flimsy steps and tapped on the door. There was no reply. I opened it a crack, and instantly the smell of sickness flowed out to greet me. I pushed the door fully open and went inside.

The sick man lay in the bed furthest from the door. Two further beds had been placed either side of the door, as if their occupants wanted to be as far away as possible. The man was elderly and lay in a half-sitting position, pillows behind him. His face was deathly white except for two spots of colour on the sunken cheeks. His eyes were shut and I could hear the crackle of his breathing from where I stood.

I went over to him, kneeling down beside the bed. He was struggling for each breath and the effort was exhausting him.

'I need very hot water in a wide bowl, and a cloth,' I said quietly to the woman – she had crept to stand just behind me – 'and send someone to fetch white horehound oil.'

'White horehound oil,' she repeated, 'yes, I'll send the boy, and I'll put water on to heat.'

I would put drops of the oil into the hot water and hold the bowl before the old man's face, I was calculating, and the cloth draped over both the bowl and his head would mean he'd inhale the steam, and—

But then the man's dark eyes flew open and he stared right at me. I thought for a moment that it was fear that was twisting his features but then I realized it was anger. Fury.

He shot out a hand and grabbed my wrist. Even in his high fever he was strong. He muttered something in a foreign tongue, the words indistinct, then said abruptly in English, 'Who are you?'

'Gabriel Taverner,' I said. 'I'm a physician.'

The fury erupted. 'I do not *want* a physician! I *told* them, I—'

'You may not want one but you need one,' I interrupted calmly.

He looked at me for a long moment, his face working. Then he said in a very different tone, 'Where are they? Am I left here alone?'

In a heartbeat he had changed from resentful aggression to the pathos of sick old age.

And as he leaned forward against me I thought I felt him sob.

I stayed with him while obediently he breathed in the steam from two successive bowls of steaming water laced with white horehound oil. The congestion in his chest seemed to ease, and as his tired old body relaxed he settled against his pillows and fell asleep.

The woman said she would repeat the treatment later, and I undertook to return the next day. As she saw me out she whispered, 'Will he die, Doctor?'

'I hope not,' I replied. I thought at first that her concern was for her business – it doesn't encourage trade if dead bodies are observed being carried out of lodging houses – but then I saw the deep pity in her eyes.

'Poor old man,' she muttered. She reached into the purse at her belt, but I stopped her.

'No need,' I said quietly. She had been the one running up and down the stairs, and she'd paid for the horehound oil.

She nodded her thanks. 'I only hope the other two come back soon and take over the care of him,' she said worriedly. 'It's not right, truly it isn't!'

With a murmur of agreement, I hastened on my way.

The afternoon was now well advanced. I was very hungry and I wanted to see Celia. She had still been upstairs in her own quarters when I'd left that morning, and I hadn't yet apologized for having left her and Jonathan so abruptly the previous evening. Not that she'd appeared to mind, I thought now as I urged Hal on. Neither had he, come to that.

I wanted to be back well before nightfall.

I hadn't forgotten that strange moment late the previous night when I'd thought I heard the hiss of a whisper. And there had been the earlier incident out in the yard, where I'd run at a phantom intruder with a muck fork. I'd told myself repeatedly that I was allowing my imagination to get the better of me, but my unease seemed to have lodged in my mind.

However, it was only a short detour to call in at Tavy St Luke before I went home, so that was what I did.

Jonathan was in his church. He was standing quite still, looking up at the stained-glass panels set into the top of the wall between the body of the church and the side chapel dedicated to St Luke.

'They still fill me with joy,' he said without turning round, 'even though we know their story and its sorrows.'

'How did you know it was me?' I said, going up to stand beside him.

'It's the determined way you walk,' he replied.

'I'm sorry I had to abandon you last night.'

'No need for apologies. Did the man survive?'

'Yes. He was well enough to slip out of the room in the coroner's house where he'd been left and make his escape under cover of night.'

'Escape? He was a wanted man then?'

'No, not really. It's true he climbed a wall into the rear yard of a private house, but I don't think anyone had it in mind to accuse him of any crime.'

'Then why did you say he escaped?' Jonathan repeated.

'Because he was one of the fugitives from the *Falco*.'

There was a brief silence. 'You are sure?'

'I am.'

Jonathan nodded slowly. 'So you wanted to talk to him.'

'I did, very much.'

There was another, longer, pause. Then he said, 'Gabriel, I am uneasy in my mind about that ship; more accurately, about who, or what, hid down there in the deepest hold. Their presence . . . *haunts* me. I dream of—' But he stopped abruptly, apparently not willing to share the secrets of his sleeping mind with me. 'You will think me foolish and over-imaginative, I suspect, but sometimes I think someone's watching me. Following me while I go about my daily round, and always keeping just out of sight, so that when I spin round and call *who's there*? there is no reply and nobody – nothing – to be seen.'

I sighed. 'I do not think you're either foolish or

over-imaginative, Jonathan. For one thing, I don't think either fault, if faults they are, is characteristic of you as I'm coming to know you. For another, I've been experiencing exactly the same thing myself.'

TWELVE

Jonathan and I left the church and went to his house, where he poured measures of brandy for us both.

'I too have the sense that somebody is watching me,' I said as we settled either side of the hearth. Jonathan had stoked up the fire, and the heat and, more importantly, the light were providing their age-old comfort and reassurance. The brandy, however, was the best restorative. I have often wondered who provides our vicar with such fine French brandy; someone, presumably, who values him as much as I do.

'And as soon as you mentioned dreams,' I went on, 'I knew we had to speak.'

'You too?' he asked.

'Oh, yes.'

There was a pause, then he said cautiously, 'Would you like to talk about them?'

I wasn't sure where to begin, so I started with the prosaic. 'They began the night after I'd first gone to see Captain Zeke on the *Falco*, so that's . . .' I thought back. 'Roughly a week ago.'

Jonathan shot me a sympathetic glance. 'If your experiences have been anything like mine, that is a long time to have suffered,' he said quietly.

'I haven't dreamed every night,' I replied. I smiled briefly. 'Only most of them.'

'To describe what you see might help to disempower its force?' Jonathan said tentatively. 'And I take it that you have not mentioned the dreams to – to anyone in your household.'

I assumed he meant my sister. 'No,' I agreed. Then, for I felt he might ascribe my reticence to some fallible quality in Celia, I added, 'I share many things with my sister, Jonathan. More, perhaps, than I should, but she is a strong woman and has endured much without breaking.'

Almost inaudibly he murmured, 'I know.'

I stored away that soft, revealing comment, for it was not the moment to respond to it, and anyway I wasn't sure Jonathan had intended me to hear.

'The reason I have not confided in her concerning these wretched dreams is that I am ashamed,' I plunged on. 'Ashamed of my terror, ashamed of the instinct that would have me keep a light burning all night; most of all, ashamed of my new reluctance to close my eyes and yield to sleep because I am so afraid of what will come to me when I am helpless in the dark.'

Oh, but it was good to speak of it at last. I had been keeping it to myself as a way of pretending it wasn't really happening, and the strain had been considerable.

'You describe it well,' Jonathan said. '*What will come to me.* It is precisely what I feel, too.' He paused, thinking. 'Something lurks, patiently waiting, until I cannot fight it, and then it slips into my dreams and it is as if somebody is pushing it.'

I nodded eagerly. 'Yes, precisely that. I see a huge animal, just out of sight among a tangle of trees and undergrowth – a jungle, for there's a sense of great heat and humidity. It moves with the sinuous stealth of a great black snake, but when I turn to look at it I see two brilliant pale green eyes staring straight at me, and then I can see it's a panther.'

He nodded. 'Go on.'

'I see myself within the dreams, but I seem to be performing acts I have never performed in life, nor had any desire to. I make strange potions, I blow a cloud of some weird dust into people's faces, so that they cannot help but breathe it in through nose and mouth. I am *cruel*, Jonathan; I use others for my own sinister purpose, and it is this aspect that disgusts me most. That and the dead bodies.'

'Ah,' he breathed. 'Yes. The dead bodies.'

'I watch as the ground opens and the dead crawl back up to the surface,' I plunged on, barely registering his quiet comment. 'Then it is no longer I who am in control, and I am helpless to resist as the figure in white commands me to—' I stopped. 'And then I am neither the controller nor the instrument but the victim, and that is the worst of all.'

Silently he reached out and poured more brandy into my cup.

'What you describe is horribly familiar,' he said quietly after a long pause, 'for I have seen similar violent and disturbing scenes. I believe,' he went on, the confidence returning to his voice, 'that some power which came here on the *Falco* is indicating its presence to us; to you and me.'

'Why us?'

'Because we are the most involved.'

'What about Theo?'

'You are quite sure he is not being sent these dreams?'

'Yes, he'd have—' I stopped. 'Well, no, I'm not sure, I suppose. I'm just assuming he'd have told me.'

'Yet you have not told him.'

'True.'

'Let us assume for now that he is free of this horror, as I fervently hope he is,' Jonathan went on. 'If it is only the two of us, then I suggest it is because we are closest to whatever lies at the dark heart of the matter: you because you have examined the bodies of two of the fugitives—'

'Three,' I interrupted. 'Only the third one wasn't dead.'

'Ah, yes. The man you treated last night. And, of course, you studied the tiny female corpse that was left on board the ship.'

'So that explains the interest in me,' I said. 'What about you?'

'I entered their alien world,' he replied. 'Down in that dark little hold, I had to approach whatever lurked there in order to communicate the wish that it should leave. I think—' But he did not go on.

I recalled what he'd said as we rode home after the purification ceremony. He'd described two battling forces, one that was protective and the other malign: powerful, ancient, sinister, dangerous, and emanating from the darkness.

Dear God, and he had opened himself to it, whatever it was, and now it had latched onto him . . .

'Jonathan, this is appalling!' I said urgently. 'You came to carry out the ceremony at my request, and it has brought to you this terrible danger! Have you no means of protecting yourself?' I stared wildly round the little room, as if searching for a sword or a dagger.

And Jonathan said calmly, 'Of course I have, Gabriel.'

I turned to face him. He was holding up the wooden pectoral cross that hung on a leather thong above his heart.

'I will admit, however,' he added with a wry smile, 'that I have been spending a great deal of time in the church of late.'

'I might just come and join you,' I muttered.

'You would be most welcome.'

After a moment I said, 'Why are we being visited by these dreams?'

'The power that has come here is showing us its strength, perhaps. Letting us know that it is not to be lightly dismissed.'

'No fear of that,' I said. Then I was struck by a new thought. 'Jonathan, what of the fugitives? Do they have the dreams, do you think? Are they as afraid as I am?'

'As we are,' he corrected. 'I imagine so. I sense that these poor souls are in torment. They succeeded in their aim of reaching England – if, indeed, that was their destination, and—'

'It was,' I interrupted.

'How can you be sure?'

'Because it seems likely they seek particular people. Their presence has been recorded in two very specific places: the residences of Richard Hawkins and Thomas Drake.'

I watched as Jonathan absorbed that. 'Both of whom have strong links with the Caribbean, which was the point of departure for the fugitives,' he observed.

'Yes, and those links are of long standing,' I responded. 'Sir Richard's father was trading in slaves from the early 1560s, Sir Thomas's brother joined him a few years later. The young man whose body was found near Buckland Abbey had African blood,' I added quietly. 'As, I suspect, did the man I treated last night, although his eyes were blue.'

'Do we postulate, then, that the fugitives are a band of runaway slaves?'

'But two of those I have encountered are not of fully African blood and the man in the barrel appeared to have none at all,' I said.

Jonathan frowned. 'Is there intermarriage between slaves and slave owners?'

'I cannot answer that,' I said. 'Perhaps not marriage but, human nature being what it is, I would assume there is sexual congress, wouldn't you?'

'I would,' he agreed, 'and, again taking into account human

nature, especially man's nature, I fear that a child born by a
slave woman to a white master might not have been conceived
at the will of both partners.'

It was a roundabout way of expressing it, but I knew what
he meant. 'I fear you are right,' I muttered.

'Is this about revenge, do you think?' Jonathan said suddenly.
'Does a son born of rape seek retribution?'

'I have heard no rumour of involvement between any man
of either the Drake or the Hawkins family and a slave woman,'
I said. 'They were in the Caribbean for gold and treasures,
not for—' I held back the crude expression I'd been about to
utter.

'No indeed, and you are quite right to point out that they
are very probably blameless in *this* respect.' His words, and
the very way he said them, carried the strong implication that
he did not hold the men of either family quite as innocent in
other matters. He was a man of God; in his compassionate,
humane eyes, slavery would be an abhorrence. 'And yet, Gabriel,
I feel the presence of the ancient, dark homeland of the
Caribbean slaves in this. I sense—' He did not continue.

'I do too,' I said.

And I told him how, after we had cut down the young man's
exsanguinated body from the tree above the river, I had gone
home and sought out my Caribbean notebooks. I also told him
what I'd written in them.

'They brought their fearsome gods with them when they were
torn away from their homeland,' Jonathan said reverentially
when I had finished. 'They found comfort in their faith, and
who can blame them? Their lives were brutal, they were in an
unknown land, and so they turned for help and support to the
only thing nobody could take from them.'

I was surprised to hear a man such as him defend an alien
belief. 'But their gods are not our God,' I said.

He looked at me for a long moment. I thought at one point
he was about to say something, but he shook his head and kept
silent. Eventually he said, 'I too have studied this faith.'

'You have?' My surprise increased. 'But—' I was about to
ask how on earth he'd come across it, but realized I would
sound impertinent. Even more so, I further realized, than I must

already appear by having lectured him on something about which he undoubtedly knew far more than I did . . .

'I was at Cambridge,' he said, and his eyes held amusement at my discomfiture. 'Trinity Hall.'

'Yes, so you once told me.'

'I was to have read law, but my path was diverted. I studied instead the law of the Church, which we know as canon law.'

'And that included vodou?' It seemed unbelievable.

He paused, then said, 'The great masters who were our instructors were wary of the religion of our country's enemy at the time.' The Spanish, I thought. Jonathan was being very diplomatic in not naming them. 'To defend oneself against an enemy it is advisable to learn all you can about him, and—'

'But the Spanish are fervently Catholic!' I interrupted.

'Of course,' he said impatiently, 'but by the time I was at Cambridge they were already in possession of much of the Caribbean, and they had sent their priests to root out the secrets of men's hearts. Those priests encountered the faith that the slaves had brought with them, and they discovered how one dark, ancient belief system met and absorbed elements of another; one that pre-existed among the indigenous peoples of Central and South America. The priests wrote of their findings – and they were brave men, those Spanish priests, and their accounts are frequently harrowing – and, writing as they were for their masters and ultimately their king, they did not hold back.'

I wondered how on earth the writings of Spanish priests in the Caribbean had come to be read by a young ecclesiastical student in Cambridge. Looking at Jonathan's expression, however, I didn't ask.

He glanced at me. 'I know what you're thinking,' he murmured. 'You are very interested in how it was that I read the papers and the journals I pored over, and you are absolutely right in the conclusion that I am not going to tell you. Men risked their lives to acquire and disseminate this perilous information, Gabriel, and I will not endanger them.' He looked around at the darkening room. 'Even here – especially here, just now – I fear being overheard.'

'I understand and I'm sorry,' I said.

'No need to be sorry, for you managed not to ask the question burning in you,' he said lightly. Then, frowning in concentration, he added, 'We were speaking, were we not, of the fugitives, and whether they too were experiencing the same dreams that haunt us?'

'We were indeed.'

'Yes . . .' He thought some more. 'You have suggested that England, and this specific area of England, was their intended destination since they have been to both Buckland Abbey and to Sir Richard Hawkins's Plymouth house. They have, it seems we must conclude, something extremely powerful with them: a dark force that can enter men's dreams and make him see visions from another world.'

'There are potions and powders that can instigate these visions,' I said.

'Yes. And the adepts of vodou and its associated faiths are well practised in the making of such potions. So, the fugitives leave the *Falco* and for some reason are not able to take with them the dried corpse that they took on board. It – she – was, however, so important to them that they stole her back from Master Davey's house.' He paused. 'Is it theft when you take back what belongs to you? Is it right to say that a power object such as that tiny corpse can *belong* to anybody?' He shook his head. 'But those are questions for another time.'

He turned to me, looking me straight in the eyes.

'Gabriel, there is great danger here. We cannot know what the fugitives' purpose is, but we must conclude that, taking into account the strength of the weapons they have brought with them, it is potentially very, very harmful.'

'*Weapons*? But—'

He made an impatient sound. 'Oh, *think*, Gabriel! I do not refer to swords, knives, muskets, well-armed ships with canons and well-trained archers lining the upper deck. Those are not the only weapons, nor, indeed, are they the most formidable.' He lowered his voice and said quietly, 'You know the danger to which I allude, for you have just told me how something – some malign and very powerful spiritual force – enters your mind as you sleep.'

'Enough!' I said quickly.

But I didn't think he heard; if he did, he took no notice. Leaning forward in his fervour, he went on, 'And I have experienced the same danger, I too have been terrified so that I fear to go to sleep, and, believe me, I would *far* rather face a flesh and blood enemy pointing his sword at my throat, or the iron and wood threat of a vast ship bristling with guns – something that I can see, hear and feel with my everyday senses – than what presently haunts my dreams!'

In the few moments before he brought himself back under control and was once more the cool, detached figure of the vicar of Tavy St Luke's, I glimpsed just how afraid he was. And I understood, for I felt exactly the same.

I reached the safe confines of the Rosewyke yard before it was fully dark. I had not enjoyed the short ride home. Even before my talk with Jonathan, I had already become far too aware of my surroundings when on my own; far too willing to ascribe to every innocent countryside noise a sinister and dangerous meaning; the hissing whisper was but the latest example. The relief I experienced at seeing Samuel's impassive face and Tock's permanent expression of mild bemusement made me realize just how twitchy I had become.

Celia and I ate supper together. She had looked at me with a slight frown as I came in and I was aware of her watching me while we ate, but her conversation was of light, mundane matters and, as she described her encounter with an elderly woman friend who fussed her like a hen with one chick, she even managed to make me laugh.

Later, however, as we sat together either side of the fire, the shutters closed against the night, a good fire burning and Celia's beautiful embroidery spread over her lap as she calmly sewed, I sensed from the sudden tension I observed in her that she was preparing to speak on more vital matters: to ask me why, perhaps, I was acting so oddly.

To forestall her, I said, 'I called in to see Jonathan on my way home, to apologize for having abandoned you yesterday evening. I *am* sorry, Celia. I hope it wasn't awkward in any way after I'd gone?'

She looked up. 'Awkward?'

I thought I detected a slightly mocking tone. 'Well, you know.'

'In fact I don't know, Gabe. I can assure you, however, that being alone with Jonathan was in no way *awkward*.' This time there was no doubt about it.

'Oh. Well, good.' She was still looking at me, her eyebrows raised. 'And it was an enjoyable evening?' I plunged on.

'It was, thank you, Gabe.' As she bent over her stitching, I thought she was smiling.

'I hope you found enough to talk about,' I said. I've never truly learned the art of when to stop an unwise exchange, particularly with my sister.

'Without your scintillating presence to provide interesting topics of conversation?' she said somewhat acidly. 'Indeed we did.'

'Jonathan is a man of much learning and he has an enquiring mind, so no doubt you—'

She put down her embroidery and glared at me. 'Gabe, if you wanted details of every little thing we said to each other, then you ought to have stayed here and not gone dashing off to attend to your patient!' she said. 'Jonathan was a delightful guest, he expressed appreciation for everything Sallie put before him – well, you observed that for yourself since you were here – and we enjoyed a glass or two of brandy in the library after the meal, we talked without a pause for at least two hours, whereupon he exclaimed that it was late, he was sorry to have outstayed his welcome – I assured him he hadn't – and he thanked me very much for a rare and delightful evening and expressed the hope that we might do it again.' She stopped, panting, slightly flushed. 'And that is absolutely *all* I'm prepared to say!'

I reflected, as I picked up the book I'd been reading and pretended to return to my study of its pages, that she had said a great deal more than she'd probably intended.

And I wondered just how soon she would realize.

But when, a little later, she broke the silence, it was not to refer back to what we'd just been saying. Instead, an anxious expression in her eyes, she said, 'Gabe, what's the matter?'

'Nothing!' I said before I'd had the chance to think how unwise it was.

She tutted. 'Something *is* the matter. You keep looking up and staring around. You jump at the small, normal noises. You look pale, and although you said you were very hungry earlier, you only ate half your food.' She leaned closer. 'You're my dear brother, we've shared much that we'd far rather not have shared and I had the idea we were close. You helped me when I very badly needed help, and I would like to believe that means *you* can ask *me* for my help, such as it is, when you are in need. Please, Gabe, tell me?'

Her earnestness touched me, as did the honesty and courage I saw in her face and her warm hand reaching to take mine. 'Your help is invaluable,' I said quietly, 'so no more of this *such as it is* rubbish, and in any case modesty doesn't suit you.' She grinned. 'I am indeed troubled, Celia,' I went on. 'It's hard to explain, but I believe—'

'It's the ship, isn't it?' she interrupted. 'Something to do with what was found on the *Falco*, and Captain Zeke asking you to help, and Jonathan going on board and saying prayers to purify the secret hold where the fugitives hid.'

'Yes,' I said. 'He told you about that?'

'Well, *you* certainly didn't,' she said shortly. Then she added, 'Sorry.'

'I didn't want to—'

'Worry me?'

She said it lightly, but I knew how it irked her to be treated like a fragile little woman who had to be sheltered from life's rawness and violence. Considering what she had endured, it was hardly surprising.

'No, not that,' I said. 'There was something very badly wrong on the *Falco*. I think, by not telling you about Jonathan's purification ceremony, or any of the other things that have been happening, I was actually trying to protect myself rather than you.' I met her eyes and attempted to smile. 'I wanted to keep *here*' – I waved a hand around the cozy room – 'safe. Inviolate. Untouched by the blue ghosts and whatever it is they've brought here with them.'

She nodded. After a moment she said, 'Jonathan is frightened.'

'He told you?'

'He didn't need to. I went out to the yard with him when he left and just as Samuel was bringing out his horse, a barn owl flew low over the house. He jumped as if I'd stuck a needle in him.'

Poor Jonathan. 'He is afraid,' I said. 'So am I.'

Then I poured out more brandy, took a deep breath and told Celia everything that I had been holding back.

THIRTEEN

'So as I clearly recall saying to you before,' Celia whispered over breakfast the next morning – Sallie was out in the scullery, but my sister and I knew from long experience that her hearing is equal to that of a bat, if not better – 'what we really need to find out is what brought the fugitives to this part of England, and why they've been lurking round the residences of Drake and Hawkins.'

'Yes.'

'If you don't mind me searching through your books, your notes, your maps and everything else up in your study, shall I see what I can discover?'

'I don't mind at all, and yes, please do.'

Having been taught by our formidable grandmother Graice Oldreive, Celia's knowledge of many subjects – most subjects, in fact, that are not to do with medicine or the sea – far exceeds mine.

'What are you going to do today?' she asked.

'I have several patients to visit, I should call in on Theo to see if the man bitten by the dog has been found, and—'

'I don't think you will find him,' she put in.

'Why not?'

'Because wherever it is that these fugitives are hiding, they have chosen the spot well. Nobody has reported strangers, have they? And they took back the tiny corpse that was left behind on the *Falco*, and that hasn't been found either.'

'So, you envisage some out-of-the-way place where they have found shelter, where they've hidden the little corpse and where the dog-bite man fled back to so that his companions can look after him?'

'Precisely that.'

'But how could they—'

'Oh, for goodness's sake, Gabe, we live on the edge of a vast moor with great tracts where nobody goes and where there are the remains of abandoned dwellings, not to mention outcrops of rock that provide shelter and concealment! If you were going to say how could they stay undetected, then I would reply, very easily!'

I grinned, for she was quite right.

'So, let me remind myself,' she went on. 'There are, or were originally, at least four of them: the old man whose body was in the barrel, the young man who was found at Buckland Abbey, the dog-bite man and a lithe person who was small enough to clamber through Theo's little window. Is that right?

'Yes.'

'And the old man was English but the two others you've seen were of mixed blood.'

'Yes.'

'And all of the men you've seen have blue hands and forearms,' she murmured. Then she gave me a dazzling smile. 'Oh, I *love* a challenge!' she said, getting up. 'See you later.'

As I left the house and went to collect Hal, it occurred to me, not for the first time, that Celia didn't have enough to do. Considering how much she had to offer, I thought that was a great pity.

I took Flynn with me. He is an obedient dog, and two of the patients I was going to visit were children, one only three years old; the presence of a good-natured dog with gentle manners was often a distraction while I did things that hurt.

I told myself that was my reason for having him with me and that it was nothing to do with the fear of ominous presences lurking in the shadows.

When finally I arrived at Theo's house, Flynn was tired and very willing to lie down in the yard. I went on into the house and found Theo in his office.

'Jarman Hodge has gone up onto the moors,' he said, not bothering with even the briefest of greetings; I gathered from this that he had made no progress in his investigations into the two deaths or the mystery of where the tiny corpse had gone, and that he was becoming deeply frustrated at his failure and increasingly short-tempered as a result. I knew him well enough to be aware he never took out his ill humour on his wife or his children, so I resigned myself to being the recipient.

'Gone to look for the fugitives' hiding place,' I remarked.

His head shot up from the document he was studying. 'How do you know? You've seen him?'

'No. It was only a guess – Celia suggested the same thing this morning, and she reminded me how easy it would be to hide on the moor.'

He nodded. 'Yes.' He looked down at the document. 'I've already got two dead of consumption and a stillborn child to process and now there's this!' He picked it up and waved it violently in my face. 'The body of some old man has washed up on the banks of the river and the dear God above knows what I'm to do about him since half his face has gone, one of his hands is missing, he's as naked as the day he came into this world and not even the mother who bore him would recognize him.' He swore, at length and without repetition, for some moments.

I knew about the dead consumptives, who had both been my patients and whose deaths had been anticipated. The stillbirth might well have been one of Judyth's patients. Theo, I guessed, wanted to devote his time to the responsibilities presently before him and did not welcome this new distraction.

'Want me to go and have a look?' I offered.

'Not your job, strictly speaking, but mine,' he grumbled, but he was looking at me shrewdly, hope in his bright blue eyes.

'One of your men can come with me and we'll take the cart,' I said. 'I'll have a good look at the body and act on your behalf.'

'You have the time?'

'Yes.'

'Then thank you, Gabe. I'd be grateful.'

The body had washed up on our side of the river, which made collecting it an easier task. It lay on a befouled stretch of shore and it was covered in the thick, stinking mud that was soon to coat both the lad who'd driven the cart and me. The lad had brought a bucket – I guessed he knew the location and had been prepared for the muck – and fetched water to sluice over the dead man where he lay. Examining him, I determined that he was old, as Theo had said: well over sixty, his skinny old body bent and worn out. It was not clear yet how he had died. There

were no obvious wounds nor signs of sickness, but he was very
thin so it could easily have been from starvation. He had been
in the sea for some time. Sea creatures had eaten away most
of his face, his left arm ended above the elbow and one foot
had gone. The lad chucked another bucket of water over him,
washing away the mud from his right side, and as his hand
appeared I saw that what remained of his flesh was stained blue.

I stood up.

We had found another one.

I wasn't looking forward to breaking the news to Theo. The
lad and I carried the body into the house and were heading for
the cellar when Theo bellowed from his office, '*Not there!* Take
him to the house up the road.'

We shuffled back again. Theo came to stand in the doorway,
glaring at us. 'I've had the body from Buckland taken there to
join the man from the barrel,' he said gruffly. 'The pair of them
may as well lie together, since they got here the same way.'

The lad opened his mouth to speak and I guessed he was
going to tell Theo that a third fugitive was about to join the
first two. I shook my head at him, and he kept quiet.

'I'll come back and report to you when we've settled
him,' I said to Theo.

He grunted something and went back into his office.

As the lad and I carried the corpse up the road, I said, 'Sorry
I stopped you.'

The lad grinned. 'I don't mind, Doctor T. I'd far sooner you
told him than me.'

Down in the crypt of the empty house, the two bodies lay
on trestles. I held the third corpse while the lad set up another
one, then we laid him down.

Tacky mud still covered much of his torso. Looking down
at myself, I saw how dirty I was. The lad grimaced at me. 'Want
me to wash him properly while you go home and clean up?'

'Yes please. I'll be quick.'

I rode home as fast as Hal would carry me, Flynn running
beside us. Both of them were fresh – much fresher than I was
– for they had rested and been well looked after in Theo's yard,
and we were soon at Rosewyke. I washed in the yard, abandoned

my outer garments for Sallie to deal with and rushed upstairs for fresh linen and a clean tunic and hose.

'Is that you, Gabe?' Celia called out from my study.

'Yes.'

'Come in here, I've found—'

'Can't stop,' I yelled, 'I've got a body waiting for me.'

She was standing in the gallery outside the study as I hurried back to the stairs. 'Is it another one? Oh, Lord, it is, isn't it?'

'Yes.'

'Go on!' she urged, gesturing with her hands as if to shoo me away. 'I'll tell you later. *Hurry!*'

I hurried.

Celia listened to her brother pounding down the stairs, his impatience to be gone and his urgency to get back to his task almost visible presences. It was, she mused, as if a wildly-spinning wind had briefly hit the house, erupting up the stairwell and stirring the still, calm air to frenzy. She heard him race across the hall and through the kitchen, yelling something in reply to Sallie's question, then he was down in the yard and Samuel was handing him Hal's reins. There was more shouting, then Hal's hooves clattering across the hard ground as Gabe kicked him to a trot, then a canter, and they were off.

'Phew!' Celia exclaimed softly.

Then she returned to Gabe's study and dived back into what she had just been doing.

She had found the map that Gabe had shown her a week ago. She had studied it for some time, reminding herself of the details of the *Falco*'s last voyage: how she had circled the Caribbean, sailing along the north coast of Venezuela and north-west past Panama to Guatemala, heading on eastwards for Cuba, Hispaniola and her last port of call. Then, with the map open on Gabe's desk, she had investigated his books and journals and found three different accounts of travels in the Caribbean islands and the Spanish Main. There were bookmarks in all three, each marking a relevant section, and she realized that Gabe had recently done exactly what she was doing.

He has already been through this material, she thought. And yet still he is distracted, worried and uneasy; which suggests he has found nothing very helpful in terms of discovering what is happening . . .

She closed the books with the book marks, stacking them and putting them aside.

Then she returned to the densely-packed bookshelves to see what else she could find. Not long before Gabe's brief eruption into the house had distracted her, she had found something rather interesting.

Now, once more seated at his desk, a clean piece of parchment before her, pen and ink horn to hand, she returned to the work that had snagged her interest. She read on, captivated, pausing from time to time to refer to the map and sometimes spending a frustratingly long time trying to locate a specific place. She was an orderly, disciplined scholar – her grandmother had ruthlessly instilled good habits into her – and she managed to control her impatience, refusing to allow herself to go on with the fascinating tale until she had carefully studied the map and seen the locations described in the text.

And, as so often seemed to happen when her imagination had become engaged, finding out one thing led instantly to an urgent need to find out about another. So she went back to the bookshelves and found a work that comprised the writings of several men who had sailed with Francis Drake in 1577 and returned three years later after circumnavigating the world. That, naturally, sparked the desire to see it for herself, and so she climbed up on a stool and very carefully took down the globe – one of Gabe's most treasured possessions – that stood on an upper shelf. She located England, then traced the voyage of those little ships down the west coast of Africa, across the Atlantic to South America, south to the Magellan Straits and up the other side, up, up, ever north as Drake – according to some – attempted to find the elusive Northwest Passage and return home across the north of the great land mass that separated the two vast oceans.

Unable to find it, he had instead turned west out across the Pacific.

She stared down at the enormous, almost empty space of sea that seemed to occupy a third of the sphere. How did they do it? she wondered. From where within themselves did they find the courage?

Because they knew it meant money, came the answer. They did it for wealth, and the power that invariably accompanies it.

The words in her head were spoken in her grandmother's voice, and Celia smiled in gentle reminiscence.

And the voyage had indeed turned out for the good. Drake's little ships, laden down with gold taken from the Spanish back on the other side of the great dividing land, had not had to risk being relieved of it in their turn on the way home by those who had originally stolen it. Instead, Drake had made his way to the Spice Islands, amassing a cargo almost as valuable as gold to take back to England.

Drake, naturally, had come home a very rich man . . .

Celia replaced the globe. She put the book of collected writings back in its place. She sat down at the desk, thinking. About sailors and danger; about early explorations in strange and perilous lands; about the Spanish, and how they had looked upon the Caribbean and all the lands around it as their own fiefdom until a handful of cocky little upstarts from Devon had demonstrated how wrong they were.

About the men who had managed to return home, vastly richer than when they'd set out.

About those who didn't.

She told herself the idea was nothing but a foolish fancy. She wrote sums on her piece of parchment; could it be possible? Really? She thought about hardship and deprivation, and the devastation these factors would have on a human body. She thought about resentment hardening into something much more dangerous; about envy; about just how much a man – a group of men – might be willing to risk in pursuance of a goal. She thought about the weapons they might employ and whether they would—

'Mistress Celia?'

The voice – Sallie's voice – penetrated her intense concentration. 'Mistress Celia?' It came again. '*Mistress Celia!*' And again, this time rather more loudly, for Sallie had puffed up the stairs – still calling out – and was now lurking in the doorway to the study.

'Sallie!' Celia exclaimed, feigning surprise. 'Were you calling me?'

Sallie gave her a sideways look. 'Well, yes, Miss Celia, that I was.'

'I *am* sorry.' Celia stood up, closing the book she'd been studying and covering the map with her parchment of scribbles, sums and notes in a casual gesture that she was sure didn't fool Sallie for a moment.

But, with an indulgent smile, Sallie said, 'Sorting out the doctor's papers and that? Good for you, Miss Celia, I'm always on at him to let me come in here and do a bit of dusting, only he always tells me not to and says he'll never find anything if I tidy up.'

Celia bit down the curt reply that no, she hadn't been tidying, sorting or dusting, she'd been reading, because women could read as well and quite often a lot better than men and they also had a brain, so were perfectly capable of studying and learning and working out solutions to challenging problems, thank you very much.

There was no point whatsoever in expressing such opinions to Sallie. In her view, men did the thinking and women fed them, looked after them and cleared up after them, and that was that.

So she just said mildly, 'Yes, it is a little dusty in here, isn't it?' and Sallie rolled her eyes in sympathy.

'Did you need me for something?' Celia added; Sallie was staring round the study as if just itching to fetch a feather duster, a bucket of soapy water, roll up her sleeves and turn out the study while its habitual resident was out.

With a visible effort she turned her attention back to Celia. 'Did I . . .' She frowned, then, her face clearing, she said, 'Yes! Indeed I did – do – need you, Mistress Celia!' She leaned closer, and Celia registered the smell of baking and sugar that always seemed to float around her. 'There's that *person* downstairs,' she confided, a disapproving frown knitting up her forehead. 'Wants to speak to the *doctor*, if you please!'

'Well, a doctor does indeed live here,' Celia pointed out, 'so it isn't so unreasonable, is it?'

'Oh, she hasn't come here to ask for advice or treatment!'

Sallie said scornfully. 'She sees to all that sort of thing for herself.'

For a moment Celia wondered hopefully if the caller was Judyth Penwarden, straight away dismissing the idea; Judyth appeared to be one of the very short list of people who had won Sallie's approval (the others being Theo Davey and Jonathan Carew and precious few others) and the housekeeper wouldn't have sounded so disapproving of Judyth. She certainly wouldn't have referred to her as a *person*.

'I'd better come down, Sallie,' Celia said. 'I will explain that we don't know when Gabe will be back, and offer to take a message. Who *is* it?' she added as she followed Sallie back down the stairs. 'You still haven't told me.'

Sallie gave a huff. 'No, indeed I haven't, Mistress Celia.' She turned, giving Celia a baleful look. Then, dropping her voice until it was all but inaudible, she mouthed, '*Black Carlotta.*'

'Black – oh!' Celia stopped dead. She had just met the old woman, only the other day, and she was aware both Judyth and probably Gabe too had occasional – perhaps even frequent – contact with her; Judyth, indeed, made no secret of her admiration. But Celia had always been wary and, now that it seemed she was about to meet her alone, wariness was threatening to turn into fear.

'I won't let her hurt you,' Sallie said staunchly. 'Wants to speak to the doctor – well, it'll be you, him not being here – in private!' She made a sound eloquently expressing vast indignation.

'It's all right, Sallie, I'm sure she—'

'Just you receive her in my kitchen,' Sallie hissed, 'and I'll be close and handy in my little room; you can yell out if you need me.'

Celia watched as her sturdy, courageous housekeeper squared her shoulders, strode into the kitchen, said disapprovingly, 'Here is Mistress Palfrey,' then went on into her room and pointedly closed the door.

Celia looked at the black-clad figure standing in the middle of the kitchen. She brought a sense of the outdoors with her; Celia caught a faint and heady aroma of hedgerows, of foliage, of living things. She was staring at Celia with an expression of lively interest and she looked neither dangerous nor threatening.

'Good morning, Mistress Carlotta, we meet again,' Celia said politely. 'My brother is not at home, but perhaps I may help you?'

'Know why I'm here, do you?' the old woman said.

'No. Not really. As I said, Gabe isn't—'

'Doesn't matter.' She went on studying Celia, and there was a look of deep compassion in her shining eyes. 'Doing all right, are you?'

'I am, thank you.'

Black Carlotta nodded. Then her expression darkened and she said, 'Tell the doctor I came. Tell him I said to watch out, for, like I said afore, there's danger here.'

'Danger,' Celia repeated softly. Then she heard herself say, 'I know.'

'Feel it, do you? Good, that's good. Means you'll believe me and take heed.'

'But *what* danger?' Celia asked urgently; she thought Black Carlotta was about to go. 'And how do we take heed? How do we protect ourselves?'

Black Carlotta said nothing for some time. Then she murmured, 'It is something I have not encountered before. I was sensing it when I came to tell you the first time, but now it is . . .' She paused, frowning. 'This is a great and ancient evil, and it has been awoken far away and brought here. There is another force besides – it is small but its power is intense and it stems from the female principle, and its force is protective . . .' She closed her eyes, swaying to and fro, gently at first and then with increasing speed and violence. Celia, afraid for her, leapt forward and took hold of her shoulders. It was like wrestling with a powerful and determined ewe, and one of Black Carlotta's flying hands caught her across the cheekbone.

But she held on, and presently the swaying slowed and stopped.

'Thank you,' Black Carlotta said faintly. She glanced at Celia. 'I hurt you. I am sorry. It was not deliberate.'

'I know it wasn't.' Celia resisted the urge to put a comforting hand up to her throbbing cheek. 'What – er, what was happening?'

'They – it – knows I'm here. Knows I can sense its presence,' Carlotta said shortly.

'*It?*' Celia felt a chill of dread snaking down her spine.

'Seems it doesn't like folks nosing around,' Black Carlotta said. 'Even more, it doesn't like having an opposing force standing over those it would target.'

'Opposing force . . .' Celia thought she understood. 'Please,' she said urgently, 'you mustn't endanger yourself for our sake, it's not right for you to be hurt protecting us, and—'

But Black Carlotta laughed.

'Bless you, I am not referring to myself,' she said quietly. 'I'd do what I could if I had to, make no mistake, but it's not me that's standing between you and the dark power.' She raised her head, listening, looking around as if she heard or saw something undetectable to Celia. 'It's her,' she whispered.

'Her?'

Black Carlotta nodded.

And, for a mere heartbeat, Celia thought she saw the white-clad figure of a tiny woman, brown skinned, dark eyed, a strip of pure silver hair visible under the smooth headdress.

'Who is she?' Celia gasped. The tiny figure was there again, flitting in and out of her vision like a child playing hide and seek.

Smiling, Black Carlotta shook her head. 'Don't know, lady. But I'll tell you this: she's mighty powerful whoever she is, and she won't let you come to harm if she can prevent it.'

Celia reached blindly behind her for a chair, sank down on it, tried to focus on the elusive white shape, blinked to clear her vision—

And, for all that only the briefest instant had passed, when she looked again the white shape had vanished.

And so had Black Carlotta.

FOURTEEN

When I got back to the crypt beneath the empty house, the lad – whose name, I learned, was Ned – had not only given the corpse a thorough wash but also wiped down the trestle, swept and mopped the floor, as well as finding the time to spruce himself up, wash the filth from his hands and face and brush down his clothes. He was a bright boy, as no doubt Theo had already spotted, and I resolved to tell Theo what a help he had been today.

'Do you want me to stay, Doctor T?' Ned asked as I rolled up my sleeves and stared down at the body waiting for me on the trestle.

'No, Ned, thanks – nothing else I need from you just now.'

He looked disappointed. 'I've already taken the horse and cart back to the coroner's yard,' he said. He was looking at me, an appeal in his brown eyes.

'Would you like to stay?' I asked.

He nodded eagerly. 'Yes!'

'It's not pleasant work,' I warned him. 'I shall be examining every part of the body, searching out its secrets, determining how this man lived and, more importantly from the coroner's point of view, how he died. I may have to cut into him. Will you be able to witness these tasks, do you think, without fainting or bringing up your breakfast?'

Ned grinned. 'Reckon so, Doctor T. My father butchers pigs.'

'But this was a man, Ned,' I said gently. 'He lived, breathed, loved, hated, laughed and cried just as you and I do.'

He swallowed. 'Willing to give it a try, Doctor, with your leave.'

'Very well, then, Ned. I will tell you what I'm doing as I do it, what I conclude, if anything, and why. The instant you feel you've had enough, take yourself off and I will think none the worse of you. All right?'

'All right!' echoed my new apprentice, with what, under the circumstances, I considered admirable eagerness.

'Then we shall begin. This is the body of a man of advanced years who has had a very hard life and, latterly at least, nowhere near enough to eat. He suffered from scurvy – see the swollen gums and the missing teeth? He—'

'How d'you know he was old?' Ned asked.

'Mainly from the state of his bones, his joints and his teeth. He'd have—'

'He'd have walked with a stoop and maybe a limp, like my old grandfather,' Ned put in.

'Yes, quite.' I had spotted something: the corpse was missing most of its clothes, but there was a wide leather belt around his shrivelled hips and it had saved at least that part of his flesh and the organs that lay beneath it from the hunger of the crabs and the fish. I unbuckled the belt and opened up the lower abdomen. I heard Ned give a couple of dry retches, but he controlled himself.

'What are you looking for?' he asked presently. He was leaning over my shoulder.

I pointed. 'This.' There was a sheet of muscle in which there was a stoma – a hole – through which a fist-sized piece of flesh bulged. 'It's a hernia.'

'Was it how he died?'

'No, hernias are hardly ever fatal. Many men have hernias – women too – and they are particularly common amongst sailors because they have to do so much heavy manual work.'

'Hauling on ropes and sails and anchors and that,' Ned remarked vaguely. He didn't sound like a lad with experience of the sea.

'Yes.'

'So this old gaffer was a sailor.'

'In all likelihood, yes.'

I was thinking. Ned, astute lad that he was, seemed to realize and ceased his questions.

The old man had been one of the fugitives on the *Falco*: that seemed beyond doubt, given his blue hand and arm and the place where he'd washed up. Had he died on the journey? On the very last part of it, perhaps, when those poor suffering men had almost made it. He'd have been full of hope, this old man, aware that the *Falco* was close to England now and confident he'd see his home again. But something had happened to him; he had taken sick, I guessed, because I could find no more sign of marks of violence on what remained of him now than I'd been able to spot down by the river when he was covered in mud. So, he'd fallen ill, his companions had tried to help him – *Come on, old friend*, I imagined them saying, trying to encourage him, *nearly home now! Just a little while longer, hold fast!* – but to no avail. He'd died, and the others had little choice but to chuck him overboard since they'd already put one body in the barrel and there would have been no room for a second. How had they managed that? They'd have waited until night, no doubt, but a ship never sleeps and they'd have run a grave risk of being seen. But they were almost home by then – maybe they'd decided that it was worth the risk not to be holed up with a corpse, and reckoned they stood a chance of getting ashore somehow if they'd had to leap off the ship.

They waited till England – Devon – was in sight.

Then I remembered the dead young doctor, Ashleigh Winterbourn Snell, and how Captain Zeke said the poor man had waited till he could see his homeland before leaping over the side because he wanted to lie in English waters, off an English shore.

Perhaps this old man's shipmates thought he would prefer that, too. It was the only thing they could do for him, and bearing in mind where he'd been found, they had achieved their purpose.

I became aware of Ned, becoming restless at my long silence. I stirred myself back into the present moment.

'Anything you want to ask, Ned?' I said.

'Well, yes, Doctor T.' Unknowingly echoing the words of the other lad, who'd come to fetch the Buckland body, he pointed at the corpse's one remaining hand and said, 'Why is his skin blue?'

I picked up the dead hand and examined it. 'I have no idea.' I hesitated to tell him of the other bodies who also showed staining of the hands and forearms, then I thought, why not? 'The other bodies here have the same distinctive feature,' I said. 'Come, I'll show you.'

I went to stand between the two earlier bodies, the remains

found in the barrel and the Buckland youth. I folded back the covering cloths and pointed to their hands. 'See?'

'Yes,' Ned said breathed. 'They look like they've had their hands in a pan of blackberries.'

I bent closer. He was right. I recalled blackberry picking with Celia when we were young, how our protestations that we'd hardly eaten *any* fruit were shown for the fibs they were by the blueish markings round our mouths. And when we tried to sneak a spoonful or two of the jam bubbling away on the stove, frantically blowing on it to cool it enough to gobble down before anyone saw us, we always gave ourselves away by the stains on our hands and our clothes.

'They do, don't they?' I agreed.

'Blackberry season's over,' Ned observed.

'Yes,' I murmured.

So whatever had stained these men's flesh so deeply must have been something else . . .

The day seemed already to have been interminable, and as I wearily climbed up the steps from the crypt – Ned had already gone – I realized dully that it wasn't over yet, for I still had to report to Theo and, before I turned for home, I ought to check on the sick man in the lodging house.

Theo was in his office, looking as exhausted as I felt. He was alone, although a couple of his agents were talking quietly in the front office.

'Jarman Hodge not back?' I asked.

He made an elaborate show of searching, then said, 'No.'

'I've examined the latest body,' I said, pretending I hadn't noticed the sarcasm.

'And, much to your surprise and joy, you found a tightly-rolled piece of paper shoved up his arse covered in writing and telling you who he was, who his two dead companions were, not to mention the young man with the dog bite who I allowed to vanish from under my very nose, where they came from, why they came to Devon and what they were up to lurking about at the houses of Sir Thomas Drake and Sir Richard Hawkins.'

'Sadly, no. There was nothing up his arse other than what you'd expect to find there.'

He looked at me, the angry frustration very evident in his eyes. 'No, of course there wasn't,' he said, and to my relief he was no longer yelling at me. 'Sorry, Gabe. None of this is your fault.'

'Nor yours.'

He shrugged. Then: 'What *did* you discover? Anything helpful?'

Briefly I summarized my findings. 'The blue stained hands – hand, rather, as one had gone – make it fairly certain he was one of the *Falco* fugitives,' I concluded, 'and, since he was probably even older than the man found in the barrel, I'd say he was lucky to have survived for as long as he did.'

'You reckon they shoved him over the side when land was in sight?'

'Well, it's one explanation.'

'If they'd waited till the *Falco* docked in Plymouth,' he went on, and I had the impression that he was speaking his thoughts aloud, 'they'd have had to carry him off the ship, which I suppose would have been very difficult, given they were trying not to be seen, so heaving him into the sea was a better bet.'

'I believe you're right,' I said. 'They had to abandon the little female corpse when they left, probably for the same reason, yet it must have been valuable to them because they took the great risk of breaking into your house to take it back.'

'Dear *God*, Gabe, this is a bugger of a business!' Theo exclaimed. Then, abruptly standing up, he waved a hand at me. 'Go home. Eat. Talk to that lovely sister of yours. Have a few measures of fine wine and a large glass of brandy. Sleep, and in the morning, come and tell me how on earth I am to find my way through it all.'

He came round the desk and slapped me quite hard on the shoulder. He looked tired, defeated, and I sympathized. 'Take your own advice and do the same,' I urged him. Then I added quietly, 'They are dead, Theo, or most of them surely are. They failed in whatever they planned to do at the grand residences of Thomas Drake and Richard Hawkins, and in truth I fail to see how the thin, enfeebled, emaciated remains of the group can possibly pose much of a threat to well-defended houses with gangs of servants no doubt ready and willing to defend the master and his family with any weapon that comes to hand. One fugitive was shot, remember, and one had dogs set on him.'

Theo gave a long, gusty sigh. 'Yes, I suppose you're right,' he said. 'But all the same . . .' He didn't explain his misgivings, which was probably just as well if either of us was to have any hope of sleeping that night.

He came out to the yard to see me off and we bade each other good evening. As I rode away, I couldn't help wondering what had prompted that remark of his . . . *but all the same.*

It was exactly how I felt too.

I had to face the fact that I was sorry for those poor men, as undoubtedly was Theo. More than that: I was egging them on, hoping they'd find what they sought, achieve whatever desperate mission had brought them here at such a high physical and emotional cost.

I sighed.

It had always been a faint hope. Now, surely, it was an impossible one.

I had forgotten about the old man in the lodging house.

I hesitated. Hal's head was turned in the direction of home, and I battled with my conscience. Would an early morning visit serve as well? No it wouldn't, for fevers usually rise in the evening and the thin woman who ran the lodging house might be alarmed if the old man became delirious, especially if her other lodgers started to complain.

So with great reluctance Hal and I rode down to Plymouth.

It was as well that I had decided to go, for the old man's fever had indeed risen alarmingly and he was lost in his own interior world, and a frightening place it seemed to be.

The woman had brought cold water and cloths and had been bathing his face, chest and hands until, realizing what she was doing, he had screamed at her and pushed her away. 'Told me to be gone,' she confided to me indignantly, 'and I won't soil my mouth with what he called me.'

'He is not himself,' I said, wringing out the cloth. 'In his right mind, I am sure he would only have words of gratitude.'

She looked at me doubtfully. 'I'm not at all sure about that, Doctor,' she said. 'He's a man who mistrusts and dislikes women, if ever I met one.'

Perhaps she was right, I reflected, for even in his disorientated state, the man seemed to shrink away from the sound of her voice.

'Leave him to me,' I said to her. 'I'll come and find you when I go.'

She didn't need telling twice, slipping away quickly before I could change my mind.

I sat beside the old man, repeatedly rinsing out the cloth and bathing him. He twisted and turned in the bed, his face distorted by some strong emotion, and presently he began speaking. At first the words were almost inaudible – and could well have been in a foreign tongue – but then the volume increased until he was shouting and other lodgers down on the lower floors were banging on their ceilings and yelling their disapproval.

'Hush,' I soothed him, 'be still, rest.'

He turned his head and stared right at me. 'They would not tell us!' he cried. 'We tried all our arts, we put their colleagues to the fire before their eyes, we threatened them with the same fate, but *they did not break!*'

Horrified, I wondered what terrible visions he was seeing. I hoped fervently they were nothing but the products of his delirium. I put the cloth back on his forehead, and for a moment his face relaxed. Then, suddenly furious, he shouted, 'They fled before us, and although we set off in swift pursuit, still those devils evade us!' His voice cracked and broke. I poured water, holding the cup to his lips while he sipped. 'We must find them,' he whispered.

And just before profound sleep abruptly took him, his black eyes fixed on mine and he gave me a look of such malevolence that it was all I could do not to pull away.

It was late when I finally reached home. My mind was full of what had just happened and I urgently wanted to talk to Celia. She was in the kitchen, sitting at the table while Sallie prepared vegetables for supper, and she looked up as I came in.

She was so pale that my own preoccupations flew out of my head.

'What's the matter?' I asked.

Sallie did her imitation of a hen fluffing up its feathers in outrage. 'Well may you ask, Doctor Taverner!' she said in tones of outrage. She hardly ever calls me by my name, so I knew something grave had happened. 'Poor Mistress Celia here was—'

But Celia, looking up at her with a particularly sweet smile, said, 'It's all right, Sallie dear, I'll tell him.' She stood up, went over to Sallie and briefly hugged her, then said to me, 'Come into the parlour, Gabe. The fire's going well in there, and I can't seem to get warm.' She drew a thick wool shawl around her shoulders and led the way, and I followed. I could still hear Sallie muttering indignantly as we crossed the hall.

'I had a visitor,' Celia said as we sat down; she, I noticed, had drawn her chair right up to the hearth. 'I was upstairs in your study – I'll tell you about that later, somehow it doesn't seem terribly important at the moment – and Sallie came up to tell me someone had called, and it was Black Carlotta, and when I said you weren't at home she spoke to me instead.' She paused, and her face grew even paler.

'What did she want?' I asked, then, before she could answer, 'Did she scare you? She's a little weird, I'll admit, but you know that, you've already met her, but she—'

'No, *she* didn't scare me, Gabe,' Celia replied. 'And when she revealed what she had come to tell me – us – I had the impression she was as frightened as I was.'

I left my chair and went to crouch in front of her, taking her cold hands between mine. 'What did she tell you?'

'She said we're in danger. Something very powerful and very evil from far away and long ago has been disturbed – woken up, she said – and it's threatening us. But there's another power too, a protective power, and it's a woman, or it comes from a woman – oh, I don't know, I didn't understand, and she – Black Carlotta – just said it came from the female principle, whatever that means.'

And I remembered what Jonathan Carew had said about the second, conflicting force that he had sensed in the *Falco*'s dark,

cramped hold: *The other power, very much to my amazement,
seemed to be a protective spirit.*

'I have no more idea than you,' I said, 'although this is not
the first I've heard of two opposing forces.'

'But I *do* have an idea,' Celia said in a very small voice.
Clutching my hands convulsively, she whispered, 'I think I may
be going mad, Gabe, because I do not believe such things exist,
and I have always held that the rational mind *must* hold firm
in the face of the illusions that our imagination generates, but
– but I *saw* her.'

I returned her tight hold on my hands. 'You are not going
mad,' I told her firmly. 'You are one of the sanest people I
know.' She smiled faintly. 'And what you saw – if indeed you
did see anything – is likely to have been the result of the fear
that Black Carlotta had just brought into the house.'

She thought about that. To my relief, for she has strong hands,
she relaxed her grip a little.

'Well, I thought I saw something,' she said. 'Just for the
briefest time, I had a flashing series of images of a very small,
dark-skinned woman with pure silver hair, and she was dressed
all in white.'

I met her wide, alarmed eyes. We stared at each other for a
tense moment.

Then she said, a slight tremor in her voice, 'You recognize
her from the description, do you not?'

'I – possibly.'

She clicked her tongue in annoyance. 'Of course you do,
Gabe, you must do! *I* recognized her, and I only had what you
told me to go on!'

So, very reluctantly, I said, 'Yes. It sounds as if whatever
you saw – *if* you saw it – was some sort of vision of the body
we found on the *Falco.*'

'Nailed through the throat to a rib in the side of the hold, if
I remember correctly,' Celia said.

'Er – yes.'

There was quite a long silence. My knees were cramped from
crouching, so I returned to my chair.

Then Celia said – and to my relief she sounded almost her
normal self – 'There's one thing I do not understand.'

I laughed shortly. 'Just one?'

She ignored that. 'If we are correct in assuming this little figure in white is the good, protective force – the one stemming from the female principle, as Black Carlotta would have it – then perhaps that is the reason that the fugitives took her on board the *Falco* with them, and went back for her when they had to leave her behind and she ended up in Theo's cellar. Because she protected them!' she added impatiently when I didn't instantly reply.

'Yes, that seems highly likely, but you said there was something you didn't understand?'

'Yes, I'm just coming to that.' She paused, and briefly the fearful look returned to her face. 'It's – I wondered—' She drew a deep breath and said in a rush, 'If she protected them, and they treasured her, valued her, why did they treat her so savagely? Why did they drive a nail through her throat?'

She was almost sobbing as she said the last words.

'I don't know,' I said. I too had been struck by the treatment meted out to the body, and I hadn't begun to understand back then when I first saw it that it had been a force for good, not evil. 'Perhaps because her power is too strong if she's left unrestrained?'

But then I heard what I'd just said and instantly wished I could swallow the words back down again.

It was too late; my sister had heard them.

She said in a very small voice, 'She's unrestrained now.'

FIFTEEN

I needed to talk to Jonathan.

I was all for setting out there and then, but Celia didn't want to be in the house without me – I couldn't blame her – and when I suggested she could come with me, she said, quite rightly, 'And what about Sallie? Or are you proposing to invite Samuel and Tock to bed down in the kitchen?'

So we went to bed. I didn't sleep much – as well as everything else, the sick old man down in Plymouth was still vividly in my thoughts – and I don't suppose Celia did either.

In the morning, however, there was no need to go down to the village to seek out Jonathan for, very early in the day, he came to find us.

Sallie showed him into the parlour even as Celia and I were beginning breakfast, pulling up a chair and offering to fill a platter for him without so much as an enquiring look at Celia or me to see if it was all right. Which didn't matter in the least, since it was.

Jonathan waited until Sallie had gone back to the kitchen and then said, 'I am concerned for you here at Rosewyke. There have been reports of strangers prowling around and they've been seen out this way.'

'I know,' I said.

Celia spun round to stare at me. 'You didn't mention it!' she said accusingly.

'Er – no.' There wasn't really anything else to say.

I turned to Jonathan and began to tell him what Black Carlotta had said to Celia, but Celia interrupted me, saying she was quite capable of speaking up for herself and proceeding, succinctly and unemotionally, to do so.

Jonathan said when she had finished, 'It is interesting that this woman also mentions two forces, for I have sensed the same.' He smiled at her. 'I have not had your advantage, however, of actually seeing a manifestation of this protective spirit.'

'I do not recommend it,' Celia muttered.

He looked interested. 'You felt afraid?'

She considered the question. 'No!' she replied, sounding faintly surprised. 'I was . . . shocked, I suppose, that I'd seen her – or I thought I did – and I felt a sense of her power, and it was awesome.'

'You thought you did?' Jonathan repeated.

She met his intent eyes. 'I do not believe in ghosts.'

He smiled. 'Your brother here said the same thing.'

'How can they exist, Jonathan?' Celia demanded. 'I have seen a dead body, I know that after death—' But very abruptly she stopped.

There was a short silence. Then Jonathan said gently, 'I agree, death does indeed appear very final. But what of the soul?'

'Was that what I saw?' She did not look convinced. 'Oh, I don't know *what* it was, if indeed I saw anything. Black Carlotta had – have you met her, Jonathan?' He shook his head. 'She is a forceful presence, and she'd just been telling me of this ancient evil, and I suppose I half-believed her—' She paused. 'No, that's wrong, I *did* believe her, all the while she was talking anyway; no doubt I was suggestible, receptive to the idea of spirits becoming visible, so when there was a flash of light in the kitchen, or a sudden movement, I interpreted it as a phantom figure dressed in white.' She looked at Jonathan and then at me, and there was something in her expression that suggested she longed for one of us to say *oh, yes, I'm sure that's what happened*.

Neither of us did.

After a silence which was fast becoming uncomfortable I said, too brightly, 'So, Jonathan, what of these prowlers?'

'That is really all there is to tell,' he replied. 'Two people in the village say they saw a couple of strangers acting suspiciously, although there's a dearth of good gossip at present and these reports do get exaggerated. But I've also heard that two or three settlements out on the moor and around the village have suffered thefts; a smoke-house broken into, fruit taken from where it had been left prior to storing it away. Never very much, and the more sensible of those reporting the matter put it down to children, or hungry vagrants unable to resist the temptation.'

'But you were concerned enough to come and warn us?' I asked.

'Bearing in mind what has been happening, yes.'

'Thank you,' Celia said, shooting a look at me as if to reprimand me for not expressing my gratitude. 'We—'

Too many conflicting demands and possibilities were filling my head and I could make no pattern of them all. Abruptly I stood up. 'I have a call to make, and on the way back I'm going to talk to Theo,' I said.

Jonathan stood up too. 'I want to help, Gabriel,' he said calmly. 'I have been praying for you, but what else should I do?'

I looked at him. 'Bearing in mind the nature of what appears to be threatening us, prayer is probably best.'

He smiled faintly. 'For peril to the soul, of course. I am thinking, however, of these strangers.' He paused. 'I am not unversed in the ways of violent men.'

I recalled the tale he had told me of his past. I knew he spoke truly, and also that he was not a man to hold back when need demanded he strike.

'I would value your presence, whenever you can spare the time,' I said. Then, with a nod to each of them, I left.

Hal responded to my need for speed and we swiftly covered the miles to Plymouth. I left him in the ostler's care and went on to the lodging house.

The woman greeted me with very evident relief. 'He's much worse, Doctor,' she whispered. 'Been raving, he has, and—'

'I will try to quieten him,' I said, patting her arm. 'I know my way,' I added, for she seemed on the point of coming up with me.

The sick man lay in sweat-soaked sheets and the smell in the room was awful. He was far gone in delirium, shouting at an invisible foe one moment and asking plaintively for his absent colleagues the next, sometimes speaking in English, sometimes lapsing into what I guessed must be his mother tongue. I bathed him, for all the good it did, for the instincts of all my years as a physician told me he was near death. I was holding a cup of water up to his mouth when suddenly he began to pray.

And the form of words was one that had not been heard openly in England for almost half a century.

Theo was his usual fraught, disgruntled self, but today I was in no mood to appease him.

Before he could speak I said, 'I've been treating an old man in a Plymouth lodging house. He had two companions with him and they presented themselves as merchants. The others have abandoned the sick man and he's dying. He has a high fever and amid his rantings he lapsed into prayer.'

'Why are you telling me this?' Theo demanded.

'Because I believe the old man is a Spanish priest,' I said.

'He's *what*? Dear Christ, Gabe, have we not enough on our hands without you—'

'*Listen!*' I said sharply.

To his credit, he did.

'We have fugitives from the Caribbean who are running in terror, so afraid of what pursues them that they risked the perils of the voyage in the depths of the *Falco*. We have a delirious priest who with my own ears I have heard speak of putting men to the fire, men who would not reveal some secret even under the worst torture. This priest's two companions may also be priests, and they are at large and probably hunting for the men they have pursued halfway round the world, three of whom are dead and one with his leg torn to pieces by Richard Hawkins's dogs. I may be wrong, but if not – if there's any danger of those men who have already suffered so much falling into the hands of the enemy they fear so much – then I want to prevent that happening.'

I only realized I'd been shouting when I stopped, and the echo of my words rang in the room.

Theo said into the silence, 'Jarman Hodge is back and he's found a makeshift shelter up on the moor. Whoever had been there has gone, but he followed a trail and he reckons they were heading for the river.'

'Two men? Three?'

Theo shrugged. 'Maybe.'

'The river . . . the Tavy?'

'Yes.'

He was watching me, an expression I didn't much like on his face. 'What is it you don't want to tell me?'

Theo hesitated. Then: 'He reckons they – whoever they are – have gone to ground in those woods down below your house. He found tracks leading that way.'

I turned towards the door.

'Where are you going?' Theo demanded.

'If it's the fugitives at Rosewyke they'll need protecting. If it's the priest's companions, they'll be armed. I'm heading home to fetch my sword and then I'm going to search my woods.'

He was calling out something as I left the house, his voice raised and alarmed, but I didn't stop to listen.

Judyth Penwarden was hurrying for home.

She had been up all night with a farmer's wife who was giving birth to her first child. The woman was young, scarcely more than a girl, and very frightened, and shocked to find herself in such pain. The husband – not much older than his wife – had stood in the bedroom doorway wringing his hands and looking helpless, until much to Judyth's relief the girl's mother had arrived, sent him out into the yard to find something useful to do, and then told her daughter in brusque but kind words to stop making such a noise, every other woman managed it and why shouldn't she, and to listen to the midwife and get on with it.

With calm partially restored, Judyth was able to turn her full attention to the breech birth. The young woman had good cause for distress, she knew, for the buttocks-first progress of the baby was a slow process that for a long time threatened to come to a total stop. But Judyth knew – hoped she knew – what to do, and eventually, the young wife having been encouraged to adopt a crouching pose to allow the baby's own weight to help it drop, the delivery was accomplished.

'Me, I'm all for the old birthing stools, myself,' the new grandmother declared, pacing slowly to and fro, her first grandson held in strong and gentle arms. 'Had five of my own that way, I did, and you'd not have heard so much as a peep out of me.' She shot her daughter a faintly disparaging look.

'Yes, there is much to be said for them,' Judyth said, busy with the afterbirth, 'although it us up to each mother to decide for herself. Is it not?' she added pointedly. The young mother flashed her a look of gratitude.

'Oh, yes, yes, I suppose so,' conceded the grandmother. The infant in her arms made a soft cooing sound, then tried out his lungs in a tentative cry. Apparently liking the sensation, he did it again, increasing the volume until the yells echoing round the small, stuffy room were almost as loud as his mother's had been earlier.

Judyth helped the young mother to sit up straight, pushed some pillows behind her and said, 'What that little lad needs is his mother,' and, meek as a lamb, the grandmother handed him over to her daughter.

When Judyth finally emerged, leaving the brand-new parents exclaiming in delight over their little son and the grandmother making porridge in the kitchen, it was to discover, with faint surprise, that night was long over and the sun climbing rapidly up the sky.

She set off to walk home. It was not far: she took the track that bent round to the south of Gabriel Taverner's house, then branched off it to go down to the little path that ran along beside the river. It was a short cut, and she longed to be home. It was also likely to be deserted, and she knew that to stride along beside the fast-moving water, alone with the sights, sounds and smells of late autumn, was almost as effective a restorative as the good, long sleep she anticipated.

She was past the woods that hid Rosewyke from sight and on the steep path down to the river when she first suspected she wasn't alone. She heard a faint rustling behind her, as if somebody was treading softly on the dead leaves that covered the woodland floor. She looked round. Not a sound, not a movement.

An animal, then. A deer, a fox, standing still and out of sight until she had headed off and it was safe to proceed.

She walked on, faster now, and presently jumped down the last few feet of the slope and joined the waterside path. She rounded a bend and then heard the distinct sound of someone else doing exactly what she had just done: the ground was muddy at the bottom of the slope and her feet had made a squelching noise.

Somebody is following me, she thought, not particularly alarmed. Well, more than a few people know of this short cut, so why should I be surprised? But she found that she had increased her pace.

She looked over her shoulder once or twice, but the track frequently ran beneath overhanging branches and it twisted and turned, affording far too many places for concealment.

At one point Judyth thought she heard someone panting with effort.

She walked faster, faster.

The end of the path came in sight. She saw the little settlement of Blaxton up ahead, and the jetty where the ferry ran across the river. She hurried on, emerging from the little path and joining the wider track that went the long way round. She came to the place where the path up to her little cottage branched off, running now, her bag on its strap over her shoulder banging against her thighs.

She thought someone called out. She ignored it.

She unlocked her door, threw herself inside, banged it behind her and rammed home the bolts. Safe now, she waited until the shakiness eased – fatigue, it's just fatigue, she told herself – then went through into her living area to stoke up the fire, put water on to boil and make herself a hot, restorative drink.

She was sitting in her usual chair beside the hearth, the ingredients she had mixed already doing their job, when she heard the back door slowly opening.

She sat as if frozen.

But I secured it, she thought frantically. I remember doing it, before I left last night, I—

But then she also remembered how she'd found herself out of comfrey and made a quick dash out to her still-room to fetch more.

And – the door was creaking open now, and making that noise it always made when it caught against the flagstone that stood up slightly proud – she didn't remember locking up again . . .

She tried to turn round but she could not find the courage.

Then a husky male voice said behind her, 'I do not wish to harm you but I will if I must.'

She took a breath. Two breaths.

Then slowly she turned to face him.

He was thirty or so, tall, very thin, although he had the air of a man who was once much bigger, before starvation took effect. His hair was dark, tight-curled, his skin was tawny, his eyes were blue. His clothes were little more than rags, and one leg was bare. No, not bare – she looked more closely – for it had been bandaged.

'You are hurt,' Judyth said. She was surprised how calm she sounded.

He glanced down. 'Yes. But it's not why I—'

Judyth was already on her feet. 'Sit,' she commanded, pointing to the settle set against the wall. 'That bandage looks filthy and it is starting to unwind. I have water heating and I shall fetch ointments.' She gave him a glare. 'If you permit, of course?'

He looked briefly shamefaced. He seemed to be thinking hard, calculating. Then he nodded. 'Yes. Thank you. But be quick. You *must* be quick.'

He is on the run, Judyth thought as she worked. Having her hands busy calmed her and she found she could consider her situation rationally. He fears that those who pursue him are close, but this wound on his leg slows him down.

'How did you know I would be able to help you?' she asked as she removed the bandage. It was stuck in places to the wounds beneath and she had to use hot water, and even then he winced and she sensed he was biting down to stop himself crying out.

'I've seen you. I know you're a midwife, and just now I saw you near the doctor's house.'

'But I hadn't—' She stopped. *I hadn't been to the doctor's house, I was merely passing*, she'd been about to say. But why tell him this?

She removed the last piece of the dressing, closest to the skin, and this time he did cry out.

'I'm sorry,' she said. She was horrified by what she had just revealed: a series of dog bites, some deep, some quite shallow, and the worst of them neatly stitched. It was no surprise he was in pain, and the wounds definitely required fresh, clean dressings. But there was good news too: very good news.

'I see no signs of infection,' she said quietly. 'Whoever tended you did a good job.'

This time when he spoke he sounded almost friendly. 'It was the coroner's wife first, and she bathed and bathed with water so hot it hurt worse than the original bites. Then the doctor came and helped.' Amazement in his voice, he added, 'He put *garlic* in the deepest wounds!'

Then she knew for sure that what she suspected was right. It had been Gabriel Taverner who stitched this man up. Amid every other emotion currently flooding through her there was a moment of happiness: she'd told him about the use of garlic, he'd been sceptical and made a joke about roast lamb, and she'd been hurt, thinking he'd written her methods off as riddled with country superstitions and no better than hedge remedies.

She was wrong, for he had taken it in and now used it himself.

To good effect, she thought, carefully feeling the flesh all around the bites and finding very little heat.

Then the mood changed.

She had begun on the re-bandaging, padding out the linen strips with folded cloth to protect the healing wounds, when suddenly he yelled right in her ear, 'Hurry! *HURRY,* damn you!'

She was afraid, but she was also stung to anger. 'I am trying to *help* you, you fool!' she shouted back. 'Sit still, stop yelling at me, and I shall finish all the sooner!'

She heard him muttering to himself as she wound the last strip and tied off the ends. She stood up, the bowl of dirty water in her hands, and walked across to the sink. She tipped it away, and then he was standing right behind her and she felt the point of a blade on the side of her neck.

'Leave that,' he said, his voice low with menace. 'Listen, for you must do exactly what I tell you.' He dug the cold metal into her skin, and she thought she felt a drop of blood well up. She felt her heart thumping hard in alarm.

'Tell me, then,' she said.

'Put on your cloak, then leave by the door at the front,' he commanded. 'Do not call out, do nothing to alert anyone out there of what is happening. I shall be beside you, and we will pretend that you are helping me because I am wounded.'

Clever, she thought.

'I shall have my knife just here' – swift as a snake striking, he moved his hand to the area over her ribs – 'and I shall drive it into you if you betray me.' He gave her a shove. 'Now, pick up your cloak.'

She did so, swinging it around as she put it on and wishing it had heavy stones in the hem with which to knock him off his feet.

'Out.' He pointed his free hand at the door.

She walked ahead of him, heard as he closed the door after them.

'Back the way we came,' he said softly, resting one hand on her shoulder as if for support, the other at his waist, as if clutching at himself in pain. He was on her left side and she could feel the knife, poised over her ribs. If it was long enough – she hadn't nerved herself to look – a good, hard thrust would reach her heart.

'Get going,' he said.

She obeyed.

In the taproom of an inn on a busy river quay not far away, the white-haired man pushed food and drink across the battered wooden table towards his companion. He waited until the younger man had drunk, then leaned close and said very quietly, 'What news?'

The younger man smiled grimly. 'I know where they are. Not precisely, but near enough. I have seen them, all three together and once the son on his own, and I believe I have identified the settlement in which they are hiding.'

'Good,' the white-haired man said. Then, his face tensing, 'What of—' He stopped.

'I did not see her with them,' the younger man said.

'Could they have found a secret place nearby?' the white-haired man said. His fear was evident in his staring eyes and the beads of sweat on his brow.

'Let us hope so for your sake,' the younger man muttered under his breath.

He was fighting to hide his contempt. Men such as they, rooted so deeply in the faith, had no business reacting with such terror. It was undermining; unmanly; entirely unworthy.

The white-haired man's lips were moving swiftly in a fervent, silent prayer. The younger man picked up his mug of ale, drank again and then turned his attention to his food.

SIXTEEN

He marched her back along the riverside path and up the track that skirted the Rosewyke woods. There he took a little path that opened off the main track, and they went in under a tangle of undergrowth into what was virtually a tunnel. In shadow, with dying, dusty, brittle vegetation catching in her hair and making her flesh itch, Judyth lost all sense of direction and it was a surprise when they emerged only a hundred paces or so from Gabriel's house.

She must have made some small involuntary movement, because suddenly the point was sticking into her side and he hissed in her ear, 'You are tempted to call out, to warn those within or to plead for their help. But if you give in, my knife will act far more swiftly than anyone in there.' He jerked his head towards the house, now looming up right in front of them.

Judyth walked on.

Up the steps to the entry porch. The man's fist thumping on the heavy oak door. Thump, thump, thump.

Judyth heard brisk, light footsteps crossing the flagstones of the hall. Celia, she thought, for the steps did not have Sallie's steady, purposeful tread.

Celia flung the door open, and her face lit in a smile as she saw Judyth.

'Judyth, what a pleasant surprise!' she said. 'We are all in a fluster this morning, I'm afraid, and—'

But then she must have seen something in Judyth's eyes. She shifted her intent gaze to the man, and said, 'Who is this?'

'I have a knife, madam,' the man said quietly, the smile belying the sinister words, 'and its point rests over your friend's ribs.'

'What do you want?' Celia asked. She had gone very white, and Judyth hadn't missed the quick, agonized glance she shot at her, but she sounded calm.

'To speak to the doctor,' the man said.

'He will see you!' Celia's response was a cry of protest. 'Treating sick and injured people is what he does – there is no need for this, for threatening my friend with a knife!'

But the man was pushing them inside, one hand still holding the knife against Judyth's side, the other tightly gripping Celia's shoulder. 'Get in the house!' he hissed, and he closed the door after them.

Celia shrugged him off and strode ahead, across the hall, left through the parlour and on into the library. A fire had been lit; responding to its warmth, Judyth realized how cold she was. Those few moments had apparently given Celia time to collect herself, and when she spun round to face Judyth and her captor, her expression was severe.

'If you are one of the fugitives who have been hiding in our woods, then you should be aware that right at this moment my brother is outside looking for you,' she said in a cool voice. She was staring at the man, but her eyes kept flickering to Judyth. *She is afraid*, Judyth thought. *She hides it well, but it is in her eyes.*

'Then go and call him,' the man said. He nodded towards the window, with its view over the path up to the house and the thicket of fruit trees and bushes that separated the grounds from the river, and the woodland stretching in a broad band to the south. 'Stand just there. Summon the doctor. Any hint of a warning, and you know what I will do.'

Celia gave him a look of such disgust that Judyth was half-afraid he'd stick the knife in her out of sheer anger. She risked a glance at him. His attention was fixed on Celia. 'I *have* to do this!' He hurled the words at her. 'You do not understand.'

'I most certainly do not,' Celia agreed.

She gave him one last, condemnatory glare. Then she walked over to the window, opened it and called out loudly, 'Gabe! *Gabe!*'

There was no response. She turned back to the man. 'He can't hear,' she said, 'I shall have to go and find him and—'

But just as Judyth's heart lifted in hope – for if Celia had to go outside to fetch Gabriel, then surely she would find a way to make him aware of the danger – Gabe's deep voice yelled, 'What do you want? I'm busy!'

Judyth saw Celia slump a little; she had clearly been holding on to the same faint hope.

'Come up to the house, will you?' Celia called back with just the right note of irritation. 'I need you for something.'

'Can't it wait?' Gabe shouted. Judyth thought it sounded as if he was closer now.

'No!' Celia cried.

And the three of them waited. They heard Gabriel call out to someone. One of his outdoor servants, Judyth thought, no doubt helping with the search Celia mentioned.

They heard him marching across the hard ground in front of the house. Heard his booted feet climb the stone steps, heard his heavy tread echo in the hall. Judyth found herself repeating silently, *be careful, Gabe. Please, please be careful.*

And then as Gabriel came striding into the library, despite the fact that a frightened and very determined man had a knife to her side, straight away Judyth felt safer. And, just as always happened at the sight of him – no matter how well she hid it, no matter how she denied it to herself – her spirits sang with happiness.

He looked hot. His shirt was open and she could see his well-muscled chest. His long hair was awry, as if he'd been wrestling with branches and undergrowth. The heavy gold ring in his ear glittered in the firelight. He had a sword in his right hand, its point raised and directed at the man, and a heavy stick thrust through his belt. He looked wild; alarming; and again she was aware of the instinctive knowledge that told her he was dangerous; that he would not hesitate to act with the ultimate violence if he knew it to be right, irrespective of whether or not the action was within what the law allowed . . .

She watched as Gabriel took in the scene in one swift, raking glance. He looked at his sister, still standing by the window; he looked at her, and at the man holding her so tightly. She saw a flash of fury in his eyes, quickly covered up. He said mildly to the man, 'How's the leg?'

Celia gasped. 'Gabe, you *know* this man?'

He shot a quick look at her. 'Yes,' he said shortly.

'Then why in heaven's name are you—'

Gabriel held up his hand. His eyes held his sister's, and she seemed to understand whatever message he was trying to impart.

'I will gladly look at your wounds,' he said, turning his full attention to the man and apparently ignoring Judyth's presence. 'You have only to ask, and—'

But the man shook his head, furiously, as if he was trying to rid himself of some disturbing, insistent sound that only he could hear. 'No, *no!*' he cried. 'She has already tended to me.' And Judyth suppressed a cry as he gave her a rough shake.

'I thought you were good.' The man's eyes were locked onto Gabriel. 'All of you – you, that big man, his wife. But—' He choked, quickly recovered. 'But you consort with those who want our blood.'

Judyth had no idea what he meant, and Celia looked equally bemused.

But Gabriel seemed to know.

'You are mistaken,' he said.

'Don't lie! You were seen, coming out of the lodging house. That damned Spaniard is a devil, like the others, and if you're in league with them I swear I'll—'

'I am not.' Gabriel's voice was cold. 'I tend him because I am a doctor and he is very sick. But I know what he is, and I know he and his companions have followed you from Hispaniola because you have something they want.'

'You *cannot* know!' The man sounded horrified. 'You—'

But Gabriel interrupted. 'Why are you here?' Fleetingly he looked at Judyth, then as swiftly his eyes turned back to the man. Again, Judyth had the sense of violence barely controlled.

'My father has fallen ill. I was planning to ask for your help but then we learned that you have been visiting the priests, and I—'

'You became so enraged at my treachery that you decided to make me suffer?' Gabriel suggested.

'*No!*' The single word was a cry of anguish. 'My father urgently needs a doctor and you are the man I want, but I have to *trust* you!'

'And so you hold a knife to someone I care about to make sure you can,' Gabriel said.

'I do what I must!' the man shouted.

Then, as if the fear, the uncertainty and the despair had suddenly overcome him, he dragged back Judyth's cloak, stuck the point of the knife right into the fabric of her gown – she gave a soft gasp of pain – and shouted, 'You have no choice but to do what I say! Lower your sword.' With obvious reluctance, Gabriel obeyed. 'Good. Now keep it so, or I will—'

But he didn't finish his threat. At that moment several things happened at once: Gabriel gave a long, piercing whistle, then made an urgent gesture towards Celia, and she leapt aside just as a big black shape materialized in the open window. A deep growl filled the air and the man gave a shrill scream of fear. For one instant Judyth felt the knife point press further into her – it *hurt* – then the black shape had the man on the ground, and he was curling into a ball, the knife flung away and both arms up over his face.

Gabriel strode over and retrieved the knife. Then he said, 'Off, Flynn,' and instantly the big dog abandoned the prone figure on the floor and went to his master. Gabriel reached down a hand and smoothed it back over the dog's head and down over its muzzle, murmuring words of praise, and the dog licked him affectionately, ginger brows raised as if to say, *was that all right?*

Gabriel stretched out his arm and Judyth ran to him, sagging against him and weak with the aftermath of fear. He drew her against him, holding her tightly. He felt very solid and he smelt of outdoors. He rested his cheek on the top of her head and said softly, 'Are you hurt?'

She put her hand to her side and it came away wet. 'It's not serious. I can barely feel it,' she lied.

Celia was beside them now, mastering her distress and calmly taking Judyth's arm. 'Come with me,' she said quietly, 'and we shall attend to you while Gabe deals with *that*.' She shot a furious look at the man still curled up at her feet.

But Judyth, her strength and resolve flooding back, gently disentangled herself. Standing tall, she said, 'No, Celia. Thank you, but it can wait. I want to hear what he has to say.'

Gabriel picked the man up and dumped him down on a chair. He stood considering him for a moment. 'I would bind you but for the wounds on your leg,' he said. 'My dog will make you

stay where I've just put you. Flynn, guard.' The dog came skit-
tering over, claws fighting for purchase, and sat down right in
front of the man. He shrank away, fear in his face.

'He will not hurt you if you stay still,' Gabriel said. Then,
compassion in his face, he added, 'Your recent experience has
no doubt made you wary of dogs, but mine is not as savage as
he looks.'

'You're sure?' the man whispered.

'I am.'

And imperceptibly he began to relax.

Gabriel turned to Judyth and Celia. 'Please, sit down,' he
said, indicating the chairs either side of the hearth.

'Now,' Gabriel said, turning back to the man, 'explain.'

It was all I could do not to hit him.

I told myself he was not in his right mind; that he'd been
badly hurt by Hawkins's blasted dogs, that he'd experienced
horrors and privations I could only guess at, that danger and
dire need were driving him on; that his father had been taken
ill; that I should feel compassion for him and not fury.

But he'd marched into my house and cowed my brave sister
into doing his bidding. He'd had Judyth Penwarden in a cruel,
relentless grip. He'd had a knife to her ribs and he'd penetrated
her flesh. He'd put fear in her bright silvery eyes. He'd *used* her
to make me lower my sword.

All of which added up to the strongest reason in the world
to punch him as hard as I could.

But I didn't. I just said, 'Explain.'

He looked up at me.

'You say your father needs my help,' I went on, 'and he shall
have it. But not yet.'

Still he did not speak.

I suppressed my irritation. 'I know you and the others came
here on the *Falco*, that three of you are dead, that you fled from
some terror back in the Caribbean that frightened you more
than the prospect of the voyage. I've recently come to suspect
that you were held by the Spanish – by their priests – and that
for some reason they are very keen to find you. I am quite sure
they mean you harm.' I paused, weighing my words. 'You said

earlier you thought I was good, and if by that you mean I'll help you, then you're right. I have been in the Caribbean and the Spanish Main and I would not betray any man to the priests.'

He went on looking at me for a few moments. Then he began to speak.

'We were six to begin with,' he said. 'My father Simoun Wex, poor old Philpot and Job Allcorn, they were the old men, the survivors, and you'd not believe what they'd been through. Then there was Bartholomew Noble and me – Henry Wex is my name – the sons of the old survivors, only Bartholomew's father died back on the plantation. And there was Puma.'

'*Puma?*' I echoed.

He flashed a quick grin, or perhaps it was a snarl; a savage expression made dramatic by some missing teeth. 'We call him that. He's undersized, skinny and lithe, and he said he was grandson of one of the original lot, and his father was dead, *and* his mother, who by the look of Puma must have been a woman from the mainland – Guatemala maybe, or Panama – and not a slave, and it was her that taught him about the magic.'

Magic.

Yes, of course there was magic. Not that I believed in it – or so I told myself – but others did. This man did. I glanced at Judyth, then at Celia. They met my eyes. Judyth was frowning, Celia had a look of deep interest.

'What happened?' I asked Henry Wex.

'Philpot was the first to go,' Henry said. 'On the *Falco*, not long after we'd sailed. It was hell on that ship.' For a moment he seemed to be absent, looking into the past. 'We were afraid all the time, didn't dare leave our stinking hole of a hiding place, and for all that we tried to use the barrel for our waste, that's not easy to do on a ship bouncing about like a twig on a millrace. Anyway, Philpot, God rest him, was weak to begin with and my father only agreed to let him come with us because of the old allegiance. He was sick even before we left Hispaniola and he rapidly got worse. Wouldn't eat, kept vomiting up what we did get down him, and in the end even sips of water came straight out again. Anyway, he died, and we had nowhere to put him, and he started to stink, and so we put him in the barrel.' He looked at us, his eyes pleading. 'Don't think we wanted to, but he began to rot, see, and . . .' He left the sentence unfinished.

'It went on,' he continued, more fluent now that he was deep into his tale, 'that terrible voyage went on, and it seemed it would never end. We were soon thanking the Lord above that we'd brought Puma along, because he took to slipping out in the dead of the night and coming back with something he'd filched from the ship's supplies. Usually something to eat, because hunger was a perpetual torment and we'd nothing to take our minds off it.' He paused, and the distant look came into his eyes again. 'You think your life's hard when you're a sailor, but when you're forced to endure a long sea voyage shut in a stinking little space with nothing to do and your thoughts going round and round till they drive you mad, well, then you long for the past life that you thought could get no worse.'

I pictured the secret hold in which the men had shut themselves and I imagined what it had been like. It must have been unspeakable. And as well as the terrible conditions and each other's inescapable company, those men had had the little corpse that they'd nailed through the throat to one of the ship's ribs.

'But the voyage came to an end, as voyages always do if you don't sink.' Henry smiled briefly. 'And then, just as we knew we'd almost made it, Job Allcorn went. God above, how we tried to keep him going! Puma risked his skin fetching morsels to tempt him with, he managed to get hold of the dregs of a bottle of rum, he even nicked a blanket because old Job couldn't stop shivering, but it did no good, none of it did.' He shook his head, sighing deeply. 'He was so old, and worn out. He died too, and we couldn't put him in the barrel because it was full, so Puma and I carried him up on deck one night and gave him to the sea. We could see England,' he added, his voice dropping to a whisper, 'so we told Job he'd be right, he was home.'

There was silence in the room, as if all of us there, Henry Wex, my sister, Judyth and I, were paying our respects to the dead men. And also to the ones who had endured. Who had survived.

Only to die on England's longed-for shores . . .

'Then you, your father, Bartholomew Noble and Puma

managed to get ashore without being seen,' I prompted Henry, 'but you left something behind.'

'Mama Tze Amba,' he murmured. 'Yes. That tore us up but there was no way to take her with us. We had to swim, and she—' He swallowed nervously. 'She'd have taken against that and it doesn't do to upset her.' He made a furtive sign with his right hand, as if warding off a threat.

'But you got her back again,' I said softly.

His head shot up and he looked guiltily at me. 'Aye, soon as ever we could. My father said she'd be taken off the ship soon as she was discovered, and we knew full well she'd find a way to let them know she was there.' How right his father had been, I reflected with a shiver of remembered fear. 'My father said she'd be taken somewhere safe.' Henry Wex paused. 'It's wrong to break into someone's house, especially a decent man like that big coroner, and we'd have felt really bad if his wife or one of his children had seen and been scared, but we had no choice, and Puma was in and out again like a flash of lightning.'

'Then you found your way to Buckland,' I said.

He dropped his head, covering his face with his hands. 'We did,' he agreed. 'My father said we should go there first. He had strong memories, see, and he believed the old loyalties would hold true.' He removed his hands, shaking his head. 'But it's all different now. We didn't even get the chance to explain, to say why we were there, we were driven off as if we'd come to break in and *rob* them!' His indignation was clear in his expression.

'He was shot,' he went on, his voice soft and sad. 'My friend Bartholomew, shot in the back. He was running away, he was unarmed, and that bastard shot him. Killed him stone dead, right there where he fell.'

'And then drained him of his blood,' I said.

'*What?*' He sounded outraged. 'No, no, it was *us* did that!' he said, as if it ought to have been obvious. 'Blood's sacred, see? You're a doctor, you ought to know that. It's not to be wasted, and Bartholomew, he'd have agreed with that, he'd been there when other good men died and gave their blood to benefit those left behind.' He leaned forward towards me. 'It's a way of living on, see?' he added. 'A brave man dies, and if something of him is absorbed into his friends, into those who fought alongside him, honoured him, loved him if you like, then he's not wholly dead because something of him goes on.'

Celia's quiet voice broke the stunned silence. 'Our ancient forebears on these islands took the heads of their enemies for much the same reason,' she said.

I looked at her and she smiled wryly. 'Granny Oldreive?' I said, and she nodded.

'It's as the lady says,' Henry Wex was nodding. 'It's part of what Mama Tze Amba taught us, and it's not a bad thing, like we all thought to begin with, but a way of saying to a dead friend, you're still here with me. See?' he demanded.

And all three of us murmured, 'Yes.'

'And then,' I said, 'you tried to gain admittance at the house in Plymouth.'

'I did,' Henry said ruefully. 'And it was just like it had been at Buckland Abbey: no chance to make them see it was in their interests to speak to me, to see with their own eyes what we'd—' He stopped. 'That's enough,' he said very quietly, and I had the sense he was speaking to himself.

'The master of the house was not at home,' I said, 'and the servant set the dogs on you.'

Judyth gave a soft exclamation, muttering about the viciousness of those who would do such a thing. I thought briefly what a fine woman she was. Only a short while ago she'd been threatened with this man's blade, wounded in the side by his knife point, and now she was castigating those who had hurt him.

Henry must have had the same thought. Turning, he said to her, 'I'm sorry, mistress, that I treated you so badly.'

'I know,' Judyth said quietly.

He shook his head, 'I was desperate,' he murmured. 'I *am* desperate. We didn't know they were dead!' he went on wildly. 'My father took it bad. He'd gone on hoping that one or other of them'd be alive still. *I'm* alive, he kept repeating. But you were only a boy, I'd say, and they were men full grown. But look what I've endured! my father would say.' He paused as the emotion overcame him.

'But we found out,' he went on, his voice barely above a whisper. 'Sir Francis, he'd died in Portobello back in 'ninety-six, and for all we weren't that far away, we didn't know, nobody told us! And John Hawkins was gone too, the year before.' He shook his head. 'That hit us bad, but we reckoned there was still a chance, what with them leaving descendants.'

'But you were wrong,' I said.

'Yes. It was all for nothing, and we'd lost half our number.' He dropped his head.

I was filled with pity for him. 'The bodies of your friends are in the coroner's keeping,' I said gently. 'His name is Theophilus Davey, and he is indeed a good man. Presently he will release the bodies of your friends' – I cast around in my mind – 'Philpot, Job Allcorn and Bartholomew Noble, and you will be able to pay your respects.'

Henry Wex looked up. 'You remembered.'

'Yes.'

Slowly he nodded. Then, his eyes on mine, he said, 'I was right about you the first time. I will take you to my father.'

SEVENTEEN

Theophilus Davey looked up to see one of his agents from the front office standing in the doorway, his face slightly flushed.

'What?' Theo demanded. He was busy.

'Someone to see you,' the young man said. Then, dropping to a whisper, 'It's Sir Thomas Drake.'

Theo stood up, straightened his robe, buttoned his tunic and began to smooth a hand over his disarranged hair. Then he thought, *Damn it, this is my office and if I look scruffy it's because I work too hard and have far too much to do*, and said calmly to the young officer, 'Show him in.'

He watched as his visitor came into the room. The Drake stamp was marked on his face: he looked very like his late brother and had the same short, stocky body, pale skin and patchy red beard, even barbered into the same little point. He was exquisitely dressed in a doublet of good, dark wool over expensive hose and boots, his heavy cloak looked as if it was more than equal to the worst winter weather and in his hand he carried a glossy felt cap with a curled feather stuck in it.

'Good morning, Sir Thomas,' Theo greeted him. 'Please, be seated and tell me how I may help you.'

Sir Thomas dragged forward a chair and flung himself down in it, legs splayed, then threw his cap towards Theo's desk and missed. He might dress like a refined gentleman, Theo reflected with inner amusement, but his manners haven't quite caught up.

'I believe, Master Davey, that it is I who may be able to help you,' Thomas Drake replied. 'We had a visit from one of your officers, accompanied by Doctor Taverner. My son discovered them and brought them to the house.' Abruptly he shot forward in his chair and said confidingly, 'That's my son Francis, you know, and he's at Oxford now.'

Touched by the man's evident pride in his boy, and by the

way in which he had been so eager to express it, Theo said, 'I believe I did know, yes. Splendid!' he added brightly, guessing from Sir Thomas's expression that the first part of his reply hadn't been sufficiently enthusiastic.

Sir Thomas waved a hand, smiling modestly. Then he said, 'They were enquiring about a dead man who had been killed by a musket ball, as I am sure you know as it was you who sent them.'

Theo wasn't sure he ever *sent* Gabe anywhere, but it wasn't the moment to point this out. 'Yes.'

'We told them nobody in my household fired that shot, which is God's truth. However, I believe I am now in a position to suggest who did, because he's returned.' He sat back with a satisfied smile, as if to say, *what do you think of that?*

'I hope there hasn't been another death?' Theo asked swiftly.

'No, of course not, I'd have told you straight away if so. This man – foreign, he was, spoke with a lisp and a lilt, and eyes dark as pitch although what I saw of his hair was white – came calling on me yesterday, demanded an interview in my study and in private, then asked if any rough-looking men had visited me offering a certain item for sale.' He shook his head. 'I didn't like it. Didn't like the way he asked, didn't like the look of the fellow. Foreign, like I said, face like a skull and sallow of complexion, dressed like a merchant but there was something shifty about the man and I had my doubts.' He raised his eyebrows suggestively, as if expecting Theo to grasp his meaning.

Theo didn't. 'What did you suspect he was?'

'He—' Sir Thomas frowned hard. 'He had the air of a man who conceals what he truly is,' he said after a moment. 'I can express it no better than that, Master Davey, and I do not think I should, for I might be mistaken, but I sense it as strongly as I sense you are a hard-working man with too much to do in whom I can safely place my trust.'

'Thank you,' Theo muttered. His mind was racing. *A man who conceals what he truly is.* And Gabriel Taverner had spoken of a delirious priest with two missing companions. Was the sallow-skinned foreigner who had clearly disturbed Sir Thomas Drake one of them? 'What was this item for sale?' he asked.

Sir Thomas frowned again, clearly bothered. 'He described

a box made out of some red wood, about the length of a man's forearm and a little over a hand's breadth across. Decorated with a carved pattern, he said, only the pattern was hard to decipher because the box was very old.'

'And what was inside this box?'

'Bloody man wouldn't tell me!' Sir Thomas exclaimed. 'I asked him – well, wouldn't you have done? – but he said in that smooth, silky, sibilant voice of his that if nobody had approached me trying to sell such a box, then it was better for me not to know.' He frowned again. 'Yes – I remember now – he actually said, smug bloody devil, that he *wasn't at liberty to tell me.*' He muttered an oath. 'Sly bastard.'

'You clearly did not take to the man,' Theo said.

Picking up the irony, Sir Thomas grinned. 'No, I most surely did not. Sent him on his way, and glad to see the back of him.'

'But what makes you think it was he who shot the young man found by the river?'

Sir Thomas leaned forward again. 'Because my servant saw him out – I told him to, you see, because I wanted to make quite sure the man really was leaving – and he – my man – waited by the door and he watched, he kept his eyes on the fellow right till the moment he was through the gates and on his way. He didn't like the look of him either,' he added. 'And just as the blasted man reached the road, he dived back down behind the gatepost – *my* gatepost if you please! – and picked up a bag and a long, thin object he'd concealed there.' He paused. 'Now my servant knows about such things and when he told me the long, thin object was a musket, I believed him.'

'I see,' Theo said slowly.

'Yes, I'm sure you do!' Sir Thomas said. 'Your dead man by the river was killed by a musket ball, and now we have a suspicious stranger who carries such a weapon, yet keeps that fact hidden. It doesn't take a genius to link the two.'

'It's not conclusive,' Theo said cautiously, 'but it is most certainly significant.'

Sir Thomas gave him a long look. 'I don't want this business affecting my family, Master Davey,' he said bluntly. 'My boy's at Oxford, like I just said, and he has a brilliant future ahead of him. We have a name in the county, Buckland Abbey is becoming an important venue for men of influence, among whom I number myself' – he brushed at the fine wool of his sleeve, then fluffed up the deep frill on his shirt – 'and . . . well, I would not want any echoes of the past clouding my children's future.'

Theo held his eyes. 'I understand perfectly, Sir Thomas.'

There was a heavy and slightly awkward pause.

Then Sir Thomas said softly, 'I am not proud of everything that I have done in the course of my life, but now that I have other, ah, other priorities, and a wife who reminds me daily of the fact, I am determined to put the – er – the excitement of my days sailing with my late brother firmly behind me.'

For a brief moment Theo caught a wistful expression in Sir Thomas's eyes, and he wondered how much the man would give for just one day back with the redoubtable Francis, on the deck of a fine, fast ship on a lively sea and a Spanish galleon lumbering along groaning with treasure coming into view on the horizon.

'I understand that, too,' he murmured.

And Sir Thomas Drake gave him a grateful smile.

Theo sat quite still for a while after his visitor had left. Then he went into the front office and told the lads to send Jarman Hodge to him as soon as he came in. The dark foreigner disguised as a merchant had pursued the possible trail of this very old, decorated box with its unknown contents to the Drake household, so logic strongly suggested he might also make enquiries of Richard Hawkins.

As he returned to his desk he was saying a silent prayer for Gabe out in the woods below Rosewyke.

Judyth wanted to come too, and Celia had the look on her face that I knew so well from when she was a child and feared being left out of something that promised to be exciting.

I had gone upstairs to fetch my medical bag and another piece of equipment I thought it better to have with me, and the two of them were waiting at the foot of the stairs.

'You don't know what you'll be facing and you may well need another pair of hands,' Judyth said.

'We can watch out, Gabe,' Celia said, 'and warn you if you need warning.'

I jumped down off the last stair and faced them.

'No,' I said. Celia looked mutinous, Judyth wary. I turned to my sister first. 'Celia, Judyth's been hurt.' Judyth began on a protest but I didn't let her get very far. 'If you come with me she'll come too, and she needs to rest.'

'I do *not* need to rest,' Judyth said forcefully.

I put down my bag and, not stopping to think, gently took hold of her by her shoulders, looking down into her determined face. She felt strong. 'You're bleeding,' I said gently. 'You should remove your garments and let Celia look at the injury.' The obvious thing was for me to perform that service, but neither of us suggested it and both of us knew why.

'I'll go and fetch my little looking glass,' Celia said, enthusiastic now that she knew there was a task for her to do and I hadn't said she couldn't come with Henry Wex and me purely to be bossy and awkward. 'You'll be able to see for yourself, Judyth, and tell me what to do.'

'It is *nothing*!' Judyth said for at least the third time.

I let her go. We looked at each other for a moment, and it seemed that an understanding passed between us. Then Celia said, 'Come along, Judyth, Sallie will be back by now and she shall put water on to heat.'

Finally yielding, Judyth took Celia's outstretched arm and slumped against her. As they went through the arch into the kitchen quarters, Celia turned to look at me. 'Be careful,' she said.

I reached behind me and drew out the large and very sharp knife from the stout leather sheath I'd just strapped across my back when I fetched my bag. I held it out for a moment, and she nodded. I re-sheathed it, picked up my bag and hurried outside to where Henry Wex was waiting.

He set off at a fast pace, not in the direction of the Rosewyke woods but on down the path to the road and then off towards Tavy St Luke.

'Wait!' I commanded. He stopped. 'I thought you were hiding in the woods! One of the coroner's agents followed your tracks from where you'd sheltered up on the moor, and he reported that they led here.' I waved my hand towards the trees.

Henry smiled briefly. 'My tracks did, yes. Of course they did,' he went on – no doubt my incomprehension was showing – 'I'm here now, aren't I, and I certainly didn't fly.'

'So—'

But then I understood. It was so simple, and yet it had taken me several moments to realize. 'So where are the others?' I demanded.

'Follow me,' said Henry Wex, 'and I will show you.'

We strode on down the track to the village.

The sunny brightness of the early morning had vanished. The air felt cold, and as warmth from the ground met chill air falling, mist was forming. And forming with unnatural rapidity: descending the gentle slope into Tavy St Luke was like walking into a bowl of cloudy, icy moisture. Sounds were blanketed, and it was as if the village was totally deserted. One or two lights showed in windows where lamps had been lit against the eerie midday darkness, but it seemed that they were far away and nothing to do with Henry Wex or me.

A breeze blew a sudden hole in the mist and I saw the top of the church. Then the little zephyr died away and the enfolding whiteness closed in again.

I had lost my bearings. I thought we were heading out of the village again, along a path that ultimately leads up on to the moor, but I was by no means certain. Then we came to a row of dilapidated dwellings, and Henry slowed down.

I knew where we were then. These old buildings were largely deserted now, in a very poor state of repair and virtually uninhabitable. They had been constructed centuries ago in the old style, with a basic frame made from the trunk of an oak tree with a branch at the right height and angle, cut and bisected so that the two halves were roughly symmetrical. The dwellings were the most basic form of habitation: a single room with space for the animals at one end and for the humans at the other, a hearth in the middle of the floor, one or two roughly-made sticks of furniture and beaten earth beneath the feet. The interior would be blackened from centuries of smoke slowly escaping through the straw of the roof, and the place would stink of animal and human waste and the tarry residue left by the smoke.

Henry stopped by the closed door of the last house, pausing before pushing it open. He seemed to be listening.

This cottage had been empty for almost a year and I knew who had lived here: an elderly woman and her afflicted son. He had been a deeply troubled man who had heard voices and raged his frustrated, impotent fury to the world, and almost everybody in the village had shunned him, perhaps with good reason as he had frequently been violent. Whatever had gone awry in his mind meant he was unsuitable for employment, for marriage and a family, for life itself, in truth, and his mother had cared for him alone except for Jonathan Carew, who had visited regularly. I knew this not because Jonathan had told me but because the old woman had. Desperate, too tired, too sick and too beaten down to provide the day and night watch that her son had needed towards the end, she had begged me for something to make him sleep and I had provided it.

The son had died the previous winter of a rheum that turned into a killer cough. His mother, her purpose gone with his death, died in her sleep two weeks later.

Their sad little dwelling had remained empty ever since, like most of the neighbouring ones.

Until now.

Very carefully, Henry opened the door.

It seemed that he had difficulty pushing it; as if he was encountering firm resistance. Which was odd, because the door was flimsy and hung loose on the hinges.

Then as he stood on the doorstep, he drew a breath, muttered some words I didn't understand and thrust himself forward, as if pushing against some force invisible to the eye.

Whatever it was, it broke – I distinctly heard a faint snap – and he was allowed to pass.

He stepped down into the interior and I followed. There were no welcoming bright flames – brushings, kindling and neatly-cut logs lay ready beside the hearth although no fire had been lit – but enough dim daylight seeped through the doorway into the darkness within for me to make out four human figures.

The first sat curled up in the far left corner. He was child-sized and he had a heavy woollen blanket clutched round his shoulders. His long thin legs were drawn up to his chest and he was hugging them in an impossibly tight grip with his equally long, thin arms. I had never seen a face quite like his before: the hair that fringed it was long, black and glossy, his skin was yellowish-brown, the nose broad, the forehead shallow and sloping back at a sharp angle; his eyes were very dark, set deep beneath pronounced brows. His teeth were rattling with cold and—

No.

I peered more closely, listening intently.

He was chattering to himself, gibbering, an interminable string of syllables that might have been words in an alien tongue, might have simply been noises such as an animal might make. But as I listened it seemed to me that there was a pattern: this poor, terrified boy was chanting an endlessly-repeated incantation. I judged from the look of horror he was giving me that his intention was to protect himself, and that I, along with everything else in a world turned inexplicably hostile, was the enemy.

I didn't try to touch him; in fact, I began to back away. I smiled in the faint hope of reassuring him, and murmured something that I hoped sounded soothing. He blinked a couple of times, surprised into a momentary silence, then his eyes rolled back in his head so that only the whites showed and the gibbering began again.

The second figure, an old man, lay on the opposite side of the room on a low platform roughly made of offcuts of wood. Underneath him, perhaps affording a little comfort, there was a thin, straw-filled sacking mattress. He was propped into a half-sitting position and supported by two pillows, and he too had a thick blanket tucked round him.

The third figure was almost invisible in the shadows, leaning against the cracked daub of the rear wall of the dwelling between the old man and the dark, thin boy. It was very small, stiffly upright, and it was swathed in garments of white, with a pale headdress intricately arranged on the head. A strand of silver hair lay across the forehead. Through the slits between the eyelids I thought I caught a glimmer of brilliant light.

I stared at those eyes. I couldn't look away. I was held firmly yet not uncomfortably, and I had the feeling that an intelligence was looking right inside me.

Then the sensation was gone.

The fourth figure knelt beside the old man's bed and held a coarse pottery bowl containing thin broth. The broth smelt delicious, and a curl or two of steam rose from it. The man by the bed was spooning it into the old man's mouth, slowly, patiently, waiting until he nodded his readiness before supplying the next spoonful.

Jonathan Carew said over his shoulder, 'He has eaten almost half, Gabriel, and also a piece of bread dipped in the broth to soften it.'

'It's good,' pronounced the old man in a surprisingly deep, powerful voice.

Henry Wex pushed past me and knelt down beside Jonathan. 'How do you feel, Father?' he asked anxiously.

The old man considered the question, then said, 'Better. Stronger.' He glanced at Jonathan. 'The priest here has not only brought blankets and pillows, but he knows how to cook.'

I studied him as he worked his way through the rest of the broth. He wasn't as old as I'd first thought: younger by some years than the man washed up by the river, and perhaps around fifty. He was thin, like all of them, and what little hair remained was grey. His cheekbones stood out from the filthy skin of his face and he was missing many of his teeth. He too had suffered from scurvy, but I did not think that was the worst of his complaints.

I crouched down next to Henry. 'Have you been eating fresh vegetables or fruit since you got here?' I asked the older man.

He grinned. 'Oh, yes, Doctor. We know how necessary it is to do so,' he added, 'and, believe me, such foods were what we most craved when at last we had some choice over what we ate.'

Jonathan moved away from the bed head, and I took his place.

I looked down into the sick man's light eyes.

'I was a ship's doctor,' I said. 'I have spent many years treating sailors, which I assume you once were, and now I look after landlubbers too, so whatever is wrong with you, I expect I'll be able to treat it.' He was staring up at me and I thought I saw amusement in his eyes. 'As long as you're not pregnant,' I added.

'I've delivered a few babies, but I'm not well versed in the arts of the midwife.'

Now the old man was smiling. 'Reckon you're safe on that one, Doctor,' he replied. Under the blanket he made a pretence of patting his belly, then said, 'No, as I thought,' withdrew his arm and held out his hand to me. 'Simoun Wex,' he said.

As I took it, I noticed that his hand and forearm were stained deep blue.

Jonathan and Henry withdrew discreetly to the far side of the room while I examined Simoun Wex. As I had begun to suspect, the trouble stemmed from his heart, and its beat was faint and irregular. Mentally I went through the contents of my bag. Yes, I had the right potions with me.

'I need hot water,' I said.

'No fire!' the old man said firmly, and I heard Henry mutter something similar.

I looked down at Simoun Wex. 'I understand that you wish your presence here to remain a secret,' I said. 'But you are sick, you need a preparation for which I require hot water, the mist is gathering outside and the temperature is rapidly falling. Without heat you will probably die.'

He stared up at me for a long moment. Then he nodded. 'Light it, Henry,' he said.

I thought Henry would protest but he said nothing, merely stood up and set about making the fire. And I knew, if I hadn't before, just who was in command here.

I knelt by the swiftly-waxing fire and opened my bag, flipping through the folded papers containing prepared herbal mixtures until I found what I wanted. It was my usual cardiotonic and contained among other substances digitalis from foxglove leaves, dried and powdered flower stems and leaves of lily-of-the-valley, valerian and lime to reduce anxiety and promote a sense of calm. Henry had suspended a battered old pot over the fire and fetched water from the well behind the row of dwellings, and as soon as it was hot enough I took one of the old mugs from the crooked shelf over the bed, rinsed it well and then prepared the potion.

I made it strong. The old man's heart was stuttering and he needed help. He drank his medicine slowly, grimacing at the

bitter taste. I spoke softly to Jonathan, and, nodding, he got up
and left the dwelling, returning a short time later with a bottle,
four cups and a platter of thick slices of bread spread with
butter and honey.

Jonathan Carew is proving to be a good village priest, despite
the unsuitability for such a role which others may suspect but
only he and I know of with certainty, and the villagers' favour-
able opinion of him is demonstrated in the little gifts they leave
outside his door. Jonathan has no need to keep bees, bake bread
or make butter for himself, and I am all but sure he doesn't
acquire his own brandy.

Henry fell upon his share of the food and welcomed Jonathan's
proffered brandy as if he were a man dying of thirst and unex-
pectedly given a sip of water. Simoun too ate the bread and
accepted a few sips of brandy. The long thin boy, however,
would not be drawn out of his corner.

'He should eat,' I said, to no-one in particular.

'Aye, I know,' Simoun said heavily. 'But he's deep in the
magic.'

The magic. Yes, I thought, there was something strange in the
atmosphere here, although I couldn't recall being aware of it
other than as a sort of background hum since that weird moment
when I'd first come inside. I risked a glance at the tiny, white-
clad figure. Perhaps she was asleep, or deep in meditation, or
even . . .

I pulled myself up sharply. She wasn't *anything*. She was
dead.

'He won't touch food or drink until he's released and it is
permitted,' Simoun was saying, nodding in the direction of the
silent figure in the corner.

'Permitted by whom?' I demanded.

But the old man shook his head. 'You can't use your science
and your logic here, Doctor. It won't do any good.'

'But—'

'Puma will eat when he's ready,' Simoun said, with such firm
finality that I knew it was no good arguing.

I sat with my back against the old man's bed, realizing
suddenly how tired I was. The sweetness of the honey, the
nourishment in the good bread and the strong alcohol seemed

fishermen and sailors took us where we wanted to go. Us and
. . . *her.*' The last word was a whisper.

Then, before I could ask him to explain, he looked at Jonathan
and at me and said, 'Got any idea, Doctor, Father, what it's like
on an indigo plantation?' Both Jonathan and I shook our heads.
'It's hell. Hot as hell, leastways, only the air's so full of moisture
that it's a wet hell, not a flaming one, and your skin never dries,
you're always running with sweat, and then your flesh gets thin
and peels off your body at the slightest touch and you get this
fungus growing on you.'

I was about to make a comment, for I'd come across such
conditions in the Caribbean, but Simoun Wex spoke on.

'It's a pretty plant, indigo. Dark green leaves, oval in shape,
flowers like little butterflies that develop into pea pods. It's the
leaves you need, see, because the dye comes from them.
Apparently it grows in India – a Spanish priest told me that
– but they don't produce enough to feed the growing market
and so the priest's fellow countrymen decided they could line
their purses with gold by cultivating it on the Spanish Main.
Guatemala was the focus of their endeavours, and that's where
we were sent.'

He stopped to take a sip of brandy. Henry was watching him,
a worried expression on his face, but Simoun gave him a nod
of reassurance.

'The hardest months are July, August and into September,' he
resumed, 'which also happen to be the hottest, just to make
conditions even better.' He gave a bitter laugh. 'They need a great
deal of labour for the cutting, and the locals do that because the
Spanish masters discovered pretty quickly that they're not tough
enough for the fermentation vats and all the sicknesses that lurk
in the foul, stinking air that clouds above them, and too many
of the locals kept falling down dead. Nowadays it's the slaves that
extract the dye, and that usually means the black slaves brought
from Africa.' He paused. 'Them, and us.'

'How long were you there?' I asked. I could hardly believe
what I was hearing: that a group of Englishmen, two of whom
were in that very room, had survived when men indigenous to
the country had perished. It could only be, surely, because they
had not been there for long . . .

But, 'Oh, years,' said Simoun Wex indifferently.

'You were sold into slavery?' I queried, again struggling with my incredulity.

'We were, Doctor. And, bearing in mind who sold us and where we'd been before, we were glad to go.'

'What could possibly have been so bad that enslavement was preferable?' Jonathan asked, his voice full of anguish.

Simoun peered round me to look at him.

Then he said very quietly, 'The Spanish had us, Father.'

'The Spanish . . .'

'Their priests, to be exact. Furthermore, they believed we had something they very badly wanted, and they had their own ways of trying to make us tell them where we'd hidden it.' He paused. 'It was just seven of us – Job Allcorn, Philpot, Arthur Noble, three others and me – who were sold and sent to the indigo plantations, but there were quite a lot more of us when they first took us. They gave up on us.' He gave a gaunt smile of grim satisfaction. 'Even they tired, in the end, of trying to extract from us something we kept insisting we didn't know.'

'What happened to the other three you just mentioned, who were sold with you?'

'They died on the plantation, Doctor, just as Arthur Noble did only sooner,' he said. Then, in a soft voice that sounded full of pain, he added, 'And before that, eight of us from the original group died under the priests' tortures, three more lasted long enough to get as far as the indigo plantations, then they died as well.' He drew a shaking breath. 'Now Job Allcorn, Philpot and young Bartholomew are dead too, and it's just my son and me, and Puma there. We are all that is left.'

And he dropped his face into his hands.

EIGHTEEN

'It all began with such high hopes,' Simoun Wex said, picking up his tale. 'We set out together, Philpot, Job Allcorn, poor old Arthur Noble and me, and so many other men and boys whose faces I still can picture, for all that it's half a lifetime since I saw most of them. I first sailed with John Hawkins when I was ten years old, and it was two years later when we set off on what was to be my final voyage. Mine and that of so many more.' He shook his head sadly. 'Philpot was five or six years older than me, Job Allcorn a couple of years older still, and he – Job – was a man already, in body, mind and experience, and he took care of Philpot and me while we found our feet. We were all Plymouth men, see.

'So, there we were in our great convoy. Two royal ships led us, the *Jesus of Lübeck* – and she was huge, and the old king, God preserve him, purchased her from the Hanseatic League and converted her to a fighting ship – and the *Minion*, and four other ships besides, and one of those was the *Judith*, and she was Francis Drake's ship. It was Hawkins's third triangular voyage – you know what that means?'

'Yes,' I said. Jonathan frowned.

He nodded. 'Aye, of course you do. You told me you were a navy man. He was a man brimming with confidence, was John Hawkins. He took such pains to find out what he needed to know; he had eyes and ears everywhere from the Thames to the Spanish Main, and he used the intelligence they provided to the utmost. He knew how to get what he wanted out of people, and as a leader of men he was in a class of his own. Well, that's what we all reckoned, anyway, and although I was young and green, I'd seen enough of other captains to recognize a good one when I saw him.

'We sailed from Plymouth and as soon as we were rounding the long nose of Brittany the bad luck began. The nimbler, newer ships fared well enough but the *Jesus*, God bless her memory, was an old lady by then, riding so high on the water and far too big for the job she was now being asked to do. She was meant for brief, fine weather jaunts in her own waters, and now here she was rolling and pitching in heavy seas, every timber strained to its limit and caulking spewing out everywhere you looked. We all thought we were doomed, Hawkins ordered us to pray, and how the old *Jesus* survived I'll never know, unless it was the fervent and desperate prayers of a hundred and fifty men . . .' He smiled reminiscently.

'We sailed on, past Spain and Portugal until we were off West Africa, and there we collected our black gold and sailed for the Caribbean. But our masters didn't have it all their own way once we began trading, for the Spanish devils were wary of us by now and in most of the islands and the mainland ports the governors were under strict orders to have nothing to do with us. But Hawkins and Drake had golden tongues, both of them, and they knew well enough how to exploit a man's weak spots, which were usually closely associated with his greed. In the end, Hawkins made it all turn out the way he wanted, and our ships were groaning with gold and other precious cargo and we were ready to go home.

'But it had all taken too long; far too long. The hurricane season was on us, and there we were on the *Jesus of Lübeck*, a battered old ship totally unsuited for what we were putting her through, and every one of us haunted by the memory of how nearly we'd come to grief back off Brittany all those months ago. Great God above, I'd never been so frightened in all my young life – the stern planks were breached, and the wild waves flooding in and out filled the hold and we found fish swimming above the ballast as if they were out in the open water.' He shook his head, his old face deeply troubled.

'By the time that storm abated and we had time to collect ourselves,' he went on after a moment, 'we knew we were lost. We were all but out of supplies and we tried eating hides, and even cats and rats, only we sicked most of it up again. We had to put in somewhere for food and clean water and to set about urgent repairs if we stood any chance of sailing back to England. So when a Spanish ship directed us towards a port that was close enough for us to limp to, that was what we did, and we sent up prayers of gratitude because we reckoned we'd been saved. But salvation came with a warning: the place we were heading for was where the Spanish amassed their purloined gold and silver before shipping it back to Spain. They'd be on their guard, it stood to reason, for the reputation of the English went before us and no Spanish governor or ship's captain was going to welcome us with open arms when they had a flotilla of treasure ships amassing in their harbour.

'But Hawkins, he had a plan. He *always* had a plan.' Simoun smiled briefly. 'We sailed the proud old *Jesus* into San Juan d'Ulúa under the royal standard, because he – Hawkins – knew full well that from a distance it resembled the Spaniards' own flag, and the only fire that greeted us as we sailed into port was a welcoming salute from the shore batteries. They thought we were the vanguard of the treasure fleet.' He grinned savagely.

'When they realized it was the dreaded Juan Aquínez, as they called Hawkins, their fear overcame their common sense and they threw down their weapons, abandoned the big guns and fled. Hawkins told the commander we were friendly English ships only there to re-supply and that we'd sail first thing in the morning, as soon as we had what we'd come for. But our luck changed, for morning brought the treasure fleet, and, for all that Hawkins held the port and the shore batteries, keeping Spanish ships from entering their own harbour would be an act of war. So he decided to negotiate.'

Simoun paused, took a drink, then collected his thoughts and resumed. 'We won't stop your ships coming into port, Hawkins tells the commander, as long as you permit us to finish our repairs before we leave. It looked like the commander was agreeing, but behind our backs he sent to Veracruz for more men, and heavily-armed men at that.

'We reckoned we would be all right. The ships of the Spanish treasure fleet were packing into that narrow harbour, sure enough, but we were lined up on the other side, the *Minion*, us on the *Jesus*, the *Grace of God*, then Drake's *Judith*, the *Angel* and the *Swallow*, and between us and the Spanish there was an old hulk of a vessel, deserted but for the rats.' He paused. 'Only it wasn't, because that crafty bastard of a Spaniard was secretly sending his newly-arrived reinforcements aboard. Oh, John

Hawkins challenged him, only to be fobbed off, but then one of our Spanish hostages was discovered with a hidden knife, and that was that. Hawkins fetched his crossbow and shouted his challenge, the Spanish on the hulk came out from their hiding places and Hawkins loosed a bolt at the Spanish vice admiral. Then it all started in earnest. The Spaniards overran the *Minion*, which was the closest ship to the hulk, and up on the *Jesus* – which towered over all the other ships – we got the perfect view as the fighting swarmed up onto our own decks.

'Hawkins was prepared, just as he always was, and straight away he issued the command, at which we cut our cables and began to warp out of that hellhole of a harbour.' He paused, glancing at Jonathan. 'Are you still with me?'

Jonathan shook his head.

'Doctor?' Simoun said. 'Want to explain while I take a breather?'

'Warping is a way of clearing harbour,' I said. 'You send out a boat on which you've loaded the anchor, secure the anchor some distance away and then the crew back on the ship haul on the anchor cable and in this way move the ship up to the anchor. Then you pull up the anchor, take it further away and repeat the process, and go on doing so until you're in the open, and the tide and the wind take over.'

Jonathan looked at Simoun. 'And you managed that, under those conditions, with your six ships?'

'We did,' Simoun replied, and the pride was still vivid in his voice. 'Once we were in our proper element we could bring our guns into play, and that was where us on the *Jesus* showed our worth because we had the mightiest fire power, we all knew what we were doing and we pounded those Spanish vessels until we hit the vice admiral's ship right in her magazine and tore her apart.

'But it did for the old *Jesus*, and soon we all began to realize it. Hawkins was right there with us in the thick of it, yelling himself hoarse and watering his throat with draughts of ale from his special silver mug, telling us not to be afraid because God was with us – hadn't the almighty saved him from the shot that had just blown away his silver mug? – and that deliverance would be ours.

'And we had to witness the poor old *Jesus* as she died.' Simoun's voice broke on the words. 'Hawkins knew she was done for and he used her to shield the *Minion* and Drake's *Judith*, onto which we'd loaded all our gold and treasure. But we didn't give up, and our gunners kept to their posts, and we went on firing even while the rest of the cargo was carried from our holds to the *Judith* and the *Minion*. But then the Spanish sent in the fireships, and that was our cue to leave, and we leapt from the *Jesus*'s high decks down onto those smaller ships, and John Hawkins was the last to go.'

Briefly he fell silent, perhaps out of respect for his brave captain.

'We might have had the *Judith* and the *Minion*, but we'd lost every other ship, and it was a terrible, terrible day,' Simoun went on heavily. 'We'd made off with the Spaniards' treasure, for sure, but we'd suffered many casualties, lost the beloved *Jesus* and far worse was to come.' He paused, looking round at his audience one by one, as if assuring himself he had our full attention. 'Because next day we discovered that under cover of the night, Drake had set off in the *Judith* and sailed for England. Oh, he was right to do so, and we all knew it, for his ship was badly damaged, in no condition to take on the Spanish again, and although the *Judith* was loaded – overloaded – with treasure, there hadn't been time to stock her with food and drink. For all that every man and boy of us crammed so tight on board the *Minion* cursed Drake that morning for aban-doning us, we all knew he'd done the right thing – the only thing – and, moreover, that his own chances of making it home were slim at best.

'John Hawkins covered up his fury, for it did no good to rail and fume when it wasn't going to change anything. He knew the *Minion* had no hope of getting back to England seriously overcrowded as she was with two hundred men and hardly any food, so he said that half of us had to go ashore and try our luck on land. We wouldn't be deserting, he told us, because there he was giving us permission, and, believe me, it was hard to decide where giving permission stopped and issuing a direct order began.

'So there we were, a hundred desperate English sailors on a

northern Mexican shore, Philpot, Allcorn, Noble and me among
them, and we stood and watched as our ship, our only link to
home, hearth, kith and kin, safety, security – to England herself
– sailed away and left us.

'Very soon we were attacked by the jungle tribes that lived
there, and we made up our minds that we'd be better off handing
ourselves in to the Spanish.' He shook his head again. 'And what
a mistake *that* turned out to be. Some of our company got shipped
off to Spain to work like the slaves we'd just been importing
to the Caribbean. We thought at first that we who remained were
the lucky ones, for what could be worse than the fate of those
who had gone? But then the Inquisition turned up.'

I looked at Jonathan. He had gone pale.

'I was still only thirteen years old,' Simoun went on, 'and
Philpot reckoned I'd likely be sent off with the other boys to
work in the monasteries with the black-robed priests. But I was
big for my age, and when the priests came to select the lads
they wanted, I stood up straight and threw my chest out and I
was passed over. Dear Lord, I recall so well how I was *glad*!'
His eyes widened in remembered amazement. 'I thought it
had to be better, to stay with the men I knew, and Philpot, he
leaned close and said, don't worry, lad, you'll be with Job and
me and the others, and we'll take care of you. But, of course,
he – they – couldn't take care of me any more than they could
of themselves.'

He paused briefly, and I had the sense that he was steeling
himself for what was to come.

'Lord, but they knew how to hurt a man, those damned priests
of the Inquisition,' he said softly. 'And all in the name of the
vicious, cruel and narrow-minded God they worshipped,
although even in the very worst of it I remember asking myself
what Our Lord would make of it all when he'd said so often
that we were to love one another. *Love!*' Simoun's suddenly
harsh expression suggested he might have spat had it not been
for Jonathan's and my presence. 'They dispatched those they
didn't want.' His voice was louder now, full of ancient anger.
'You got strangled if you were lucky, burned alive if not. The
ones they had a use for – the strong ones – were sent to the
galleys.'

He looked down at his blue-stained hands, once again gathering himself.

'For us, they reserved their most refined methods of information extraction. They knew, we reckoned. They knew damned well that we bore a secret; that an object of great importance to the Spanish had been entrusted to us as we left the *Judith*. Somebody must have pointed the finger, and if it was in order to end the same tortures that were being meted out on us, then I can't say I blame him, whoever he was, and I'd have given up a name myself if I'd had one to give.'

'But you held out?' I said, my voice hardly more than a whisper.

Simoun's mouth stretched in a terrible smile. 'I did, Doctor, because the name I'd have screamed out was my own.'

There was a long silence. Then he said, his voice infinitely weary, 'In the end they gave up. We were shadows of the men we'd been by then, myself especially – they *knew*, those fucking Spanish priests, they knew, but I'd made my mind up I wasn't going to tell them and I never did. And, like I said, they gave up. They sold us to the owner of an indigo plantation in Guatemala, and that's where we stayed for the next thirty years. Some of us took wives and begat sons – I did, so did old Arthur Noble before he died, and he called his son Bartholomew – and we made as good a job of living a normal life as we could. As any man can, when he is enslaved and has no choice over his own fate.'

His eyes had been roaming round the room, and now they rested on Puma.

'And there we might have stayed, Job Allcorn, Philpot, my son and I and Bartholomew Noble, and there we might still be, except that one day *he* came into our lives.'

Simoun gave a deep sigh, and it seemed to me, watching him, that of a sudden he was exhausted. His eyes had closed, his thin face had sunk and he leaned back into his pillows as if all strength had left him. I looked at Henry, who had quietly come to crouch beside me.

'There is more, I know,' I said to him softly, 'but for now your father has talked for long enough. He needs sleep most of all, and also food and clean water, and—'

'And another measure or two of that brandy,' Henry said.

Jonathan stirred from whatever deep thoughts held him captive. 'I will fetch all that is needed,' he said. 'And also more firewood.' He took in Henry's worried face. 'Yes, I know you want to stay in hiding, but you are under my protection now, and I will look after you.'

He didn't say how, or from what or whom, but the very tone of his voice seemed to inspire confidence, and Henry simply nodded.

'You need water to wash with,' Jonathan went on, studying the three men in turn, 'and you urgently require new clothes.'

'I may be able to help with the clothes,' I said, thinking of my sister and the chests full to bursting that she had brought with her from the marital home after the death of her husband.

'Good, thank you,' Jonathan replied.

I stood up. 'I must be off, in any case – I need to go home to Rosewyke and make sure Judyth is all right.'

Henry hung his head. 'Please tell her how sorry I am,' he muttered.

'I will. I'll make haste, I'll find some clothes for you, then—' There was something else I had to do, but I was tired now too and my brain was turning sluggish. Glancing out through one of the many cracks in the door, I noticed to my great surprise that it was dark. No wonder I was tired.

Rapidly I revised my plan.

'It is late, and we all need sleep, not just him.' I was addressing Henry, and now I inclined my head towards his father, eyes half closed as he lay back in his bed. Henry nodded his understanding. 'Before I go home I must ride down to see Theo Davey,' I said, 'for there is much to tell him.'

Henry's head shot up. 'But you can't—'

I put my hand on his shoulder. 'I have no choice,' I said. 'But you can trust him. That I promise you. I shall return here early in the morning' – I sent up a silent prayer that no patients would arrive at my door needing immediate aid – 'and bring more medicine for your father, and what new attire I can lay hands on.'

'But—' Henry protested. Then, appearing to slump suddenly,

he said, 'Very well. Thank you, Doctor, and we shall expect you in the morning.'

As I hurried away, I heard Jonathan say quietly, 'God go with you.'

I found Theo still in his office, although all his officers had left. The appetizing smells of the coroner's supper that came sneaking down from the family's quarters made my mouth water and my stomach rumble.

Theo was sitting at his desk and leapt up as I went in. 'You are unharmed?' he asked urgently. 'No sword fights with foreigners in your woods?'

'I'm unhurt, and I don't think they were ever there. I'm sorry it's so late, but—'

He waved away the apology. 'You have news for me, Gabe,' he said as we sat down, 'as have I for you. I'm going first, for I have news of those very foreigners.'

And he launched into an account of a visit from Sir Thomas Drake, concerning a dark-eyed stranger who demanded a private audience with him and asked about a red wood box whose contents he would not divulge, and how this man had hidden a musket in the undergrowth by the imposing gates to Buckland Abbey, which was enough, apparently, to convince both Sir Thomas and Theo that this stranger had been the man who had shot the dead man found by the river. Bartholomew Noble, as I now knew.

'So I sent Jarman Hodge to seek out Sir Richard Hawkins,' Theo went on before I could begin on my own tale or even comment on what he'd just told me, 'and Jarman says he's returned to his Plymouth house, although his wife and family remain at Slapton, and what do you think?'

'I'd guess from your expression that he too has received the same enquiry from the same dark-eyed stranger,' I said, 'and that in all likelihood he also sent the man on his way.'

'You'd guess right!' Theo exclaimed triumphantly. 'This vexing puzzle begins to reveal its heart, Gabe, and—'

I let him ramble on for a few moments. Then, interrupting him in mid-flow, I said, 'I know where this red wood box is, Theo.'

He looked dumbstruck. He frowned, as if momentarily cross that I appeared to have overtaken him on the road to the truth, then he whispered, '*How* do you know?'

So I told him.

'I believe,' I went on, 'that whatever the box contains, it is very valuable and very, very secret. Simoun Wex stole it, I think, although he himself maintained it had been entrusted into his care. He knew what it was and where it was, and he kept back the information even under great torment.' Briefly I told Theo what Simoun had told me, and he looked as horrified as I had been.

'Those poor men,' he muttered. Then, frowning, 'So this foreigner pretending to be a merchant who is asking after the box . . .?'

'I would guess,' I replied, 'he belongs to the organization from whom the item was stolen. Not when it came into Simoun's possession, but when the English sea dogs originally took it.' I hesitated, then said, 'I believe they are Spanish priests, and that what was stolen was something of very great importance, and that they have sent some of their own to fetch it back.'

Theo shook his head as if to clear it. 'So Hawkins or Drake took something from the Spanish priests, and it was given to Simoun when he was put ashore and left behind . . . Why?' he demanded.

'If it was in truth given to him,' I replied, 'then I can only think it was because whoever handed it over reckoned he had a greater chance of surviving than anyone aboard a vastly over-crowded, damaged ship trying to sail home across the width of the Atlantic.' I noticed Theo's expression. 'No, I don't really believe that either. I think Simoun Wex used the confusion aboard the *Minion* at San Juan d'Ulúa to steal the box and its contents. Or maybe he'd already stolen it before that.' I shrugged. '*I* don't know!'

'Hmm.' Theo looked at me shrewdly. 'And what does he propose to do with it?'

'He's probably hoping a member of the Drake or the Hawkins clan will buy it. They were both there, you know, that day.' I had told Theo a little about what happened at San Juan d'Ulúa, and now I told him some more.

'D'you think they're here for vengeance?' he asked softly. 'An eye for an eye, not with Francis Drake or John Hawkins because they're dead but with some close relative? Or maybe they'll demand a vast payment in exchange for not spreading the story?'

'It had crossed my mind,' I said, 'but I think I was wrong. What you've just said about the foreigner disguised as a merchant, and the lengths he's going to, convinces me just how valuable this item in its red wood box must be. I reckon that's all Simoun Wex and his son need to assure their future. Provided,' I added, 'Thomas Drake or Richard Hawkins wanted to buy it, which it appears they don't.'

Theo sat back in his chair, a distant expression in his eyes. 'What do you imagine it is, Gabe?'

'I have no idea.'

But, I thought as I got up to go, I intend to find out in the morning, as soon as Simoun Wex has recovered sufficiently to take up his tale again.

Judyth had left by the time I finally reached home. I had been secretly hoping she might have stayed to see me, but given the late hour, it had become more and more unlikely. 'She was truly all right?' I demanded of Celia as she came to greet me.

'Yes, Gabe, it was only a shallow wound and I helped her to patch it up. She was much more cross about her gown,' Celia added, 'which now has a neat little cut in it.'

I will buy you a new gown, I said silently to Judyth. *I will buy you a gown of pale silvery silk to match your eyes*. The memory of how she had felt when I'd held her in my arms was very vivid.

Celia was clearly waiting for me to speak, a wry expression twisting her mouth. So I just said, 'I'm sure she's handy with a needle and will be able to mend the tear,' which was about the dullest, most lumbering remark I could have come up with, as my sister's face clearly told me.

'I said she was welcome to stay and have supper, and to spend the night here,' Celia said, 'but she clearly preferred to go home. I offered to send Samuel with her, or to lend her my mare, but she was adamant.' She raised an eyebrow. 'She's a very independent woman, isn't she, Gabe?'

'Yes,' I muttered. Then, unable to stop myself, 'She really was all right?'

Celia tucked her arm through mine. '*Yes*, Gabe. Now, listen,' she went on, her eyes alight with excitement, 'because I've been going through your papers and your books and journals and I've discovered something *really* interesting, and I think I now know where your *Falco* men were abandoned and why, and although I don't know what happened subsequently I feel I can make a very good guess, and—'

I hated to do it. Hated to spoil her moment. And, even as I prepared the words, I was thinking how hard she'd worked, how brilliantly she'd done, and that she'd discovered right there in my own study what it had taken me so long to find out, and I'd only done so because a father and son had just told me their story.

I put my arm around her, hugging her to me. I dropped a kiss on her smooth hair and said gently, 'Dearest Celia, I already know. Now, I'm going to need some of those spare clothes of yours.'

She recovered so well. When she understood the full extent of the plight of the *Falco* fugitives, she swallowed her disappointment over not being the one to enlighten me and threw herself into offering a different kind of help.

I was quite surprised that she had indeed brought more than a considerable amount of Jeromy's clothes with her, and she must have noticed.

'They are made of very good fabrics, Gabe,' she said briskly as we knelt side by side up in her little sitting room rooting through the largest chest. 'And he hadn't even worn some of these garments.' There was a defensive tone in her voice. 'I wasn't going to waste them!'

We selected fine linen shirts, simple wool tunics, hose, cloaks, a pair of boots. 'Outfits for three men, you said?' she asked as a thorough search revealed no more footwear. 'Then they'll just have to fight over these.' She shooed me out of the room. 'Go and get something to eat – Sallie's long turned in for the night so don't wake her – and then for heaven's sake go to bed, Gabe, you're worn out.'

'But—' I gestured feebly at the pile of garments and the boots.

'I'll see to those,' Celia said firmly. 'I'll pack them up and have them by the door when you're ready to leave in the morning. *GO!*' she said with mock anger.

I did as she commanded.

NINETEEN

'**P**uma's mother was a vodou priestess – a *bokor*,' Simoun Wex began.

Then he fell silent, looking round at his audience as if allowing time for that remarkable statement to sink in.

We were back in the deserted house, Simoun, Henry, Puma, Jonathan and I. It was the middle of the morning of the next day. I had hoped and intended to be there sooner, but I'd had callers at my door even as I gobbled down a hasty breakfast and it had taken some time to attend to them. Once again there was that gloomy, darkening mist outside, but the fire was burning brightly, chasing the shadows into the far reaches of the room. The dark, thin boy was alert now although he still kept to his corner, knees drawn up, arms wrapped around the lean torso as if in self-defence, hugging his blanket tightly to him.

Puma.

As if he felt my thoughts bent upon him, suddenly he turned his head and looked at me. His dark eyes were so shiny that they appeared like tiny mirrors reflecting the flames of the fire. I had the sensation that the inside of my head was being . . . raked, was the best way to describe it; it was as if minuscule probes were searching through my mind, hunting out the very nature of me. The sensation wasn't exactly painful but it was hard to endure nonetheless. Just as I was about to protest, or to move away so that those brilliant eyes were no longer looking right into me, it stopped. Puma dipped his head in a swift nod, and I saw what could have been a smile briefly cross his dark face.

Simoun, I thought, had observed the exchange. He waited, watching Puma and me, and as Puma lowered his head, he resumed his story.

'She was a powerful woman, much respected, much feared,' he continued. 'She had strange symbols painted on her body, black eyes that burned into you, and she had power over the dead.'

He had spoken in so matter-of-fact a tone that it took a moment for the meaning of what he'd just said to penetrate.

'She – *what*?'

Even as my exclamation rang out, I felt Jonathan's hand on my arm. 'Wait, Gabriel,' he said very softly.

'But he speaks heresy!' I hissed back.

The pressure of Jonathan's hand increased. '*Wait*,' he repeated.

I stared at him in amazement, a dozen questions filling my head and demanding to be asked. But his expression was stern, and I bit them down. I turned back to Simoun, and he took this as a signal to continue.

'You find such claims hard to stomach, Doctor? So did we, but we had the advantage of hearing them when we lived alongside those people on the indigo plantation, and we witnessed such things with our own eyes. Puma's mother was called Atashua.' Puma looked up sharply at the sound of his mother's name, and Henry muttered a brief reassurance. 'She controlled people brought back from the other side of the grave by means of her magic. She was her son's teacher, and he in turn spread her teachings to his friends the English sailors on the plantation. He was a solitary youth, always left well alone by his own people because of who he was, and we had befriended him, and Henry here and Bartholomew were his friends when the boys of his own people shunned him because they were afraid.'

I opened my mouth to protest, for Puma was a boy even now and Henry was a grown man. Simoun, smiling, forestalled me.

'I know what you're thinking, Doctor. Puma is not what you imagine him to be. He looks like a boy but he is not.'

I nerved myself to look at Puma again. He was already staring straight at me as my eyes fell upon him. And I saw what Simoun meant.

Puma was slim, built more like a girl than a boy, and not very tall. His face was unlined, the skin smooth and showing no signs of a beard. But the eyes, those large, deep, dark, shining eyes, were as old as time. In a flash of alarming insight, I realized something: they reminded me of the glitter I thought I'd seen between the dead and desiccated eyelids of Mama Tze Amba when she was still pinned to the rib in *Falco*'s hold.

Moreover, now I came to think about it, there was a resemblance in the facial features . . .

Another frightening thought struck me, but once again Simoun picked up my thought before I could put it into words.

'No, Doctor,' he said very softly. 'An ancestor, of that there is no doubt, but from a very long time ago.'

My heart was beating uncomfortably fast. I took a deep breath, trying to steady myself. Jonathan murmured something – I wasn't sure what it was – and I muttered curtly, 'I'm all right.'

'Both mother and son responded to the men's interest,' Simoun resumed. 'It was a novelty for Atashua to find foreigners who wanted to listen to her, for otherwise she and the other practitioners were reviled by those who claimed to be their *masters*' – he poured a world of venom into the word, his voice loud and full of passion – 'and who utterly refused to recognize that their beliefs had any value; who dismissed the *bokors* as trash and their followers as ignorant savages quite incapable of recognizing or understanding the deep mysteries of faith and the abstractions of the spirit world.' He paused, his anger having made him breathless. 'Denying their faith, of course,' he resumed, 'makes it easier for the masters to treat them as if they were not human. To all those vicious, cruel soldiers, priests and overseers, they are just slaves, brute animals.'

He stopped. His words were still ringing in my ears.

Presently Jonathan said calmly, 'What is the essence of this faith, Simoun?'

Simoun turned to him, surprise on his face, as if he was saying, *you of all men should ask that?* Jonathan met his questioning eyes with a smile.

'It is not easy to sum it up, Father,' Simoun said after a while. 'In brief, seems to me it's to do with trying to understand the natural processes of life, and in particular our own spiritual nature. The ancestors, the animals and their spirits . . . there's life in everything, see, and it all needs to be in harmony. When it isn't, the rupture has to be healed, so that we live in peace with ourselves, with one another, with God.'

'Amen,' Jonathan said softly.

Animals . . .

I heard myself say, 'When I was in that secret hold with – er, with the lady' – I indicated the tiny white-clad figure – 'I had a vision of a beautiful female face that slowly turned into a crocodile.' I looked at Simoun.

He glanced at Puma, then back to me, surprise in his face. 'Did you, now,' he murmured. 'Then you—' He stopped, and after a moment said in a different tone, 'They revere all creatures. The snake is important for it represents earth, and the rainbow is heaven. All men and women have their spirit animal, and the crocodile is—' But Puma made a sound – a swift, violent sort of cough – and Simoun did not go on.

'To continue answering your question, Father' – Simoun turned back to Jonathan – 'the faithful believe there is one Almighty God, and that it is abstract. Below it, spirits called Loa rule different aspects of the world, made manifest via natural elements such as wind, rain, thunder and lightning, rivers, oceans . . . anything you care to think of. They appeal to the ancestors for guidance and protection, and a specially-trained person known as the *griot* memorizes long lists of family history, as well as the legends of the people.'

'And you and your fellow exiles learned all this?' Jonathan asked.

'Aye,' Simoun replied. 'The men were willing pupils and some of them became adept. We had nothing to lose, remember, and the way we'd been treated by those fucking Spanish priests had turned us brutally away from the faith we were born into.' Once again his voice had risen in anger, and we waited as, breathing hard, he brought himself under control. 'I apologize, Father, if I offend you.'

'You do not,' Jonathan said quietly. 'Please, continue.'

Simoun sighed heavily. He glanced briefly at his son, then at Puma, but if either knew what he was about to say – and I guessed they probably did – neither tried to stop him.

'Trouble is, there were bad things to be learned along with the good,' he said heavily. 'I can only say in our own defence that we were desperate. We'd been left in an alien land, the Europeans we'd gone to for help had turned on us, beaten us, tortured us, burned and hanged our companions, enslaved the rest of us, and we were full of fury, willing to grab at anything that offered the chance of revenge. No,' he corrected himself, 'we weren't after revenge, we were trying to survive. So many of us were already dead.'

He dropped his face in his hands, and I saw his shoulders shake as he remembered and his grief briefly overcame him.

Jonathan said, 'They are gone now, beyond their pain and suffering, and let us hope they have found their way to a kinder place.'

Simoun nodded. 'Aye. Thank you, Father.'

Presently he lowered his hands and went on.

'They taught us their ways, and how to use the power to intimidate, terrify, overcome. They knew how to send a person into another's dreams, so that one man may achieve control over another.'

I made as if to protest, but again Jonathan stopped me.

'We were afraid of the power,' Simoun whispered. 'All of us; we were overawed and horrified at what we'd unearthed in ourselves, and I reckon that Atashua and the other *bokors* regretted what they'd done, for none of them had understood how deep our anger ran.' He drew a shaky breath. 'When they did – when it was demonstrated one moonless night just what they'd brought about by stirring us up, and they saw the extent of the awful, horrible, *wrong* things we now could do, they knew they had to act. They were responsible for this wild new evil force, and because they were good people – they were, they *were!*' he cried, although neither Jonathan nor I had suggested the contrary. 'Because they knew they had to protect us from ourselves – us and others, oh, yes, even more vitally, protect others – they provided us with a counter force.'

I was lost. Bemused by this talk of an alien faith, of powers that everyone else in the room seemed to believe in while I felt like a lone voice of logic and reason, vainly crying *It cannot be so! Such things are not possible!*

But Jonathan wasn't lost.

Even while I was struggling to understand – to *begin* to understand – he said calmly, 'And so they provided you with Mama Tze Amba to be your guardian spirit.'

Simoun spun round to stare at him, so fast that I heard the

joints in his neck crack. 'You know this!' he whispered, wonder in his voice. 'You—' But, overcome, he couldn't go on.

'You brought her with you on the most difficult journey imaginable; a journey when sense would dictate you travelled as light as you could,' Jonathan said. 'You pinned her to a rib in that terrible hold, controlling her awesome power as I imagine you have often been driven to control her when her fierce protection of you threatens to have the opposite effect?'

'Yes, you are right,' Simoun said, glancing across at the motionless white-clad figure. 'She is terrible in her full power, Father. We suffered so badly on that ship, and when poor old Philpot went, she was like a great white flame, searing through the hold, about to blast out through the lower decks and upwards, and it wasn't only discovery we feared but that she'd likely set the whole ship afire and we'd all perish.' His face was alive with remembered horror. Henry reached out and briefly took his hand.

'And that was when we had to fix her to the rib,' Simoun concluded after a moment. 'It was appalling, and we drew lots for who did it, and poor old Job Allcorn drew the short straw, and afterwards we wondered if—'

'No, Father,' Henry interrupted. He took Simoun's hand again. 'She'd have known why. She'd have understood. We told her, didn't we? She always knows.' He too turned to look at the tiny figure, giving it – her – a bow.

And then suddenly I remembered that Jonathan had spoken of two conflicting forces. It had been when we rode away from our visit to the *Falco* after he had carried out the purification ceremony, and he'd said that there were warring powers down in the hidden hold. I heard his words in my head. *One was powerfully aggressive, evil, malign; it had its origins far away and a long time ago, for it carried the darkness and the cold damp of the deep earth. The other power seemed to be a protective spirit.*

I turned to him now. 'You knew,' I whispered. 'You picked it up, that day we went to the *Falco* together. You—'

'I didn't know, Gabriel,' he whispered back, 'any more than I know now, for these are deep matters of great antiquity and require a lifetime's study.' And briefly I saw a light in his strange green eyes; a hunger for knowledge, for *knowing*, a fierce desire to pore over abstruse writings and ancient texts, devouring them, taking them inside his own soul, using the sparkling intelligence and the keen insight that his Maker had bestowed upon him for their intended purpose. Yet here he was, vicar of a tiny parish in a far corner of England, dispatched here by those who well knew his worth and for this reason – because his qualities meant he maintained a dangerously open mind – had bound, controlled and exiled him.

I realized in that moment how very much I valued him.

'I am very glad you are here,' I said impulsively.

I doubt very much that he had any idea what prompted the remark, but he smiled anyway.

'We have gone down on our knees in gratitude for Mama Tze Amba many a time, I can tell you,' Simoun resumed, 'and during the short time when she wasn't with us, when we had to leave her behind and Puma here fetched her from that house, we—'

But Puma had made another of his strange noises. We all turned to look at him. Huddled in his shadowy corner, his blanket clutched to him and now held up over his face so only his eyes showed, he was all but invisible. His eyes shone briefly as he returned our anxious glances and he held up a hand, asking for silence.

Henry hurried to his side, speaking to him in a strange-sounding language. Puma answered, frowning as he tried to go on listening at the same time.

And presently I too heard what he had heard.

Footsteps, on the track outside.

And Puma quietly raised the blanket higher and somehow managed to extinguish the light in his eyes.

I lunged for my sword, lying just inside the door, and Simoun pushed that hidden object deeper beneath his pillows. I almost had my hand on my sword hilt when the door burst violently open, its leading edge catching me across the brow so that I was knocked aside and I saw flashing stars of bright light as pain seared through my head.

Two tall figures stood in the doorway. Swiftly they stepped inside and the second one closed the door. They were clad in black robes over which both wore heavy cloaks of good cloth coloured with costly dyes; one was deep blue, one dark brown. They had fashionable caps on their heads. To the casual glance they looked like prosperous merchants on a mission to seek out new trade. But I had a pretty good idea that in truth their nature was quite different.

The one in the brown cloak seemed to be in charge. Trying to focus, my vision still disturbed and my head throbbing with pain, I saw a man of perhaps sixty years, a little over average height, broad in the shoulders yet lean and sinewy. His face was heavily lined and his skin was sallow. It could have been that he had lived for years in the hot sun but I suspected he had been darkish from birth, for his white hair still had strands of black and his deep-set, small eyes and his eyebrows were dark as soot.

Even before he spoke, I had him down as a Spaniard.

His colleague, still leaning against the closed door, began to say something to him, but he silenced him with an abrupt movement of his left hand. His right hand, I now realized, held a narrow, wickedly-pointed sword and, as I studied the pair of them, the second man drew a long dagger from its sheath. He was watching us, cold contempt in his dark eyes. He was younger than the first man by perhaps twenty or thirty years and he too was dark, his hair black. His lips were full and sensuously curved. He had a familiar long, narrow object at his side. It was a musket.

The thought flashed into my throbbing head with the force of certainty: this was the weapon that had taken the life of Bartholomew Noble as he fled from Buckland Abbey.

I heard something that sounded like a vicious hiss coming from close at hand. I turned to see Simoun Wex, his eyes boring into the man in brown, and Simoun breathed, 'God in heaven, I never thought to see you again, bastard priest.'

'I have been following you close, Simoun Wex, for you left too clear a trail for men who are adept at hunting down runaway slaves,' the man in brown answered, and his accent was indeed that of a Spaniard, for all that he spoke my language fluently. 'You have in your possession something that does not belong to you, and I would like you to return it to me.'

'It doesn't belong to you either, priest,' Simoun said. 'You fucking Spaniards may believe you own the Caribbean, the lands surrounding it and everyone and everything in them, but I'm here to tell you that you don't.'

The brown-clad man waved a dismissive hand. 'You always did have it,' he said in a cold voice, not even bothering to respond to Simoun's passionate protest. 'I suspected it, and even when my most persuasive efforts still met with denial, I didn't believe you.'

'Yes you did, you smooth bastard,' Simoun said. 'I know you did because you let me go. Oh, it might have been in chains to the indigo plantation, but nevertheless, I went out from your control.'

For a mere second, the man in brown looked absolutely furious. Just as quickly he smoothed out his lean face once more. 'You gave yourself away, in the end,' he said. 'You escaped, you ran, and your very flight was the confirmation I needed that you do indeed have what I always knew to be in your possession. It was not long before word reached me from those I had set to watch you. I knew for certain then. And here I am!' He feigned surprise, as if amazed to find himself there in that grim little room.

Simoun Wex was nodding slowly. 'Here you are,' he agreed. 'And what exactly do you propose to do?'

'As soon as you have given me what I have come for, I shall probably kill you,' the brown-cloaked man said. 'Yes, as you are no doubt about to point out, you are four and we but two, but we are well armed and you are not. Besides which you and your son are enfeebled from long hardship and near starvation, one of your companions is a man of God' – he shot a scathing glance at Jonathan – 'and the other is reeling from his recent blow to the head. Hmm?'

You are four.

For a moment I couldn't work out what was wrong with that statement; my head was giving me a great deal of pain and I was feeling faint. I was on the point of speaking but Jonathan drove a sharp elbow into my ribs.

Then, of course, I realized.

My three companions were far ahead of me. Henry was

slumped down against the wall as if he was as enfeebled as the priest had just said he was, Simoun was lying quite still, holding the man with his eyes, Jonathan was watchful and I held my head and groaned in pain.

The two strangers' eyes were fixed on us, the man in brown not moving his gaze from Simoun, the other one flicking his glance between the four of us. Everything about him spoke of barely-contained fury, and I had the sense that he would have elbowed his companion out of the way and taken charge himself were it not for rigidly-enforced obedience.

Unnoticed by either of them, Puma crept slowly along the side wall of the desolate little room, edged his way around the angle where it joined the front wall and then seemed to *slither* along it – there was no better word to describe his fluid, soundless, boneless motion – until he was on the far side of the doorway and just behind the man in the deep blue cloak.

He struck like a snake too, with deadly rapidity and totally without mercy. As he struck, it seemed to my bemused, bewitched eyes that he *was* a snake: long, narrow, glistening like shining black silk, with a thin, darting forked tongue that shot out of the flattened head and dived straight into the side of the throat of his prey.

The man fell as if pole-axed. He made no sound; raised not a finger to defend himself. For a few moments he twitched, there on the dirty floor at his companion's feet, then he lay still. The brown-clad priest gave a cry and bent down over him. Puma melted away.

The priest shot up and fixed Simoun with a furious stare. There was no fear in those small black eyes: not yet.

'*What have you done to him?*' he screamed. 'What devilish weapon has been used against him?'

Simoun feigned wide-eyed innocence. 'Weapon, priest? As you just said, we are not armed.' He opened his arms, spreading his hands.

'But—' The priest looked wildly around the room. '*Where is it?*' he screamed, fury making him hurl out the words in a shower of spittle.

As he looked once more around the four walls, his eyes fell

upon the tiny, white-clad figure that stood in the shadows against the wall.

And I watched as mad fury gave way to abject, shaking terror.

The priest gave a whimper, dropping his sword with a clang and then using his right hand to cross himself, over and over again, the pale fingers making ceaseless figures of eight movements. I heard him muttering prayers in his own tongue, beseeching the Lord for help. Slowly he dropped to his knees, and now he clasped his hands before his face.

He did not seem able to tear his eyes away from Mama Tze Amba.

'I believe you recognize her, bastard priest?' Simoun said in a very cold voice. 'You tried to stamp out her cult, didn't you? You tortured, maimed and murdered her priests, priestess and adherents, and you probably thought you'd won.' He paused, then said very softly, 'But you didn't.'

The priest was babbling now, and I smelt urine as his bladder failed him.

'Mama Tze Amba knows what you did, priest,' Simoun went on. 'We told her every last detail of how you killed my companions from the *Minion*.' He drew a deep breath and shouted, 'How you stuck stakes in the ground, surrounded them with dry wood, tied my beloved friends to them and burned them alive!'

'No, no, mercy, *mercy!*' the priest was screeching. 'Not I, it was not I!'

'A liar too now,' Simoun observed. 'Oh, dear, dear, and you about to meet your God, priest. Is lying really wise?' He pretended to think about the matter. Then, relentless eyes back on the priest's, he said, 'It *was* you, and Mama Tze Amba knows it. She will extract her price, bastard priest, and you will receive what you meted out.'

'*Noooooo!*' The priest's protest rose to a deafening scream and he writhed as he knelt there, his body twisting this way and that.

Then, my horrified eyes quite incapable of looking away, I understood what was happening. Beside me I heard Jonathan begin to pray, and vaguely I recognized the words of the prayer for those facing an agonizing death who had but moments left.

I could not believe what I was seeing.

It could not be real.

But it was.

Either by some power emanating from the tiny white-clad corpse, or perhaps from the superstitious priest's belief in this power, he thought he was being burned alive.

His screams were terrible. He had grasped the gold cross he had concealed beneath his black robe and now he clutched it in both hands, his knuckles white, his eyes rolling back in his head, his mouth still moving as he went on repeating his soundless prayers.

And, just for an instant, I smelt smoke and the stench of burning flesh.

I risked a look at Mama Tze Amba.

Her eyes gleamed with a light like a white-hot flame.

I think I cried out, then I fell over sideways, Jonathan caught me and I felt myself slump against the floor. Then the world turned black.

I don't think I can have been insensate for long.

I opened my eyes to find that I was lying on the bed recently occupied by Simoun Wex, a pillow beneath my head and a blanket up to my shoulders. I was shivering.

I sat up.

The priest was dead.

He lay on his back, one hand still clutching his cross, and his eyes were stark with terror. His mouth was so widely open that he had dislocated his jaw, which was what told me for certain that he was dead, for had any life remained within him he'd have been screaming in agony. He had fallen over his dead companion's outstretched legs. Simoun crouched before the two of them, Henry beside him, and Puma stood beside the little white-robed corpse, muttering as if he was talking to her.

He probably was.

Jonathan knelt beside the Wex father and son, and he was praying. They, I observed, were praying with him.

I bowed my head and waited until he had finished.

'You really feel all right?' Jonathan asked me anxiously.

It was some time later; his prayers had been extensive, but

then we had all just witnessed something extraordinary and very frightening, and I think we all welcomed the sense of God's presence and support.

'*Yes*, Jonathan,' I said with a hint of impatience, struggling to evade his grip and stand up, for I was desperate to examine the man in the dark blue cloak and see how Puma had killed him. *If* Puma had killed him, and it hadn't really been the work of a huge black snake that had somehow manifested itself in the depths of rural Devon . . .

Now Simoun, Henry, Jonathan and I stood together beside the dead Spaniards. For some time we were silent: shock can have that effect.

Presently Henry said tentatively, 'Did she – did Mama Tze Amba really do it? Burn him, I mean, and yet us not see it?'

'I smelt smoke,' I said quietly. And something far worse, I could have added.

'I too,' Jonathan said, and Simoun Wex muttered agreement.

'But—' Henry began.

'I think,' Jonathan said after a very long pause, 'that it was the priest's own faith that made him believe he was burning. All of us could see that he wasn't, couldn't we?'

But none of us replied. Like me, the others didn't seem too sure.

'He was a man of strong, perhaps fanatical, faith,' Jonathan went on. 'His religion made him do terrible things to his fellow men; his God was a ferocious deity for whom no action was too barbarous or vicious. That is not my God,' he said, his voice dropping until it was almost inaudible.

'So – so you're saying that he believed she had the power to make him burn and so he thought it was really happening?' Henry said, his disbelief ringing out.

And with a soft smile, Jonathan said, 'How else do you explain it?'

Jonathan made me sit down on the end of the bed while he gave me food and drink. Simoun was lying behind me, still pale with shock but with a smile of quiet satisfaction hovering around his mouth. Henry was crouched beside Puma, back in the corner that he had made his private domain, speaking quietly to him in that alien tongue.

I chewed my way through the bread and cheese and took a small draught of beer from the cup Jonathan held so insistently to my lips. Then I stood up – my head swam, but I ignored it – and announced to the room in general, 'I have to fetch Theophilus Davey.'

Jonathan made no protest; he knew as well as I did that I had no choice.

Simoun looked up at me steadily.

'And what do you intend to tell him?'

I met his eyes. 'That you, your son and your companion have made your way home to England—'

'To Devon,' Simoun interrupted. 'We're Devonians, from Plymouth, like I told you. Well, Henry and me, although he isn't.' He jerked his head towards Puma's corner. 'Obviously,' he added with a swift smile.

'Home to Devon, then, after terrible hardships not the least of which you suffered on the journey home. I will tell him that you were pursued by those whose prisoners you had been—'

'We were their slaves,' Simoun said sharply. 'Make no mistake, Doctor, we were treated worse than the Africans, and that's saying a great deal.'

'Yes.' I bowed my head. 'I am sorry, Simoun, I did not intend to underestimate what you experienced.'

'I know,' he muttered. 'Go on.'

'I shall say – and it is the truth – that two Spaniards in the guise of merchants trailed you to your hiding place. Master Davey already knows these men are here – *were* here,' I amended, glancing at the two corpses, 'for others have reported receiving visits from them.'

Simoun's head shot up. 'Who would that be?'

I guessed he already knew. 'Thomas Drake and Richard Hawkins.'

'Bastard priest *knew* we'd go there with the— with what we have with us,' he said. He spat on the filthy floor.

'Yes, he did,' I agreed. 'Neither Sir Thomas nor Sir Richard, however, liked the look of the man and sent him away, denying all knowledge of anyone trying to sell them any – er, any valuable object.'

'We hadn't got that far,' Simoun said. 'Our initial attempts to get a hearing from either of them did not meet with success.'

'Yes, Henry told me,' I said gently. 'I'm very sorry about Bartholomew Noble.'

'Wasn't Sir Thomas nor any of his household that fired the shot,' Simoun added.

'I know who it was,' I said.

After a moment, Simoun said, 'Then what?'

It took me a moment to realize what he meant.

'Oh – then I'll describe how the two Spaniards burst into the house – this house – fully armed, and I'll make Master Davey fully aware that I was here, I saw it with my own eyes, and I shall explain that I was the only one among those in the room to have a weapon and that I'd been temporarily disabled by being struck on the head as the door was flung open.'

Simoun nodded slowly. 'Then what, Doctor? How will you explain two dead men when none of us bore arms?'

I hesitated. 'I'll work that out when I come to it,' I said firmly. 'It is I who will examine the bodies, Simoun. I will not lie' – the expression in his eyes staring into mine told me he knew that already – 'but I do not intend to let you or your son be held responsible for murders that you did not commit.'

What about Puma?

The question seemed to hang unspoken in the air.

Just then, I had no answer.

TWENTY

I t was afternoon, yet again I'd forgotten to eat anything at midday – really, it had been the last thing on my mind – and now I stood in the cellar beneath Theo Davey's house between two trestles, each bearing a dead, naked body.

The third member of the trio who had come so far – the old priest in the boarding house – had died, I'd been informed, during the night.

Theo stood beside me, and I knew he wasn't going to budge until I'd finished my examinations and pronounced my verdict.

He was aware that something strange had occurred. My difficult and not very honourable task now was to reveal enough to satisfy Theo's suspicious, intelligent mind while at the same time not even hinting at anybody within that deserted little hovel being guilty of murder.

I decided to begin with what I believed to be the more challenging death: that of the man in the dark blue cloak, who had been the priest's underling. I had no idea how he had died. Well, I didn't know how either of them had met their end, come to that.

I positioned the lamps to best effect and leaned over the corpse.

Theo could see for himself the obvious facts such as gender, height, weight, and also the slightly less obvious ones, such as there being no blows to the head or body, no knife wounds, no shot holes or any other overt evidence of violence.

'The body shows no signs or symptoms of disease,' I said presently, 'and the man was in overall good condition. He got enough to eat and did not do any extreme form of labour.' I went on with my examination, going over every part of the body until finally – reluctantly – arriving at the shoulders and neck.

'There are two small puncture wounds in the throat, at the spot where the jugular vein drains blood from the head and down towards the chest,' I said. I hoped my voice sounded calm; that I was succeeding in disguising the fact that suddenly my heart was pounding, for the little wounds were precisely where I had imagined I'd seen a huge black snake stick its fangs in the blue-cloaked man's neck.

'Puncture wounds?' Theo repeated. He sounded, I told myself, only mildly interested.

'Yes. See?' I pointed them out with the probe I was holding.

'Hmm.' Theo leaned in closer. 'They look like insect bites,' he observed. He shot me a particularly keen glance.

'They do, don't they?' I agreed.

Theo was still looking at me. 'Reckon some little creature stung him and poisoned him, Doctor?' he said.

I made a show of studying the dead face very intently. 'No sign of vomit, although his lips look blueish.'

'He'd surely only vomit if he'd ingested the poison,' Theo said. I'd forgotten how much he knew; how swiftly and accurately he could put facts together.

'True,' I said mildly.

'So?' he prompted when I didn't go on.

I decided to tell the truth. Of a sort.

'Honestly, Theo, if I didn't know it made no sense I'd say this man was bitten by a snake whose venom is deadly poisonous and very swift-acting,' I said.

'And our only indigenous poisonous snake is the adder,' Theo mused. 'Could that be it?'

'Unlikely,' I replied. 'Adder bites often kill lambs and other small animals, and occasionally prove fatal in the case of children, but it's very unusual for a well-built adult to succumb, and with such rapidity.' I shook my head in feigned puzzlement. 'This man dropped where he stood, and I would judge he died pretty much as he hit the ground.'

There was a long, heavy silence.

Just as it became unendurable, Theo said very softly, 'Gabe, I know there's more to this than you're telling me.' He stilled my instinctive protest with a raised hand. 'But I know you well, or I think I do, and I trust you. I *like* you, damnation take it.'

'The sentiments are entirely reciprocated,' I muttered.

Silence again. Then Theo said, 'Let us proceed to the second corpse.'

I drew the sheet up over the body I'd just examined and turned to the other one.

It was much the same story – a lean but adequately-fed, fit man, this one in late middle age but healthy and with no wounds or obvious signs of disease. When I had carried out a very thorough inspection I said, 'Not even those strange puncture wounds in the case of this body.'

'So how are we to say he died?' Theo asked. Then, his tone sharp with sudden angry impatience, he said, 'God alive, Gabe, you were right there! What the fuck happened?'

So I told him.

'The *Falco* survivors had their little corpse in the house with them,' I said. 'Yes, Theo, the one they took back from right here.' Gently I thumped the trestle table before me. 'She has some power that I don't even begin to understand, and it is a power that not only the *Falco* men but also the priest – this man – recognized and understood.' I could see he wanted to interrupt but I didn't let him. 'Somehow it seemed to enter the priest's head that the figure – she's called Mama Tze Amba – could harm him. He killed so many men, and one of the most common methods was by burning. Somehow – and don't ask because I can't begin to explain it – he seemed to think she was capable of exacting revenge by meting out the same punishment on him. He – it appeared that he believed he was burning too. Before our very eyes, he fell to his knees, crying out in terror, clutching his cross, praying for his very soul, and in the end emitting nothing but one long howl of agony.' The memory was far too recent; far, far too vivid, and for a moment I felt as faint as I'd done back in the fetid little room. 'So, cause of death for this man: imaginary immolation.'

I hadn't meant to speak so harshly, but Theo, bless him, understood. He put a strong arm round my waist and held me up until my knees turned back from jelly to muscle, bone and sinew, then he said gruffly, 'Sorry, Gabe. Didn't mean to make you relive it. And you had a bang on the head, too.'

I didn't answer. It was tempting to say that I'd probably been half-concussed, and that explained my inability to describe what had happened in any credible way. But it would have been a lie and while I'm prepared to lie to quite a lot of people for a variety of reasons, Theo is among those who deserves the truth.

After a time he said, 'Do we have names for these two?'

'Not to my knowledge, although Simoun Wex knows the priest and may be able to provide one, although I imagine he's made himself erase it from his memory.'

Theo nodded. 'Well, I intend to release the bodies for burial.'

I felt a wave of relief flood through me. 'Thank you.'

There was a pause, then Theo said, 'You will swear no murder was done, Gabe?'

'Neither Simoun Wex nor his son committed any crime here,' I said.

'And the other fugitive – the long, skinny boy?'

I was tired of evasions. 'He's a grown man, his mother was a vodou priestess, he appears to have unbelievable powers I've never seen before or even suspected exist, and I *think*, although I cannot be sure, that somehow he managed to turn himself into a snake and that it was he who inflicted the fatal bite on this one.' I indicated the first man I'd examined. 'That, of course, is both absurd and totally unlikely.'

There was an even longer silence. Then Theo gave a great, gusty sigh and said, 'I'd better record death by misadventure for the pair of them, then.'

We covered up the priest, extinguished the lamps and left him and his companion lying there in the dark, cold cellar. As we mounted the steps back to the warmth and the light, Theo said very softly, 'Thanks for telling me the truth, Gabe. Appreciate it.'

Theo truly is a pearl among coroners. A pearl, in fact, among friends.

I rode home, gave my tired horse into Samuel's care and made my exhausted, stumbling way into my house.

I'd been hoping for plentiful hot water, a change of clothes, a good meal, several mugs of ale and then a long, undisturbed sleep. I had no idea what the time was – some time in the early evening, judging by the light – and I didn't care.

Celia apprehended me before I'd even got as far as the kitchen to ask Sallie for the hot water. 'Er, Gabe, actually, don't call

Sallie, because I've only just persuaded her to go to her room and stay there,' she whispered.

'Oh, dear God, what now?' I moaned.

'Sorry, *sorry!*' Celia said, and I could see her concern in her sweet face. 'There are some people here to see you and, honestly, Gabe, I think you'll want to speak to them.' She gave me an earnest, enquiring look, and pointed in the direction of the library.

'Very well,' I said grudgingly, and I followed her across the hall, through the parlour and into the library, where Jonathan Carew, Simoun and Henry Wex all stood up to greet me.

Jonathan apologized, just as Celia had done: 'I'm so sorry, Gabriel, I am sure this is the last thing you want, but really, I do not think you ought to miss this.' Also like Celia, his eyes too sparkled with excitement.

And I watched as Simoun took some object out from behind his back and placed it with careful reverence on the library table.

It was a box made of red wood, decorated with swirls and spirals, and it was so old that the beautiful design had almost faded away.

'I think, Doctor,' Simoun said gravely, 'that you have earned the right to know about this.'

For a moment I just stood and looked at it. I'd seen it before, fleetingly, hidden under Simoun's pillows in the dilapidated house. It was probably my mental state, but as I stared down at the red wood, dulled by age, it seemed to grow larger and then smaller before my eyes.

'Open it,' Simoun said.

So I unfastened the brass clasp and raised the lid.

There was a piece of parchment inside, tightly rolled and tied with a length of red silk cord. The parchment was the width of the box – eight or nine inches across – and as I undid the bow that fastened the cord and let the scroll unroll, it was revealed to be perhaps a foot and a half long.

I'd been at sea. I knew instantly what it was.

What confounded me, what made me doubt what my eyes were telling me, was that the parchment appeared to show a route through an area where all man's endeavours had informed us that there *was* no route.

I looked up and met Simoun's intent eyes.

'Is it true?' I laid a hand on the chart. 'Is this right? Is it accurate?'

'A man I trusted with my life swore that it is, yes,' Simoun said quietly.

'Who is this man?'

'He is dead, Doctor. You cannot seek him out and grill him, so you'll have to take my word for it.' He had spoken abruptly and now he added more gently, 'He was a countryman of mine and he had travelled extensively in the region with a wise and experienced native guide. He – my countryman – travelled the western end of the route with this guide, who had approached from the east to meet up with my friend.'

'And he—'

'Doctor, I shall not tell you any more so there is no point pressing me,' Simoun said firmly. 'You recognize what this is?'

'Oh, yes,' I breathed softly.

Some men called them portolans; others referred to them as rutters. They were detailed maps of coastlines, sea and ocean routes, usually created by sailors for sailors, and they were considered state secrets by the Portuguese and the Spanish. Although as a ship's surgeon navigation had not been my responsibility, nevertheless I had been strangely fascinated by the rutters of the Mediterranean and the Caribbean – even the ones of my own native shores – which my various ship's captains had shown me, for more often than not these objects were works of art in their own right. The wavy, indented lines of the coast would be marked not only with place names but, more importantly, landmarks such as churches, hills and valleys, patches of woodland; even, sometimes, some quaint local focus point such as *big yellow barn with hole in roof*. The tides were indicated and, out in mid-ocean, the mighty currents. These vast areas of open sea were covered with characteristic rhumb lines: the long, gracefully curving lines showing the windrose networks emanating from the compass rose, for the captains of sailing ships needed above all to know about the wind network when far from land.

We – the English – and the Dutch had been behind the Spanish and the Portuguese when it came to discovering the benefits of world trade, not that you'd ever catch an Englishman, especially a sailor, admitting it. Thus we'd had a good deal of catching up to do, and no sailor in our navy, from captains and probably even admirals downwards, ever missed a chance to steal a rutter from our rivals; Francis Drake, men said, had somehow got his hands on charts of the galleon route across the Pacific to the Moluccas in 1578. If you wanted to succeed in fighting, raiding and trading, you needed to know exactly where you were and what course to set for where you were intending to go.

A memory awoke in my mind of a time when, under Captain Zeke's command, we'd been involved in the capture of a Portuguese ship, the *Madre de Deus:* among the more readily saleable items such as gold and precious jewels that had been stashed away in her capacious holds, there was said to be a document that provided invaluable information on the Portuguese trade with Japan and Cathay. In all likeliness it had been a rutter such as the one I was now staring at, and it too, so they said, had been hidden away in its own precious box . . .

But the chart now spread out on my library table showed a very different part of the globe.

I dragged myself out of my fascinating thoughts.

My eyes on Simoun, I said, indicating Celia and Jonathan, 'Have you told them what this is? Have you explained why it is so vitally important?'

Jonathan murmured something, his moderate tones entirely obliterated by Celia's indignant voice. 'He didn't need to *explain*, Gabe!' she protested. 'You give me leave to read your books and your journals, and you know full well that I do so whenever I have the time!'

I did. Hadn't she only very recently demonstrated the fact by discovering for herself the story of Drake and Hawkins at San Juan d'Ulúa?

'You are most welcome, Celia,' I said to her. 'Granny Oldreive would be very proud of you,' I added softly, and she smiled. 'Go on, then,' I added.

She needed no second invitation. Simoun was watching her with some suspicion, and I guessed that what women there had been in his life had been of a very different nature from my sister. Henry was staring at her with his mouth open and his eyes full of wonder that, I thought, was poised to turn into adoration.

'England wants to trade with the world,' Celia began, 'and to do so, good, reliable access to distant shores is needed, without having to compete with the ships of those other nations who want this trade all for themselves. The Spanish and the Portuguese hold positions of power in the Caribbean, and the Dutch have control of the route around Cape Horn to the Spice Islands. For many years now, the English have been desperate to find their own way there. So, they've been hunting for a route across the Atlantic to North America, around the top of the mass of land and into the Pacific, then on to the Spice Islands via the westward way.'

She stopped, slightly breathless, and I judged from her expression that it had taken quite a lot of courage to lecture on such matters to a roomful of men. But my sister does not lack courage.

'It is known as the Northwest Passage,' Jonathan said quietly into the silence. I might have known, I reflected, that he too would be well versed on the subject. 'The existence of a northern route has been postulated from as long ago as the middle of the last century and probably further, and an expedition that I can think of in fact explored to the north *east*, when a pair of adventurers searched for a passage to the north of Russia and froze to death. In the other direction, Martin Frobisher's search for the Northwest Passage during Queen Elizabeth's reign was equally unsuccessful. John and Sebastian Cabot searched many decades earlier, and they were possibly the first men to declare that a passage through or around North America would have to be found if a short passage from England to the Orient and its wealth was to become a reality. Then—'

I felt that we might be wandering a little too far into the bottomless depths of history now, and Jonathan, I guessed, had much more to tell us if he was allowed to. 'Thank you, Jonathan,' I said gently.

'Oh!' He looked startled, then gave me a swift nod. 'Enough. Of course,' he muttered.

Simoun, his amazement at such knowledge existing here in

the library of a country doctor showing clearly in his face, straight away began to speak before anyone else could.

'The man who created this rutter revealed a great deal more to me than facts and dates and the details of unsuccessful missions,' he said. 'He *knew*. He'd been there, seen it all. They believed there was a strait called Anián that stretched between North America and Asia, and that this gave access to the Northwest Passage from the western end. Way back, the Spanish sailed along the Baja California Peninsula—'

'That's on the west coast of North America,' I interrupted, looking at Celia. 'I'll show you later, on my globe.'

'No need, Gabe,' she said curtly. 'I have already seen for myself, thank you.'

Henry Wex's mouth dropped open again.

'The Spanish thought that Baja California was an island, and that the stretch of water separating it from the mainland was the southern entrance to the passage from the Pacific to the Atlantic,' Simoun went on, watching me warily in case I interrupted again. 'They thought that by exploring from the western end, eventually the strait of Anián would reveal itself.'

Jonathan, his face alight with interest, couldn't contain himself. 'Yes, indeed, and there have been many expeditions from the eastern end too!' he said. 'Brave men have sailed around the coasts of Greenland, Baffin Island and Labrador, and only a couple of years ago one of our countrymen explored the great bay that opens up on the north east coast of America and—' Catching my eye, he subsided.

'Thank you,' Simoun murmured, not without irony. He glanced down at the beautiful parchment spread out on my table. 'Many of us believe that seeking out the western end of the Northwest Passage was what Francis Drake was really up to when he set off in 1577, and that it was only because he couldn't find it that he turned instead across the Pacific, and thus eventually came to the Spice Islands.'

There was a hushed silence while we all thought about that.

Presently I turned to Simoun. He met my stare, and I had the feeling he was waiting for this moment. 'Why are you here?' I asked.

He turned away.

'You didn't come to make harsh and unreasonable demands of the kinsmen of Francis Drake or John Hawkins. I thought at first that might be the reason, but I was wrong,' I ploughed on when Simoun made no answer. 'You're not here for vengeance on the men who left you behind to face the hell that swallowed you up, because you don't hold either Drake or Hawkins responsible for your fate. You know it had to happen; that you and your fellow sailors had to be sacrificed so the rest could make it home.'

Simoun gave a great sigh and said, 'No, we're not after revenge, and we're not seeking some extravagant pay-off to stop us spreading our story.' He stared straight into my eyes. 'Against unimaginable odds, the three of us have not only made it back to our home, but survived when our three dear companions did not, and all we want is a bit of help to settle back here in peace.' He touched the rutter with his fingers. 'We thought we had something to offer in exchange, but it appears we were wrong.'

I put that aside for the moment.

'You came home for that reason? To find peace?' I had to ask, but I was all but sure now that it was not the truth.

And the look that Simoun Wex gave me told me I was right.

'Oh, no, Doctor.' He gave a strange half-smile. 'You know, don't you?' he said very softly.

'I believe I do,' I agreed. 'Please, go on. If you are able?'

'I am.' He paused, perhaps gathering his strength, then raised his head and said to the room at large, 'We weren't running *to* England – to home – as much *from* what we left behind us.'

Nobody said anything for a few moments. Then, with an exclamation of horrified understanding, Jonathan said, 'You refer, I believe, to the magic; to the dangerous, uncontrollable dark forces that you and your companions stirred up back on the plantation. Where the thin boy's mother was a priestess, and where you fell into her ways.'

Simoun gave a grunt of laughter. 'Not sure we *fell* into anything, Father, as much as ran in with our eyes wide open.'

His face full of compassion, Jonathan said very softly, 'However it happened, you have my sympathy, and I will help you in any way I can.'

As Simoun looked at him, I thought I saw the shine of tears in his eyes. 'I'm grateful, Father,' he muttered.

It was, I reflected, something of an understatement.

'We should be all right,' Simoun went on, 'as long as we have—' But, with a swift glance at Celia, he stopped.

As long as we have Mama Tze Amba, I finished silently for him. As long as they had beside them the fearsome presence that somehow protected them from far worse magic.

But I wasn't going to mention her any more than Simoun was.

Some things are better not brought out into the open unless there is absolutely no choice.

As if perceiving that the discussion was over, Simoun rolled up the parchment, re-tied the silk cord and put the scroll into the box, carefully fastening the clasp. 'Ah, well, seems I was wrong about this,' he said, a hand resting on the box. 'Nobody in either the Drake or the Hawkins clan has the least interest in us or anything we have to offer, and that's putting it mildly.'

'Yes,' I agreed. 'They have turned respectable now and they don't want any reminder of their famous forbears' dangerous, violent pasts.' Their morally dubious pasts, I might have added. 'But I have an idea,' I went on.

Henry spun round to look at me, and the hope in his expression made me say a silent prayer that my idea was sound. Simoun went on staring down at his red wood box.

'Will you let me explore it?' I asked.

After quite a long pause, Simoun pushed the box across the table at me. 'May as well,' he muttered. Then, as if he had to part from his precious treasure quickly if he was to do so at all, he hurried out of the room and, after a final glance at Celia, Henry ran after him.

'Where will they go?' I asked Jonathan.

'Back to the derelict house,' he replied. 'It is not so bad now, and, as Simoun said, they have known far, far worse.' He hesitated, then said, 'Do you anticipate success in this scheme of yours?'

I shrugged. 'I don't know.'

*   *   *

I slept long and deeply that night, and woke refreshed and a good deal more optimistic than I'd been the night before. I rose early and was down on the quay standing beneath *Falco*'s soaring wooden sides just as the day was getting into its stride.

I should have come before, a fact that was made very clear to me by the many moments I spent listening to Captain Zeke yelling at me, swearing at me and demanding to know why the fuck I hadn't thought to give him the smallest of hints as to what had been happening. When he'd calmed down and only the last drifts of steam were coming out of his ears, I accepted his invitation to take a seat, accepted a glass from him and told him.

When at long last I had finished, he reached out a hand and grasped mine. 'I apologize,' he said gruffly. 'I gave you a bugger of a task, you did it, you came as soon as you could to give me your report and I shouted at you as if you were some worm of a raw recruit. Sorry.'

'Apology accepted,' I replied. 'So, can you help me?'

Captain Zeke thought for some time. Then he said, 'If I could relieve you of what you have in that red wood box, I'd do so. Dear God, I'd do so!' He paused, his eyes alight with the thrill of possibilities. 'But, although as you and I well know, I am a man of some means, I cannot give our fugitives the gold they require.'

'They're not greedy,' I said swiftly. 'They ask only for enough to purchase a little house. Henry will work – he is desperate to, in fact, for work will, I believe, provide the healing he so badly needs.'

Captain Zeke nodded in understanding. 'Yes, you are surely right,' he agreed. 'Poor devil's been a slave, and urgently desires to restore his self-respect. Nevertheless, Gabe, I cannot pay them what they require.' He paused. 'But I believe I may be able to direct you to someone who can.'

I went there without delay.

The house had a stately beauty and had been built, I estimated, in the middle of the last century. The small bricks of which it was constructed had mellowed pleasingly, and the gardens surrounding it were mature and well-tended. It stood some miles back from the coast, as if the former sailor who inhabited it had seen enough of the sea and her capricious moods.

It was the home of Admiral Sir Bewley Underhay, retired, and he was the brother of our local justice of the peace.

He was an elderly man now, although he still bore himself well. He was courteous and seemed pleased to have a visitor, and as soon as I had identified myself he ushered me into a pleasant room with windows overlooking woodland and fields, where he sat me down and gave me a glass of very fine wine.

When I told him what I had come for he changed.

When I produced the red wood box, opened it and unrolled the parchment inside, he acted as if Spanish spies were huddled beneath the window and lurking in the passage outside, curtly ordering me to replace the rutter in its box and hide it away.

He disappeared, and I heard him striding around in the corridor outside the room. Returning, he checked the window. Finally he came to stand over me and hissed, 'Do you *know* what you have there, Doctor Taverner?'

'I do,' I replied.

He looked as if he was about to explode. 'Then in heaven's name why have you got it? How did you come across it? Where in God's good earth did it come from? Who made it?' He puffed a bit, then said, 'How do you—'

I stopped him. 'I cannot answer those questions, Sir Bewley, for as I am sure you will appreciate, to do so would be to break another man's confidence.'

'But you *must*, you—'

Again I interrupted. 'Perhaps it will help if I say that I wish to put it into your hands. Right now, and you shall keep it when I leave.'

He gazed at me, eyes popping in his head. 'What do you want in return?'

I named the amount of money that Jonathan Carew and I believed would purchase a modest dwelling.

Sir Bewley Underhay's eyes widened some more. 'Is that *all*?' he demanded.

'It is.'

I hadn't truly anticipated that he would give me the gold there and then, but he did, in a couple of leather bags that

weighed heavy in my hands. Before he could change his
mind, I left the red wood box on the small side table where I'd
placed it and hastened away. I think he was as glad to be rid
of me as I was to leave.

On my way home I called in to see Theo.

He sat at his desk, I drew up a chair opposite to him and for
some time we simply looked at each other. He knew full well
that there were things I hadn't adequately explained to him, but
I believed he also knew that I'd told him as much as I could.
If he was left with an imperfect understanding of it all, then
so was I.

'Is it over?' he said after a while.

'I am fairly certain it is,' I replied.

'I can bury the two foreigners?'

'You can.'

'And—' He gave me an odd look, turned away and then once
more fixed me with his blue eyes. 'What of the first one?' he
said quietly.

Ah, I thought. Of course he would want to know; need to
know, in fact, for he was the coroner and it was his solemn
duty to uncover the circumstances of death for bodies found
within his jurisdiction before releasing them for burial.

So how was I to tell him that he was never going to see
Mama Tze Amba again?

'Theo, the little corpse that was removed from your cellar
needs to be with the men who brought her here,' I began tentatively. 'She isn't so much a body as a religious artefact, and—'

'Looked like a body to me,' he muttered.

'Yes, of course, and I'm not denying she was human, but
she died a very long time ago and a long way from here,' I
went on.

'You said when you examined her that she probably died of
old age,' Theo said.

'Yes, indeed I did.'

He was looking at me hopefully. 'And?' he prompted.

I shook my head. 'And what?'

'And is that still your opinion?' he demanded impatiently.

I began to understand. 'Yes.'

He frowned, clearly thinking hard. 'Then I have the cause of death,' he murmured, more to himself than to me, 'and it would serve, I suppose, to put in my report that the body was released for burial and not actually mention that it was more a matter of it being *taken* than my releasing it . . .'

He looked up at me hopefully.

It was on the tip of my tongue to say that there was no question of Mama Tze Amba being buried but I managed to bite back the words.

Instead I said, 'If you're asking my opinion, Theo, I'd say it would serve very well.'

He nodded, and I sensed his relief.

After a short pause he said, 'And the other men?'

'They will be cared for.'

He nodded again. 'Good man, Jonathan Carew.'

'He is,' I agreed.

If Theo thought that Simoun, Henry and their strange companion were to be housed in some little village dwelling found for them by Jonathan in Tavy St Luke, then so much the better. It was preferable, for both them and Theo, for the four of them not to meet again, and if what I had in mind worked out – and there was no reason why it should not – they wouldn't.

I got up to go. Theo rose too, and came out into the yard to see me on my way.

'Come to dinner soon,' he said as I mounted Hal. 'You and Celia.'

'We will. Good day to you, Theo. May we have some peaceful days now.'

'Amen to that,' he agreed fervently. Then he went back inside and shut the door.

I went back to Rosewyke, the leather bags heavy across Hal's neck. I went inside and, managing to evade attention from either my sister or my housekeeper, slipped upstairs to my study and hid the gold in a safe place. It would not be there for long: the *Falco* fugitives needed a home, and I would make sure they had one as soon as possible.

But it wouldn't be today.

Today I was tired, mentally and physically. I had seen sights

I would far rather not have seen, heard tales that told far too vividly of the brutality of men. At times in these days just past I had come close to despair, all but drawn down into the black, stinking abyss that some insist on digging across this beautiful world.

The *Falco* fugitives had a future now; I believed that I was justified in taking a few hours of absence from them and their concerns, and today I did not intend to give them another thought.

For today I had other plans.

I was going to put on fresh linen, then return downstairs to collect my horse and set out again.

I was going to ride over to the neat little cottage above the river with the door knocker shaped like an angel, because it was high time I made sure Judyth had truly suffered no lasting ill effect from Henry Wex's blade.

That, anyway, was my excuse, although I was fairly confident I wouldn't need one.

A FEW WEEKS LATER

It was a small house, in a little-used alley off a busy street in Plymouth quite near to the water. The house was unobtrusive, unremarkable, and within dwelt an old man and his mixed blood son, and the son brought in a good enough wage for the pair to live in a degree of comfort. They were attended by a long, thin servant who looked like a boy. He had strange eyes and a wild look about him. Occasionally he emerged on errands, although he preferred the safety of the little house's four walls. When he did venture out, he aroused little interest in a hectic port where exotic-looking men and women were everywhere.

The house had a main room downstairs and a scullery off it. There was a walled yard behind, and a small space for the servant just off the kitchen, warmed by the fire that was kept burning in the hearth. Upstairs there were two small chambers furnished basically but comfortably, one for the old father, one for his son.

Between these two chambers there was a little cupboard, perfectly concealed by a door that looked exactly like one more piece of the smooth wood panelling.

But this panel opened, and behind it there was a shrine. Where, propped against the wall and dressed in a freshly-washed, pure white robe and headdress, stood a tiny corpse. At her feet flowers floated in water, and the flowers were refreshed every few days. Next to the flowers, a candle burned in a red glass jar.

Although there was no longer any real need, Mama Tze Amba continued to watch over the men she had guarded for so long.

And her protection was never going to stop.